So Far Into You

Lily Malone

EasyRead Large

Copyright Page from the Original Book

ISBN: 9780857992758

Title: So Far Into You

TABLE OF CONTENTS

So Far Into You

Lily Malone

A new Australian rural romance about a millionaire wine tycoon, the woman he betrayed and the second chance neither was looking for...
When she cut her viticulture degree short and moved home, Remy wasn't thinking about anything more than making the next dollar for her pocket. Working two jobs to keep food on the table and a loan shark from the door, Remy and her mother slowly build a new life together. Then a freak storm tears through the Margaret River Wine Festival – and Seth Lasrey tears through Remy's life.

Seth is old money. She is no money. He's the boss. She's his employee. He is society connections and expectations. She is threats and bad decisions and lost dreams. They seem to be so wrong they can only be right – until a costly mistake and a timely deception drives them apart. Remy picks up the pieces of her life and begins anew. The last thing she expects is Seth to show up in her small town in South Australia, bringing with him memories that she can't escape and a damaged heart that she's not sure she can resist.

About the Author

Lily Malone would have been a painter, except her year-old son put a golf club through her canvas. So she wrote *His Brand Of Beautiful* instead. Since then she's written *Fairway To Heaven,* and the latest, *So Far Into You* for Escape Publishing. You can visit Lily at www.lilymalone.wordpress.com

Acknowledgements

Once again huge thanks to my dirty drafters: Jennie Jones and Juanita Kees, and my friend and critique partner, Kylie Kaden for help with the manuscript.

Thank you Kate Cuthbert from Escape Publishing, and editor extraordinaire, Belinda Holmes, for having such a good eye for things that could be better.

To Jarman and Breeze: more than enough dog for anyone, and too much for most.

Book 1

Chapter 1

There were prettier girls at the Margaret River Wine Festival that year but Seth Lasrey, standing inside the mouth of the marquee in Pioneer Park, had eyes only for one. She was with a group of Lasrey staff who had staked a claim on a handful of white plastic trestle tables outside the marquee, beneath a sail that would have sheltered them had there been any sun.

Her dress was the colour of a ripe slice of watermelon and she had no jacket—bloody ridiculous, he thought, given the storm that was on its way. She had her back to him, and both the dress and her hair tossed in a way that reminded him of how the waves smashed into the surf beaches all along the Cape.

Plus she was deep in conversation with his brother, Blake.

That's Blake for you. Blake wouldn't get stuck in a stuffy tent talking to a bunch of winemakers in suits when there were pretty girls in pink dresses to tune.

Seth took a quick drink of the cabernet someone had poured in his glass. Beside him, a representative from one of the French cooperages droned on about the results of their latest oak trials. As salesmen went, this guy was pleasant enough, but Seth was way too jet-lagged to be polite so when the guy drew breath he said: 'You really should have this conversation with Rina, Philippe. She's our winemaker. How we use oak is her call.'

'I will speak to Miss Stein. I will,' the salesman assured, but the look on his face said: *But I know it's you who controls the money.*

Seth excused himself and Philippe turned away, making a bee-line for the next person dressed like a decision-maker.

Which is another thing, Seth grumped. Old Joe Lasrey would have turned in his grave if he could see all the suits and ties here today. Seth's father had pioneered the Margaret River Wine Festival and Joe saw it as an opportunity for the industry to come together to celebrate everything that made it great: grapegrower and winemaker working as one. Yet every year Seth shook hands with fewer wine-stained palms and more corporate types with soft skin and slick suits.

The girl in pink tilted her chin toward Blake. Whatever she said made his brother laugh out loud and Seth took half a step forward, ready to join them.

'There you are!'

Through the muddle of bodies, his mother elbowed a path. Her perfume arrived before she did.

'Darling. I've been looking everywhere for you. I didn't see you last night.' Ailsa Lasrey lifted her head and Seth leaned low to kiss his mother's cheek.

'I only flew in to Perth last night. By the time I got down to the farm it was nearly ten. All I wanted was a hot shower and a bed.'

'You work too hard.' Ailsa rubbed her palm from Seth's elbow to his shoulder. 'Where have you been this time?'

'China. Beijing. Before that, Singapore. Before *that,* London for the second time in a month.' He glanced again toward the marquee opening. Was it darker out there? As he watched, a handful of empty plastic cups skittered off the picnic tables.

That was another thing Joe would have hated. Glass in the marquee, plastic cups outside, as if the workers couldn't be trusted not to break the best cutlery. If his father was paying any attention down in that grave, he wouldn't be satisfied with a mere turning. He'd be performing half pikes with triple twists.

'You travel too much, darling. You should stick around for a while this time, take a holiday,' Ailsa said.

'A few days off would be good.' He'd get up early, take the fishing rods. Blake said there were some good fish biting. 'But I head off again Tuesday, Bordeaux for the trade exhibition, remember? If it wasn't for the festival, I would have stayed away. It was hardly worth coming back for three days.'

'Well, at least it's a long weekend and I, for one, am glad you're here. Someone has to talk some sense into Blake.'

Seth glanced outside at his brother. 'What's he done now?'

'He said he wants to take next year off to concentrate on his *surfing.*' She said it the same way she might have said *syphilis.*

Seth shrugged. 'He's good. You know that.'

Ailsa's chin came up: 'He'll listen to you. Blake looks up to you. I'm not sure he's got people around him with his best interests at heart. Blake gets influenced so easily. He's not like you, Seth. Talk to him.'

Through the gap in the marquee, Seth saw the girl in pink laughing. Blake had his camera aimed at her and the flash was a strobe in the gloom.

Sometimes Seth envied his younger brother the freedom that came with no responsibility. Blake was happiest on the ocean, riding the waves. He worked in a logistics role at Lasrey but all he was doing was marking time, getting enough cash together to finance his next surf trip up north.

'Blake's twenty-two. He can look after himself.' It came out with more salt on it than Seth had intended but he was tired and his mother didn't know when to let up.

'Oh, don't mind me, darling. Once a mother, always a mother. We never stop worrying about our children. You'll find that out one day.' There was a pause, one in which Seth could hear the pinballs in his mother's brain falling into their slots. 'Speaking of which ... maybe you can tack on some holiday time after this Bordeaux visit, hmm? Better yet, why not bring Helene back from France with you? I haven't seen her for far too long.'

And that was a thought that needed nipping in the bud, right now. 'I don't have plans to see Helene.'

Ailsa sighed and stared pointedly out through the tent opening: 'It won't hurt the girls around here to see at least one of my sons with a girlfriend in tow. That girl in the pink dress is all over Blake.'

Seth took another look. One of her slim hands held a chunk of wheat-blonde hair at the nape of her neck, making a ponytail cascade over her shoulder. He could see why she'd caught his brother's eye. Blake was a leg man and as the wind whipped at the long pink skirt of her dress, it outlined a truly superb set of pins. She had legs like a dancer's.

She had dancer's shoes on her feet, too. Silver sparkly heels that were every bit as ridiculous as having no bloody jacket on a day like this.

'Who is she?' he asked.

'She started as Greg Trimble's viticulture trainee in March.'

'Remy Hanley.'

Ailsa's attention clicked back to him. 'I'm impressed you'd remember. But of course, Remy is an unusual name.'

Seth ignored the dig. 'Lasrey isn't so big its CEO shouldn't know all the staff by name, Mother—Dad always said that. Know their names and be the first to shake their hand.'

Ailsa bit her lip. 'We're not big enough *yet,* maybe. But we will be one day. You'll take us there. I know it.

Your father never had the vision but you do, Seth. We've had better growth in this last four years, since you took the helm, than in the previous fourteen.'

'There you are, Seth! Hello, Ailsa.'

'Rina,' he greeted. He would have shaken her hand, but hers were busy with a bottle of red and an empty glass.

'Rina, darling. How are you? You look lovely,' Ailsa gushed beside him. His senior winemaker and his mother exchanged air kisses.

When Seth looked back out the opening of the marquee, he couldn't see Blake. The girl was there though, looking lovely, if a little lost without his brother.

'Top you up?' Rina waggled the bottle at him.

He put his hand over his glass. 'No thanks. I'm driving.'

How much longer did he have to stay? Till the speeches, at least. Each year since his father died Seth had presented the Joe Lasrey Perpetual Trophy at the festival, for service to the Margaret River wine industry.

'Bugger driving. That's no fun.' Rina filled her own glass and tucked the bottle between her feet. She wore sensible black boots under practical blue jeans. Not a sparkly silver sandal in sight.

Blake jogged back into Seth's view. He had a pair of rough timber boards under one arm, like thick over-sized skis, and Seth heard him bellow to the group of Lasrey workers: 'Who's in for the plank walk with me?'

'Looks like Blake's having fun,' Rina commented, following Seth's gaze toward the park.

'He always does,' Ailsa added drily. 'So does *she.* It's not hard to see why Greg hired her.'

His mother's tone made Seth pause. It wasn't unusual to see Ailsa agitated. The word could have been her middle name. Her angst over this girl felt different. Personal. And he didn't know why. Seth didn't like it when he didn't know the 'why'.

'If there's something you want to tell me, Mother, I'm sure Rina will excuse us for a second,' Seth said.

Ailsa laughed. 'I don't keep secrets from Rina. She's like family.'

His winemaker batted Ailsa's compliment away.

'Fair enough.' Seth's patience for the festival, the marquee and his mother, ebbed. 'If Greg Trimble hired Remy as his assistant, it would be because she was the best person for the job. Take my word for it.'

'With all respect, Seth, you don't know anything about her,' Ailsa said. 'I've known girls like her all my life. They always want what they can't afford.'

'I may not know *her,* but I know Greg Trimble. I hired *him* and I don't hire dickheads. If he chose her for the job, that's good enough for me.'

It should have been the end of it. If Seth spoke to any of his staff in that tone that person would be beating a track for the door.

Not Ailsa.

She smiled sweetly. 'Ask Rina, darling. She's heard the rumours.'

'I don't give a shit about rumours. You shouldn't either.'

Blake shouted again. 'Come on, Remy. Be a sport? Lasrey won the plank walk last year, help me defend the title.'

Whatever the girl said got whipped away by the wind. Or maybe it was just that she'd started walking and Seth forgot to listen. *God, could she move.*

She kicked off her shoes, planted her plastic cup on the nearest trestle table—from where it immediately pinwheeled off—and crossed the grass to step up on the plank behind Blake. Then she bent to scoot her feet into the two elastic straps across the top of the planks before she straightened and gripped either side of Blake's waist.

Did her fingers squeeze? Or did he imagine it? For the first time Seth wondered how Blake felt about her. *Remy.* It had a nice ring to it.

'We need two more...' Blake called.

'What are you like at plank walking, Rina?' Seth said.

'Pardon?'

'Plank walking. Looks like Blake needs a quorum. No reason why it can't be us.'

'Us?' A frown dragged the corners of Rina's mouth.

'Go on, Rina.' Ailsa said. 'Think of it as good for staff morale.'

'That too,' Seth added, kicking off his shoes, putting his glass on the nearest waiter's tray. 'They're sure as shit having more fun than we are.' Seth stuffed his socks in his shoes and strode from the tent, not really caring if Rina followed.

Outside, the wind buffeted the sail above the tables, making the marquee snap like some rabid dog.

'Count me in, Blake,' Seth called to his brother.

Blake's head jerked up in surprise. His wasn't the only one. The Lasrey crowd melted out of Seth's way. He stepped on the plank behind Remy and worked his feet into the straps. He could barely wiggle the elastic past the bridge of his foot. Rina shuffled in place behind him. Gingerly, she poked her toes through the straps and took hold of his waist.

When Seth closed his hands in the groove above Remy's hips he forgot about Rina, Blake, the crowd, and the way the wind hurled through the park. Through thin cotton her hips curved warm in his fingers. How she could possibly feel warm in a dress like that, on a day like this, he had no idea, but warm she was. Vibrant and young and alive and he loved it.

Her hair chased across his chin and Seth caught a scent like summer-dry hay.

Above the Indian Ocean, leaden clouds roiled to the west. The air pulsed with energy, like a demon army cracking whips.

'*Hell and Tommy,*' Remy muttered, staring at the sky.

Hell and Tommy? Seth thought, and he smiled.

'On three, everybody. Left foot first,' Blake called over his shoulder. 'One. Two. Three. *Left...*'

Seth felt the drag through the plank as Rina struggled for balance behind him. Her hands clamped hard at his hips and he heard her swear. She didn't say *Hell and Tommy* either. He relaxed his hold on Remy to compensate for Rina's weight, not wanting to pull her off her feet.

She moved smoothly: in sync with Blake, in sync with him. Her skirt parachuted in the wind, tangled at his legs, tugged against his pants. Goose-flesh marked the deep square of pale skin between the silky pink straps that crossed each shoulder.

'Aren't you cold?' Seth asked the back of her head.

Remy peeked at him, all clear grey eyes under a flying fringe. 'F-freezing.'

He wasn't sure if she shivered, had a speech impediment, or if she'd been about to drop 'fucking' in front of 'freezing' before she'd thought better of it. He wasn't sure anyone who said *Hell and Tommy* would say *fuck.*

'There's the start line,' Blake said, drawing his attention.

***

Remy glanced sideways. Seth Lasrey's long fingers curved gently around her waist. There were no rings on those fingers, just a silver watch on a wrist covered with dark hairs. A diver's watch, she thought. At least he could keep time if they got drowned in the storm.

You could have knocked Remy over with something far less robust than this wind when Seth volunteered to be in the plank-walk team. The two brothers looked similar: olive skin from their Mediterranean heritage, tall, well built, and each had eyes dark as midnight. Apart from that, they were chalk and cheese. Blake was all sunshine. Seth was the cloud.

The CEO hadn't been around the place much since Remy started work at Lasrey Estate, but she'd had enough time to know that when Seth was in the building, the atmosphere was different. Everything moved on fast-forward: cellarhands, who might have ambled the previous day to switch on a pump or hook up a hose, suddenly got about their business with new energy.

Seth brought that intensity. The only thing Blake got intense about was having fun.

Blake lined them up with six other plank-race teams at the start of a fifty-metre grass expanse, bisected by a long barrier of rectangular bales of hay.

'Hey, Blake? What are we supposed to do about those bales? Go over? Go round?' Remy called against the wind.

'We'll worry about that when we get there,' Blake said.

'That's my brother for you,' Seth muttered behind her.

Her laughter escaped before she could rein it in. Seth laughed too, and Remy thought that she hadn't had this much fun in months. Not since she'd cut her viticulture degree short six months ago and moved home to get a job and help her mother. There hadn't been a lot to laugh about.

The starter fired his gun and Blake shouted: 'Left foot. Left!' It took them precious seconds to gain any momentum.

'Left foot, Rina!' Blake yelled.

'I'm try-*ing*,' Rina yelled back.

Remy stole a look left, they were half a plank from the lead; and to the right there wasn't a soul beside them. They had almost reached the hay bales when the storm tore the park apart.

Thick raindrops of ice-cold water slapped Remy's face, borne by a wind gust that overturned plastic chairs and tumbled tables across the grass. All around, the plank race spluttered and died. Later, Remy remembered it like an old-time war movie, with the director shooting in slow motion as soldiers fell on every side. Only in this movie there was no wash of red blood and the roar was the wind, not a machine gun spraying bullets.

The crowd flinched as the storm hit. Then everyone broke and ran for the safety of the marquee, jamming hard against those at the entrance who were watching and wouldn't budge.

Remy was drenched in seconds, cotton skirt tangling at her legs; hair plastered across her face. She could hardly see a thing.

In front of her, Blake slipped. He slipped again and there was a half-second where Remy was left holding his t-shirt as it wrenched free of his shorts. Her feet stuck fast in the bands on the plank and she swayed, hands outstretched. Then she let go of Blake's shirt and he hit the grass on hands and knees, pushing off, almost colliding with Rina. The pair lurched for a copse of gum trees on a small rise.

'Come on,' a male voice urged. Seth stood a few metres away facing the trees, hunched against the wind with his torso half-twisted toward her.

'I can't,' she said, and she laughed.

'What?'

He averted his face to keep the water out of his eyes and she thought he must think her mad because she couldn't stop laughing. 'My foot's stuck.'

Her ankle had pushed straight through the elastic binding. Short of sitting and pulling her foot free, she was trapped.

Seth swore in the direction of her toes, but started back against the wind.

'Leave me. Save yourself.' Remy swiped the back of her hand over her eyes.

'Goose,' Seth said. 'Think what it would do for staff morale if I left you behind.'

She stopped laughing because he hadn't been acting like the boss for the last five minutes but the comment about staff morale reminded her of who he was. She was suddenly terribly conscious of the clinging pink dress and her drowned-rat hair, and wasn't so sure being stuck in a rainstorm with her CEO was that funny after all. Then the first hailstone scratched a trail of blood from her arm.

'Shit. Hold on.' Seth reached her, wrapped himself around her, and stood with his body sheltering her from the storm's full force. Remy ducked her head into the depth of his chest and concentrated on not being scared, and on making herself a tiny target.

Two things happened. For the first time in a very long time, she felt safe. Someone else was taking responsibility *for her.* Someone else was being strong. She'd been the protector for so long she'd forgotten what it was like to be looked after. Then gradually, as wet skin and cold clothes met and merged, warmth flickered along all those points where their bodies touched.

Remy had time to think: *ooh, nice.*

As quick as it hit, the hail lessened and Remy risked a peek over Seth's shoulder. The group of plank walkers who had reached the trees made a second break for the marquee. Blake led the way.

'Ready to run for it?' Seth asked.

Not quite. Remy closed her eyes and pretended she hadn't heard.

***

Seth had forgotten how fast Margaret River spring storms started and stopped. It was raining still, but the hailstones petered out almost before they'd begun.

'Ready to run for it?' He asked.

There was a moment where he thought she'd snuggled even closer; and almost imperceptibly, Seth's arms tightened. She was tall, this girl, even without those crazy silver heels. The crown of her head fit perfectly into the space beneath his chin.

The rain lessened. It was time to move. Damned if he found that he didn't want to step away.

'I can't run till I get my foot out of this thing,' Remy said.

Her words whispered across his throat and the tickle of her breath stung him into action. Seth knelt to check the plank, the elastic, and Remy's lovely ankle.

'Hold on to me.' He needed two hands to get her free: one to tug at the elastic and the other to hold the plank. Remy balanced on one leg and took a death grip on his shoulder.

After a moment of careful consideration and gentle manoeuvring, he popped her ankle free.

A red welt circled the front of her left foot. He traced the crescent with his finger, inexplicably angry with the universe for causing her hurt, and flinched when he felt her touch his ear.

'You're bleeding, Mr Lasrey.'

'It's Seth.' He reached up to his ear, brushing her hand on the way. His fingers came back bloody.

Gaining his feet, he stared at the bedraggled woman beside him. A smattering of freckles dusted her nose. She had a wide mouth, full lips that the rain had left disturbingly moist, and he would bet next years' vintage that when she smiled—which she wasn't doing now—the smile would be crooked. Right now, her grey eyes looked very, very, serious. Like a scientist one DNA-strand short of a career-defining moment.

She was stunning. She was too damn young. She was his employee, and he didn't know what kind of relationship she had with his brother.

That put her off limits for so many reasons.

'You've cut your ear.' She started patting at her sides like a mother looking for a tissue to wipe her child's skinned knee.

'Forget about my ear,' Seth said, more severely than her kindness warranted, but she caused him aches in very different places and she was worried about his ear? 'Stay here, Remy. I'll be back when I've got your things. I'm taking you home.'

I'm taking you home before every man in this park gets a look at you and volunteers to play taxi. My brother included.

Chapter 2

When Seth returned with her shoes, his shoes, and a big padded jacket over his arm, she'd gathered her wits enough to tell him she'd come to the festival with Blake: freezing or not, she couldn't just *leave.*

'Blake's in no condition to drive. I told him I'd take you home.' He said it like that ended it.

Remy, however, had no intention of letting him see where she lived. 'It's too far out of your way. I'll call a taxi.'

'In the time it takes you to call a taxi, wait for it and then drive to Margaret River, I'll have you home. Look at you, you're shivering.' He touched her arm and there was something tentative about it, like he thought she might bite, or run. 'Here, put this on.' He gave her his jacket.

She gave it back. 'I'll ruin it. I'm soaked through.'

'It's only water. It'll dry.' He draped it over her shoulders and gave her a little push in the direction of the car park.

'You really don't need to do this, you know.'

'Remy, I'm not leaving you here. Do you think you could move it along? This storm isn't finished. Look at that sky.'

He had a point. Something ominous was brewing in those clouds. 'Okay. Look. Thanks. I appreciate it.'

He gave her the shoes to carry and kept walking. 'Good. Now get in.'

His car was black, low to the ground, and smelled expensive. She hesitated and he got impatient all over again: 'It's only water, Remy. Get in. Don't worry about the seat.'

'But it's such a nice seat.'

When he turned the ignition, classical music filled the car. He turned the music off.

The car was a Nissan, like her mother's. That's where the similarity ended. This car was so smooth on the road after her mother's clunky Dual Cab, even with all the blustering wind she had to keep leaning across the seat to check whether he was speeding. He wasn't.

He put the heater on, and between that and his jacket she stopped shivering. After that, she noticed little things: like the scent of his jacket and how the inner lining felt so silky on her skin, the vibration of the car on the road, the confident way he drove.

'So,' Seth said, turning the heater off.

'So, what?'

'So, I'm curious about what's going on between you and my brother. So, I'm wondering if you're going to tell me your address any time before we get to Augusta.'

'Well ... I live up past the old hospital. If you drop me at the hospital, I can walk the rest of the way.'

'And you and Blake?'

She didn't answer and his left hand tapped the steering wheel, just once, like it had done something bad.

'Blake is a good friend. Most of the kids I went to school with have all moved away from Margaret River so it's been good to find a mate here. We hang out at the beach. I mind Occhilupo. It's nothing more than that. I know the company's rules, Mr Lasrey.'

'Call me Seth,' he said again. Then his dark eyes flashed a question: 'Who is Occhilupo?'

'Blake's puppy. Blake doesn't like leaving him behind while he surfs, so I puppy-sit.'

'Puppy-sit,' he snorted, more to himself than to her. 'Why does Blake buy a puppy if he's planning to join the Pro Tour?'

'I thought that was a secret.'

Seth said: 'He must have mentioned something. My mother knows about it. So tell me, what do you think about it?'

'The puppy or the surfing?'

'The surfing.'

Remy thought it through. She didn't want to tell tales out of school but she did think it was important Blake's family knew how serious he was about his surfing. 'I think he should do what he wants. He said it's always been a dream. What about you? What do you think about it?'

'It's a pipedream.' His voice was flat.

'I've seen him in the surf, he's really good—'

'That's not enough. Do you have any idea how many *good* surfers there are in Margaret River?'

Remy held her ground. 'I do, and I think you're underestimating him.'

'He's too old.'

'Twenty-two is *not* old. I'm twenty-three.'

Seth laughed. It was short and sharp and not particularly pleasant. 'Most of the guys, if they're going to get a start on the tour, they're in their teens.'

Remy couldn't answer that.

She liked going to the beach with Blake, but once he joined the line-up she couldn't tell him from the other surfers in the water. She liked watching the surfers ride the waves but she could only handle so much of that before she lost interest. That was when it was nice to have Occhy to take for a walk.

After a time, Seth changed the subject. 'Do you know who Occhilupo is?'

'Of course.' She did know, *now*. 'Mark Occhilupo was Blake's idol.'

'He had so many posters of Occhy in his bedroom when he was a kid.' He smiled and Remy decided it made his face so much nicer. 'Did you know who he was, or did Blake have to tell you?'

'I knew,' she said indignantly.

Seth eyed her across the car. 'Liar.' Then his gaze returned to the road.

They were inside the town boundaries now and he'd slowed crossing the bridge. It was Saturday afternoon and town was busy with tourists, like always. Judging by the puddles over the road and the height of the river, the storm had hit hard here too.

Seth stopped on the main road and waited for oncoming traffic before he could turn up Tunbridge Street. 'Where did you say you live?'

I didn't. 'Just drop me at the Old Hospital. I'll walk from there.' The houses opposite the Old Hospital were actually quite quaint.

'I am not dropping you at the Old Hospital. It's still miserable out there. Just give me directions.'

'It's fine. I like the walk.'

'Barefoot? Or would you put those shoes back on for the hike?'

'Oh, fine.' *Hell and Tommy.* 'If you turn right past the hospital, then first left. I live up there. There's a big hedge out the front.'

'That wasn't so hard now, was it?'

Actually, it was excruciating. The houses on her street weren't any kind of quaint and her place was the worst of the lot. It was right at the end of the cul-de-sac and it might as well have had a sign out the front that said: renovate or detonate, or just plain kill me now.

'Here?' Seth said, slowing as Remy pointed to the overgrown photinia hedge.

Next door's blue heeler barrelled out to the adjoining fence, barking at Seth's car. A soccer ball bounced after him.

Remy started to shrug out of Seth's jacket, but he said, 'Keep it till you're inside. You can bring it to the winery on Monday.'

'It's a long weekend.'

'Then Tuesday.'

'Are you sure?' What if she snagged it on the doorway? What if there was a break-in? That jacket would be the most expensive item in her house.

'I'm sure. I have to get back to the festival to present a trophy, so if you don't mind...'

'Oh, I'm so sorry. Why didn't you say?' Remy scrambled out of the passenger seat, clutching the jacket around her throat, clutching her shoes as the wind tried to spirit them away. 'Thanks for the lift, I really appreciate it. I'll look after the jacket, I promise.'

'See you when I'm looking at you,' Seth said.

Remy watched his car turn in the cul-de-sac and speed back down the hill. She watched till it turned the corner, trying to snap her brain away from the scent and warmth of Seth's car, into the reality of misty-grey slush and puddles.

Next door, her neighbour screamed at the two boys who'd chased after the soccer ball and the dog. 'You kids! Get the hell *out* of the rain.'

They were ten and twelve, those kids. The youngest on the verge of turning sullen, the eldest: already there. She was sure they'd kicked their ball after the blue heeler so they could get an eyeful of Seth's car. Cars like that never turned up this street.

The not-quite-sullen kid waved as Remy snuck between the fence and the Dual Cab. The other kid ignored her. The dog growled.

***

Seth drove north with the window open and Tchaikovsky loud in the speakers. The icy air cleared his head. The music filled it. Clear or fill—he didn't care. What he needed to do was keep Remy out.

Every time she'd breathed in, right there on the seat beside him, he could have sworn the air in the car moved. Like she was the moon, and he'd been sucked into her gravitational pull.

Seth scrubbed a hand through his hair. Maybe he needed that holiday more than he'd thought, or maybe he had the worst case of jetlag in living history. An hour with this girl and she'd seriously messed with his head.

He thought about what she'd said: about Blake, about the puppy. Then he thought about *how* she'd said it. She had a wonderful voice: slow, soft, considered.

Seth gave up on the icy air—all it was doing was freezing his nuts—and buzzed up the window.

He needed to talk to Blake, see where his brother's head was at, but he believed Remy when she said there was nothing going on between them. She was a good kid with a kind heart, he was sure of it. Nothing trained a man to judge character like running his own business.

Yeah. And if I keep calling her 'kid' long enough I might even believe it.

Thank God he'd had a jacket to throw over that 'kid' or he might have crashed his damn car trying not to stare at the way her nipples fought the fabric of that pink dress.

Seth slowed near the park. The crowd had thinned and it wasn't hard to find a slot for the GTR near the marquee. All he had to do now was get in, present his father's trophy and get out.

***

'You're home early,' her mother said, as Remy shucked Seth's jacket from her shoulders and draped it over a kitchen chair, fussing at the sleeves to stop them creasing. 'You're just in time for the second half. Eagles are up.'

Lexie Hanley had a plate of sliced apple and cheddar cheese on her lap. A glass of cheap and cheerful white wine balanced against her thigh. In the pot-belly stove, the fire glowed low and the room was cosy enough that Remy didn't miss the jacket's warmth. Losing the silky texture and the divine Seth smell was a different matter.

'So, how did it go? Did you get hit by that hailstorm? I thought our roof was going to blow off for sure. I couldn't hear the game it was so loud.' An advert came on and she tore her eyes away from the television. 'Oh my goodness, love! What happened?'

Remy waved her soggy, grass-stained shoes at her mother. 'We got caught in the storm. Go on, you can say I told you so, I know you want to. You didn't want me to go to the festival with Blake.'

'I told you so.'

Remy stuck her tongue out and Lexie laughed. 'Get changed, love.'

Once the dress was in the washing basket and she'd brushed the grass off her shoes, Remy made herself a hot chocolate. Chocolate appealed to her more than sauvignon blanc.

'Did you have a good time?' Lexie asked, turning the volume lower. 'It's such a long time since you went out and did something for yourself. You've been working so hard.'

'So have you, Mum. Hopefully after a year or two of this, we'll have paid Doug Mulvraney back. It won't be like this forever.' *I won't have to work two jobs forever.*

Remy put a cushion over the hole in the worst side of the orange couch and sat next to her mother, tucking her feet beneath her. She'd put a pair of thick socks on because her feet refused to feel warm.

'Seth Lasrey was at the festival. He gave me a lift home,' she said.

Lexie's eyes narrowed. 'I thought you went with Blake?'

'I did. He had a few too many drinks and we got caught in the storm because my foot got stuck when I was trying to do the plank walk'—she didn't have to look at her mother to know her eyes were goggling—'and Seth was kind of ... there, and he just offered to bring me home.'

Lexie scowled at the jacket draped on her kitchen chair. 'So I guess that's his?'

'He lent it to me. I got soaked.'

'Please tell me it's not Armani?'

'I think it might be.'

Lexie let out a low whistle. 'Make sure we lock the doors tonight.'

'Like a locked door would keep anyone out of this place. They can just climb through any window.'

'That reminds me, love,' Lexie said. 'The property manager rang this afternoon about the flyscreen—'

'She rang on a Saturday?' The property manager hadn't returned her calls all week. It was hard to imagine her ringing on the weekend.

'She apologised for not getting back to you. She said the landlord has been interstate and she hasn't been able to get a hold of him. She said that he'd authorised her to get a handyman around here on Monday afternoon and she asked me to remind you not to try fixing it yourself.'

'At least the job gets done if I do it.'

'I know, love. But last time you almost fell off the roof when the gutter broke, remember?'

'I remember. If they hadn't taken so long to get someone around here, I never would have had to get up there in the first place.'

Lexie took another sip of her drink. The final quarter was about to start. Remy had half an eye on the muscled men in short shorts but it wasn't the footballer's bodies that slid through instant replays in her head.

Hell and Tommy. Remy shivered as her mind ran away with her ... until she pulled herself up short.

He's the boss, Rem. Fantasy was all it could ever be.

She needed this job. Lasrey Estate paid the bills and kept food on the table and fuel in the fire. Any kind of affair with her boss was a one-way track to a termination letter.

When her father died, he'd left gambling debts: dogs, horses, even money he'd borrowed from Mulvraney to speculate on a hot stockmarket tip or three. All their married life, Lexie said, Wayne Hanley had been a sucker for a get-rich-quick scheme. Sharks like Mulvraney preyed on men like Wayne. Remy and her mother had found out the hard way, those debts didn't stop at the grave.

Chapter 3

Seth woke late Sunday morning and in the time it took him to work out the hum on the roof was rain, his thoughts turned to Remy—

He swung his feet out of bed, pulled on trackpants and a shirt, made coffee and toast, hands flying. Turned on the radio, sang along, did anything to keep his mind off—

He slurped his coffee, spluttered as it burned his tongue.

Seth drank the brew staring over the vines, standing on the blackbutt flooring in the front room of the log cabin that was as much a home as he had anywhere in the world. This time of year the bright green growth spiked up from the trellis like a punk's haircut.

The cabin had been built for his mother's parents, so Joe had somewhere to get Grandma and Grandpa Hindle out of his way. When Ailsa's parents hadn't been using it they let it to friends. When he and Blake were young there'd always been people here. Seth's father built the cottage on the prettiest spot on the farm. Up on a small hill, flanked by jarrah and marri trees. The front room and deck overlooked the vines and the small blue dam where they'd fished for marron when they were kids. Back then the dam had a canoe in it that leaked. He and Blake were forever bailing it out. The canoe hadn't been there for years.

In the skies to the west, remnants of yesterday's storms rolled through. They lacked the intensity of Saturday. The rain fell straight, melting on the roof rather than hurling against it.

He wondered how Blake's head was this morning, grinned as he bit into another slice of toast. Little brother was probably out in the water. Blake always reckoned nothing cured a hangover faster than a surf. Except sex.

Was Remy with Blake?

Was she running on some lonely wild beach, chasing Blake's puppy along the shore?

The vision seared his brain before he could block it. Remy's golden spray of hair blowing in the salt breeze; her feet digging into the heavy sand, gorgeous legs working overtime.

Not good. He banged the empty coffee cup on his hip.

Seth couldn't remember a time when the most important thing in his life wasn't work: the next deal, the next acquisition, the next export push. That had changed in less than twenty-four hours and his world felt off-kilter as a result, but brighter. Like Tinkerbell had sprinkled him in fairy dust and he couldn't shake off the glitter.

For the first time in a long time, he wanted to empty his suitcase and hang the stuff in the cabin in the big wardrobes he never used. He wanted to know if his fishing gear was still in the shed out the back and whether the boat would start if he kicked the engine over, whether there was bait buried in the bottom of the big chest freezer.

He wondered if Remy liked fishing.

Seth packed his breakfast cutlery into the dishwasher, threw a week's worth of jocks and socks in the washing machine and contemplated the day ahead. His head felt thick, whether from lack of sleep or too much of it, he wasn't sure.

How did Remy spend her Sundays? Her work mobile number would be in the staff list on his computer. He could ring her. Find out.

Or not.

It went on like that for a while. He weighed the pros for seeing her again outside of work (of which there were few) stacking up against the cons for not calling her (of which there were many). They included the mountain of emails and paperwork he had to get through before he left for Bordeaux on Tuesday.

The pros were by far the more tempting.

Then a vehicle on the driveway into the cabin snagged his attention.

It was Blake and judging from the surfboards on the roof-racks, he'd already been for a surf. He'd be hanging out for a coffee. Pity the cabin pantry wasn't stocked or Seth could cook him bacon and eggs. For now, toast was the best he could do.

***

Seth filled ten minutes or so answering Blake's questions about his latest overseas trip and he was itching to get to the harder stuff. *Remy.* He knew how she felt about Blake. Now he wanted to know how Blake felt about her. If Blake intended to make a play for Remy, Seth would step back, no questions asked.

Blake had seen her first. It was the honourable thing to do.

'So, big day yesterday?' Seth said, when they each had a coffee cup in their hands and sat sprawled in the two cane chairs in the front room.

'Too big.' Blake downed the last of his coffee in a gulp and let out a deep groan. 'I needed that.'

'Things kicked on after I left?'

'Kicked like a steel-capped mule.' Blake made a face. 'A few of us ended up back at my place. Busted out a bottle of Jimmy Beam about two o'clock.'

'Glad I went home.' Seth was glad he'd taken Remy home, too. She didn't need to get caught up in Blake's circle. Those boys partied hard. 'So, I got a few questions for you, bro. Are you up for 'em?'

'Shit.' Blake winced. 'What did I do now?'

'Mum and Rina cornered me yesterday at the festival, about you and Remy Hanley.' Seth tried her name on his tongue and found he liked it.

'Me and Remy?' Blake scrubbed his salty mess of hair. Grains of sand somersaulted to his shoulders then the floor.

'Yeah.' Seth held his breath, waiting for Blake's answer.

'Sure I kind of sussed her out the first few weeks, when she started working for us. What guy wouldn't? She's gorgeous.'

He had to stop himself nodding agreement. He waited. Waited some more. Blake would fill the silence eventually. He always did.

'But you know? I never got the sense she was interested not really, and shit, man—' Blake crossed his opposite foot and rested it on his knee, knocking more grains of sand that had stuck to his foot. 'I mean, you wrote that damn workplace policy for all the staff. No bonking in the barrel hall, remember? No personal relationships in the workplace. Remy needs her job. I don't want to make that hard for her. She's had a rough enough trot as it is.'

'What sort of rough trot?' It annoyed him that Blake knew Remy best. It annoyed him that Blake knew her at all. It shouldn't, but it did.

That annoyed him too.

'Her old man died at the start of the year. Now there's a bloke that you wouldn't piss on if he was on fire.'

'Why?'

'He drank everything he ever earned, and pretty much everything Remy's mother ever earned. He wrote himself off the night he crashed his car. Remy says they're just lucky he didn't take anyone else with him. She cut her last year of viticulture at university short to come home when he died.'

The conversation lapsed while Seth thought that through, and then he remembered his original thread: 'So there's nothing going on between you and her? When you take off surfing full-time next year, you won't be zipping her in your board bag or anything?'

'She wouldn't come with me. I just told you she needs her job. She's serious about her career.' Blake squinted across the space: 'And who told you about the surf tour anyway?'

'Ailsa,' Seth conceded absently, as the knowledge Blake and Remy weren't a *thing* pulsed through him. 'But you've talked about it before. No surprises there.'

'So what do you reckon my chances are?'

Seth shrugged. 'You'll have to get your shit together. Quit partying.'

'That's easy if I've got something to work for.' Blake's eyebrows quirked. 'What? You don't think I can do it?'

'On your best day you can mix it with anyone. But day in, day out? Big surf, crap surf? Whether you're in the zone, or not? That's another thing. You've never stuck at anything long enough to find out how good you could be.'

Blake launched into the same theme Seth had heard for years. How this time he was serious. How this time he was sure.

Seth tuned out. His brother cycled through life. Every six months or so he'd decide to knuckle down at something, whether that was surfing or work or study, then next time they spoke it would be travelling through Europe that was the hot idea, or buying a motorbike and riding around Australia. Blake was a spinning top. You never knew what he'd turn to next.

Seth crossed his right ankle over his left leg and the two men sat there for a while, mirror images, thinking. Although Seth guessed they were thinking very different things.

'Ailsa and Rina say Remy's only after one thing, and it's not your body,' he said.

'She's not after money,' Blake snorted. 'Not Rem.'

Rem. The familiar way Blake shortened her name annoyed Seth too.

Blake said: 'I can't even buy her a cup of coffee without her getting all huffy. I took her fishing to Augusta in your boat a few weeks back and she wanted to pitch in for the petrol.'

'You took my boat to Augusta?' What Seth really wanted to say, so hard it hurt his chest was: *you took her fucking fishing?*

'Hey, it's been sitting in the shed most the year doing nothing. I thought I was doing you a favour.'

Seth forced himself to relax. He couldn't shake the feeling this was something else his brother got to do with Remy first. 'Did you catch anything?'

'Half a dozen whiting, some crabs. It was fun. She baits her own hooks. Casts like a pro. She guts her own fish. She bought me a beer at the Augusta pub after and then she beat me at pool and won her fuel money back. She likes dogs. Powderfinger is her favourite band. She never orders pineapple on pizza but she loves anchovies and extra chilli.' Blake rose from the cane chair, stretching his back. 'Remy's a mate. I like her a lot. Don't think I don't know when you're on a fishing expedition of your own, big brother. I may look like a surfer dumb-arse, but I'm not stupid.'

'I never said you're stupid. Dumb-arse, on the other hand—'

Blake wasn't finished. 'Mum never thinks any girl we meet is good enough, going way back since school. You know that. And if Rina saw what I saw yesterday at the park, she'd be filthy about it too.'

'What the hell?' Seth's foot slipped from where it had been propped against his knee and met the timber floor with a thump.

Blake put his cup on the kitchen countertop. 'Rina has been trying to work out where her toothbrush could fit in your bathroom from the day you hired her. I might have been pissed yesterday, but that doesn't mean I missed your superhero act with Remy. Neither did Rina. Count on that.'

'Bullshit,' Seth said.

'Bullshit nothing,' Blake declared. 'You and Mum think the sun shines out of Rina's pointy little arse. You don't see what I see, or what the rest of the staff put up with. She takes credit for ideas that aren't hers. You guys promoted her into the executive team—against my vote by the way—and now she uses that to intimidate people. Staff are worried if they do anything to piss Rina off, they'll get the sack. Everyone knows she sucks up to you and Mother like you wouldn't believe—'

Frustration brought Seth to his feet. 'Don't chime in now after swanning around in logistics for a few years pretending to work. You and Rina don't see eye to eye because you are polar-fucking-opposites. You take a sickie if you stub your big toe. Rina'd have to be dying before she didn't show up for work.'

'How many female winery staff has Rina employed since she's been with us?' Blake said, his frustration matching Seth's, voice rising.

'Jesus, I don't know, Blake. Not many, but what the heck? It's a male-dominated industry.'

'She hires men because she doesn't want any women working around you on the off chance one of them catches your eye. If hiring Remy had been Rina's decision, Rem wouldn't be here.'

'Rina is the reason I've been able to spend the time growing the brand this last few years. I don't have to worry about the day-to-day winemaking program anymore because she handles it. She's damn good at her job—'

'Whatever, dude. Saint Rina lives. At least I've said my piece,' Blake put his hands up in mock resignation, but clearly he was ready to go. As he walked out the door he looked back and added, 'For what it's worth, I think you and Remy would be good together. You need someone who can lighten you up a bit, make you laugh. Thanks for the coffee.'

'You think I don't laugh enough now?'

'Seth ... come on, man. It's me here. You don't laugh at all.' And he was gone, leaping down the front steps to his car.

Seth shut the door behind him.

It was fine for his brother to take life as a big fuck-off rainbow. Blake didn't have a multimillion-dollar wine business to build. He didn't have twenty staff dependent on him making good decisions about that company's future growth.

So he didn't laugh enough, hey?

In the end, it made the decision about what to do with his Sunday easy. Seth grabbed his jacket from the hook beside the front door. A minute later he dug a picnic rug out of the linen closet in the cabin's spare room, and snatched up his wallet and keys.

***

Remy was in the sunroom, contemplating the broken flyscreen and the flies caught between the wire and the glass, when she heard the dog bark next door. Then one of the kids shouted, 'Hey, Leo, that car's back again. The black one.'

'The black one? Sick!'

Dashing through the kitchen, she peered out the front window and was in time to see Seth's GTR nose behind the hedge. Seeing it was enough to start the rapid thud in her chest. Thank heavens for the dog and those boys. Seth's car was so quiet she'd never have known it was there.

His car door slammed.

Hell and Tommy. He's coming in.

Remy ran to the kitchen and grabbed a grey plastic shopping bag. Then she ran to get the jacket from the back of the chair and folded it, laying it carefully inside the bag. She contemplated the resilience of the package for a full two seconds then ran back to the kitchen, grabbed a second bag in which to wedge the first, and fled for the front door. That put her on the porch clutching the precious bundle before Seth reached the steps.

'Hi,' she said, knees like jelly, heart like a hammer, hoping with every breath that Seth wouldn't look too closely at the house or at her. She had no make-up, no jewellery. She must look as much of a wreck as the house.

'Hey.'

They spent a mini-age just looking at each other before he smiled. Not a proper smile, more a tilt of his lip and a light in his eyes, but it was sexy as all hell and it made her smile too.

'Did you need your jacket early?' she asked him, holding out the package. She couldn't think of any other reason why he'd come here.

Seth took the jacket, but said: 'No. Not really. I came to see if you'd like to take a drive with me.'

'A drive?'

'Yeah. I thought maybe a picnic.'

'A picnic?' What did that mean exactly?

'Picnic.' He said it nice and slow, like he was teaching math to the dog next door. 'We take a rug and some food and a picnic basket. Except all I have is a cardboard box. I've been to the markets at the Old Hospital. I have crackers and brie, olives and a smoked salmon dip, and I bought a container of dolmades.' He stopped. 'Do you know dolmades?'

'Of course. I can tell you the difference between sushi and sashimi too.' The minute she said it, she kicked herself for showing off. Pride would be her ruin—wasn't that what her mother said? Sushi was raw fish, and sashimi was a style of raw fish. Wasn't it? Something like that?

It didn't matter anyway, because he never asked her to substantiate her raw fish know-how.

Remy stared at her feet. They were bare, which was the norm when she was at home. She was wearing a white t-shirt, because it was warm and she'd been about to start work. Making phone sex calls for White Knights was water off a duck's back after two and a half years, but that didn't mean the sexy storytelling didn't get her temperature up. She'd paired the t-shirt with three-quarter denim jeans that had butterflies stitched on one thigh.

She shouldn't go on a picnic with Seth, she had work to do. They needed the money and White Knights paid well. But she sure as heck didn't want to stand here on this awful rickety porch, looking at weeds in the driveway while the boys next door ogled his car ... she had to get him out of here.

Remy cleared her throat. 'It won't get us in trouble? I mean ... I signed the memo. You know ... the workplace relationships one.'

'Blake calls it the *no bonking in the barrel hall* policy.' He was teasing, and it was gentle, but even then she could feel the heat creep up her cheeks. 'We're not in the office now, and it's just a picnic. Don't worry about the memo, okay?'

Remy glanced down at her clothes. 'Am I okay like this?'

'You're fine.'

'You're a liar.'

The boys from next door tired of ogling Seth's car and Remy saw them file back inside. The dog sat on their porch, nose on his paws.

'Can I bring anything?' she said, wracking her brains for what was in her fridge. *Coles brand cheddar, anyone?*

'I've got it covered.'

'What about shoes?'

He joined her in checking out her feet. 'Have you got any walking shoes?'

She nodded. There were joggers on the porch. She left them outside so she wouldn't track sand through the house. Remy slipped them on her feet, not bothering with socks.

'Do you need to leave a note?'

'My mum's working. She won't be back till late.'

'She works Sunday?'

'Yeah,' Remy said. *Stacking supermarket shelves pays time and a half on a Sunday.*

He waited for her to elaborate and when she didn't, he said: 'Okay then. Let's go.'

***

'What does your mother do?' he asked, once she was buckled in the car and they were driving. He'd thrown the plastic bag with the jacket into the back seat. *Thrown it.* Remy was mortified.

'She trained as a nurse. She used to work at the Margaret River Hospital before she had me.'

'She doesn't do that now?'

'She lost her confidence. She thought hospital technology had passed her by.'

He drove for a while and Remy tried to think of something that might change the subject from her mother's work, and wasn't about *his* work.

She settled for: 'Have you seen Blake today?'

He nodded.

'How's his head?'

'Not as bad as it should have been.'

'I bet he'd been for a surf.'

'He had. Hey, Remy?'

'Yes?'

'How about we don't talk about my brother.'

Her gaze leapt to his face. His hands on the wheel were relaxed but there was something tight about his jaw. He asked: 'Why don't you want to tell me what your mother does?'

Remy blew out a noisy breath. 'She works in the supermarket. She stacks shelves. Night shift.' Her tone added an inaudible, *so there.*

'What was the big deal about telling me that?'

She shrugged. 'There's no big deal.' *We just don't broadcast it to everyone. I don't tell everyone I spin phone sex fantasies for a second job, either.*

Seth turned right onto Caves Road and soon after, turned left into the driveway that led to one of the area's boutique guesthouses. The gravel road split into three, one of which turned hard left and uphill into the accommodation. The other two forked off the path ahead. Seth chose the left fork and started up the hill. Soon they were driving in an avenue of white-trunked Tasmanian blue gums. At the crest of the hill the road narrowed, before it curled down the other side.

'We should have brought my ute,' Remy said, as the GTR hit a pothole and muddy water flew.

The track got narrower and more rutted, before it finished at a gate where a sign said private property.

There was a small flat area of grass by the track and Seth parked. They both got out of the car.

They were under tall, thick peppermint trees that flanked a meandering stream. The gurgle of the water and the whistle of birds were all she could hear. Everything smelled like rain.

'It's pretty.'

'That's the Ellen Brook.'

'Is it private property?'

'That place there is,' he indicated the gate. 'Where we're going, it's all National Park.'

He fished his picnic box out of the back of the car and put the contents in a backpack that he slung over his shoulders. 'Come on, we go this way.'

He nodded toward a narrow bridge that crossed the stream and opened into a paddock beyond.

***

Seth glanced at Remy. Most of the time her gaze was on the bush by the track as she walked easily through the thick yellowish sand, even though they tramped steadily uphill. Sometimes he'd catch her taking a deep breath in, like she was sifting all the sights and scents of the bush through her lungs, and she'd smile as she'd breathe out.

'Look out, Seth.'

She'd said that a couple of times now, because he'd been watching her and not where he was going and he'd been about to trample some little plant she thought precious. 'You get any closer you'll step on that cowslip.'

She pointed out a dainty yellow flower. An orchid, she told him, a triple-header. She said it with something close to reverence.

He felt like he could talk to her for a year and there'd still be more to learn. She intrigued him and he didn't know why. So what if she was easy to look at? So what if she glided at his side, natural as the stream slipping beside them.

He'd known plenty of stunning women with a walk that could stop traffic. Those women didn't have him contemplating making a call to Rina to ask if she would go to Bordeaux this week in his place.

Seth didn't believe in fairytales. The only thing he'd ever loved at first sight was a Monaro and when he'd loved that car, he'd been seventeen.

'There's a double spider orchid.' She'd stopped a few steps behind him with her finger on the stalk to display it. He felt almost guilty for missing it.

'Yeah. It's beautiful.' *So are you.*

'You didn't even look at it,' she admonished him. 'It's so fleeting, wildflower season down here. You can miss it by a week. We're so lucky to see this.'

He stepped over a log that had crashed on the path during last year's controlled burns and held out his hand to help her.

'I'm okay. Thanks though.' Her gaze was on his face in that second before she returned her attention to the track and the bush and the flowers.

'When did you last take a girl on a bushwalk and a picnic?' She asked him.

He didn't have to think about it: 'I took a girl called Leeanne to a waterfall at Moses Rock.' He'd kissed her there, spread out on the blanket while the casserole he'd made cooked in a camp oven. He'd been damn proud of that casserole.

'Did you kiss her?'

'I did.'

'Did you like it?'

'It was okay.'

'Did she like it?'

'She let me do it again.'

Remy blushed, and found a bunch of donkey orchids to show him.

'What about you?' he said. 'Who was the last man you kissed?' *Don't say Blake.*

'I don't think I've ever kissed a man.'

That got his attention fast, but there were another couple of bushwalkers heading their way up the path. The man used a stick like a ski pole, pushing the ground as he came through the sand. The lady had her camera pointing off into the bush. They were slow walkers.

'When we get round that corner down there, there's a spot where we can get off the track and have something to eat,' Seth said.

'Sounds good to me. It's so beautiful in here. Thanks for showing me this place.'

'No problem,' he said.

'Pretty, isn't it?' the bushwalking woman said as she passed.

'Beautiful,' Seth agreed.

Remy said, 'Stunning.'

The path turned into deep shade where the trees changed from tall jarrah and marri to peppermints shot through with creepers and ferns, and the earth smelled rich and green. There were arum lilies everywhere, white heads popping up like a thousand swans. They were noxious weeds in the South West—conservationists hated them—but they were so pretty when they were like this, Remy couldn't find it in her to hate them.

Seth put his hand behind her back to guide her and Remy all but jumped out of her skin. *Hell and Tommy.*

'I didn't mean to frighten you. I was going to say, it's this way.' He led her off the track and into the bush, through a faint path in the arum lily forest.

Remy tried to still the racing hum of her heart. The small of her back felt warm where his hand had pressed. She could feel the imprint of his fingertips on her skin.

He didn't frighten her, but her body's response was kind of terrifying all the same.

She'd had crushes before. In school and in university. At uni it had been Mr Southby. He was tall and slim. He had kind eyes behind his glasses and a passion for vineyard ecology that overflowed every lecture he taught.

This was different. This was bone-jarring, stomach-clenching different and it made each breath skip from her lungs faster than the one before it, until her head and heart felt so loose parts of her might fly right off.

'It's just here,' Seth said.

Remy followed him around yet another gnarled peppermint trunk. He stepped back to let her pass, held out his hand to show her, and asked, 'What do you think?'

The Ellen Brook cut about fifteen metres beneath them, snaking to the sea. They were standing in front of three vast peppermint trees growing so close, it was hard to see which boughs belonged to which giant.

Seth pulled off the backpack, spread the blanket and sat with his back against one of the trunks.

Remy hadn't finished staring at the dell. The creek rippled where water cascaded through tangled snags and leaves. Orange and black butterflies flitted in the patches of filtered sunlight, and a dragonfly zinged forward and back. Birds sang songs Remy didn't know.

Seth snapped the lid off the dolmades and offered the plastic container up. She took one with a mumbled thanks, biting into the spiced rice mix.

'It's beautiful here. How did you find this place?' She looked for a spot to sit that wouldn't make her feel she was crowding him. He was so big, legs spread loose like that, and the blanket was so small.

'My old man knew of it.'

Remy chose another dolmades. Chased it with an olive stuffed with chilli and feta. On the second olive, she smoothed a patch of blanket and sat, shuffling backwards until the tree met her spine.

'Blake said you like fishing, and you shoot a mean game of pool.'

Remy slathered the cracker with too much brie, and chewed. 'It's not fair, you know. I don't know anyone who could tell me stuff about you at all.'

'Ask me something.'

She thought about it. 'Why don't you ever smile?'

'I smile.'

'No you don't. You hardly ever smile at all. Everyone is scared of you. When you joined that plank walk yesterday, you could have knocked all those people over with a feather.'

'I like to think I'm hard but fair. You can't get too friendly with employees in my job.'

Remy laughed. 'And you don't think this is friendly?'

'This is different. I want to get to know you better and I don't have a lot of time. I'm supposed to fly to Bordeaux on Tuesday.'

'Bordeaux,' she breathed. It sounded so far away. It made *him* sound so far away.

'It's in France,' he supplied.

'I know where *Bordeaux* is.'

'Sorry. Course you do. I keep comparing you to my brother. I'm never sure if Blake knows what day it is, let alone what country I'm talking about. His head's always somewhere else, but you,' he paused, searching for the right word. 'You seem so grounded.'

Paying off debts to a loan shark does that to a girl, she thought, but she didn't say it.

'So where do you see yourself in five years, Remy?'

Not selling phone sex as a second job while my mum's working night shift, that's for sure. Not living in a weatherboard rental with holes in the flyscreen and bills on the fridge. 'I'd like to be a senior viticulturist somewhere, I guess. I'd really like to be my own boss. Have my own vineyard.'

'Land costs a lot down here.'

'It does.' Unspoken between them was the knowledge the cost of the land would most likely kill Remy's dreams.

'What about the fishing. What's the biggest fish you ever caught?' He asked quickly, as if he regretted bringing money into their glade.

'I caught a Samson fish on a friend's boat in Geographe Bay. That was years ago. I mostly fish for herring off the beach. I'm not fussy. Fresh fish cooked in butter in a pan when they're just out of the ocean. That's pretty special.'

Remy had grabbed a cracker and was about to slap brie on the wafer-thin biscuit. Her hand shook and the cracker split. Seth caught one of the broken pieces. Reaching for Remy's hand, he added his half of the cracker to hers, making the biscuit whole. Then he took the morsel from her and held it toward her lips.

Remy leaned forward and bit the cracker. It split immediately, showering crumbs across his stomach and the blanket, and she laughed as she took it from him and put the second half in her mouth.

He let her finish chewing. He waited till she stopped laughing. He helped her wipe crumbs from his shirt and from the purple butterfly stitched on her jeans. Then he put his hand on her cheek and drew her face toward his.

As kisses went, it was very gentle, very soft, but not so quick as to be over before it started. If soft could equal thorough, that's how Seth kissed. He made every cell inside her sigh for more.

She pulled back for a moment to meet his gaze. His eyes were dark and deep and filled with more questions than she wanted to answer.

'If you're going to get me fired, you might as well make it worth my while,' she said.

Then she kissed him again.

Chapter 4

Seth rang Rina on Monday morning. It was a long weekend and she didn't need to be at the winery, but that's where she said she was when she answered her phone.

'I'll come in,' he said. 'I'm at the cabin. Five minutes.'

She had coffee ready when he got there. He drank it with her in the lab.

'You don't have to impress me anymore, Rina. This working on a long weekend...' he smiled as he said it, thinking of Remy's comment about him not smiling enough.

It was wasted because Rina had her eyes on the lab charts, not on him. 'These tests weren't going to run themselves. I know they're right if I do it.'

His smile vanished. 'Why? Isn't Stuart measuring up?' Stuart was the lab technician. If he'd been getting things wrong, Seth wanted to know.

'He misses a few things here and there. Don't worry. I've spoken with him about it. He says he'll take more care. I had some free time this morning. I'm going out for lunch later.'

Seth got straight to the point. 'I'm supposed to fly to Bordeaux tomorrow tonight for the Vinitech exhibition. I don't suppose your passport is up to date?'

Rina put the charts down hard enough to swirl dust motes from the lab bench. 'Sure, my passport is up to date. Why? Have you got space in your suitcase?'

Seth moved closer, sneaking a glance at the pH results from old habit. Nothing out of the ordinary there. 'I only got back from China on Friday night. Be nice to stay home for a while. Bordeaux would be new for you. It's an interesting place ... the old part.'

'You're asking if I want to go *instead* of you, not with you.' She turned her back to him, fiddling with her papers, making neat edges as she formed the pile. 'For a moment there I thought you were asking me to go *with* you.'

'We can't both be out of the country at the same time, Rina. Who'd run the place? Blake?' He laughed, but he couldn't help thinking about what Blake had said: that Rina liked him in more than a professional way. Could his brother be right? Was she seriously thinking an invitation to visit Bordeaux meant anything other than business? If that was the case, he'd have to say something about it. Nip it in the bud.

Rina turned, and the moment Seth saw her face he relaxed. There was no sign Rina felt anything for him at all. Not disappointment. Not hurt. Her expression was smooth.

'Blake wouldn't be the best choice you ever made, Seth. He'd give the cellar boys the afternoons off if the surf was up.' She shrugged an apology. 'Now I think about it, I'm not even sure where my passport is. It's probably buried in a box at the back of my shed. It could even still be in the cupboards at Mum's place in the Hunter Valley. Maybe next time, hey?'

'Yeah. I knew it was short notice. Dig your passport out or get a new one, Rina. The company will pay. It'd be good if you did a few of the international trips next year. You'd get a lot out of it, and retailers like to see the winemaker's face. They must be sick to death of seeing my ugly mug.'

'I'll look into it.'

Rina picked up Seth's coffee mug and her own, turned her back to him again and washed them in the laboratory sink. She took her time about it, rinsing, drying the mugs, hanging them on the branches of the lab's coffee-mug tree. A couple of times the mugs clanked, hard enough Seth thought they might chip.

'Everything else okay with you, Rina?'

'I'm fine. I always reckoned the dishwashing liquid they buy here makes everything slippery. Late night last night, that's all.' She steadied the last swinging mug and turned around with a bright smile. 'So where were we? We better catch up on the oak program if you're going to Bordeaux.'

***

For the first time since she'd met Seth Lasrey at her job interview, Rina couldn't wait for Seth to leave her alone. It was too hard trying to feign indifference while he dominated the small laboratory space, all smouldering eyes, broad shoulders and that Mediterranean combo of olive skin and black hair she found sexy as hell.

It had been so near impossible to control her reaction when she thought he'd invited her to Bordeaux, and she was mortified she'd almost let it slip, shown him how much she cared.

Somehow she masked the disappointment that burned like acid at the base of her throat. Somehow she answered his questions about toast levels and flavours and discussed how much new oak she'd need for the upcoming vintage. Whatever she said must have made sense because Seth didn't look at her like she'd grown an extra head.

That was the problem. Seth didn't really look at her at all.

She shivered, clutching the two flaps of her lab coat together at her stomach.

Seth wasn't paying attention, and he missed it. She could probably have opened the lab coat, like a flasher, and he wouldn't have raised an eyebrow.

'So I think that's about it then, Rina, thanks. If you think of anything else, put it in an email to me. I fly out Tuesday night. Hey, have a nice lunch.'

Lunch? She blinked at him blankly. 'Oh, yes, lunch today with the girls. Thank you, I will. You too. Have a good afternoon.'

When the lab door shut, Rina sat back on the counter, gripping the edge so hard her hands hurt. She sat like that for a long time, but she didn't cry.

Like everyone else on the Lasrey staff, she'd heard the stories about Seth's relationship with the French wine heiress Helene Bouchard. Ailsa made no secret of how much she'd like to see Seth marry Helene, merging the two wine companies. The French woman with the posh-sounding name didn't worry Rina. Perhaps because Seth never talked about her, and if she'd ever overheard him mention Helene's name in response to a media or business question, it was to say he and Helene were just old family friends. She'd even dared consider at night, in her dreams, that Seth was coy about Helene because really, it was Rina he loved...

Helene was far away. She wasn't in Rina's face, not like Remy.

Remy.

What wouldn't Rina give for Seth to look at her just once, with half the emotion she'd seen in his eyes when he held Remy in that rainstorm on Saturday?

Who did Seth think he was kidding? *Now* he wants to stay home for a while? He never wanted to stay home before. Usually his feet barely touched Australian soil before he was off on another trip, rustling up new business opportunities around the globe.

This wasn't about Seth spending time at home. It was about being near *her.*

It wasn't fair.

Remy Hanley had been on the scene six months ... first cuddling up to Blake and then, seeing all Blake was interested in was surfing, she'd turned her attention to Seth. Ailsa had said as much in the festival marquee: Remy didn't care which of the Lasrey boys she caught, as long as she hooked one of them.

Seth was only human, and male to boot. Rina had to save him from making any dumb decisions. It was her job to watch Seth's back at Lasrey. If she had to extend her help into Seth's personal life, so be it.

Ailsa would thank her for it, and the day would come when Seth would thank her too. Hopefully as he gazed into her eyes and told her she was the only woman he'd ever want, and the one woman in the world who made his life make sense.

She had to find a way to get rid of Remy.

With that decision reached, Rina felt better. She tidied her papers, cleaned up the lab and when she locked the door, a smile touched her face.

***

Seth hadn't intended visiting Remy again Monday—he didn't want to crowd her—but after his meeting with Rina at the winery, his thoughts drifted to Remy time and again.

In the park on Saturday it had been the physical things that fascinated him. Her legs, her walk, her laugh and, when he'd gotten close enough to look into them, her eyes.

Yesterday afternoon had shown him another side. Remy's joy in something as simple as a bushwalk and a picnic. He couldn't remember the last girl he'd spent time with who would have found more wonder in a double-headed yellow lady donkey orchid (or whatever the hell she'd called it), than in a diamond ring, or a new pair of shoes.

And then there was the kiss.

That first kiss told him much, but the second told him so much more. That Remy could be bold when she wanted to be. That she wasn't afraid to break the rules. That her lips were wide and warm and the bottom one was even softer than the top.

There wasn't much he wouldn't give just to kiss her again.

In the end, he put his laptop aside; didn't return the emails that were lining up in his inbox. Instead, he climbed into the GTR and drove south, listening to a Tchaikovsky sonata he'd heard a hundred times and finding new depth to the music. Heart on fire.

The boys and the dog from next door were kicking their soccer ball in the park as he turned into Remy's street.

Her driveway was empty. A tail of smoke wisped from the chimney but her house had the shut up look of a primary school at end of term.

He'd bought two takeaway coffees. They sat in the cup-holders on the dash and looking at them, he felt like a bit of a dick.

Hey. I was in the area, Rem. Thought you might like a coffee.

He'd come this far. He had to see if she was home. He turned in the cul-de-sac and parked on the opposite side of the street. The hedge hid Remy's house.

Skirting a murky brown puddle, Seth started up the driveway. His was so engrossed in watching the house he already wasn't paying attention to where he stepped, but the second he saw movement in the window, he forgot about his feet.

It was Remy. He knew by the way her left hand trapped a flick of blonde ponytail at the nape of her neck. It was how he'd first seen her in the park, standing with her back to him.

His foot crunched gravel. Instinctively, Seth moved to the edge of the driveway where heavy weeds masked his step. Remy's posture *felt* private and he didn't want to scare her.

As he neared the timber steps he slowed again. There were voices. No. He could hear *a* voice—Remy's voice—quite clearly. But it was different: lilting, almost singsong, as if she might be reading poetry, or rehearsing a scene from a play.

He tested his weight on the bottom step. When it didn't creak or groan he gained the next two levels and approached her front door. His knuckles were poised to knock when he heard, clear as day: *'Spread your legs. I want your tits rubbing that wall.'*

Seth's knuckles, his whole arm, might well have turned to stone.

He floundered for some context, but all he could come up with was: *what the fuck?* Who was she talking to? Was there someone else in the room? *A girl?*

That thought blew his mind for five incredibly horny seconds. Two girls, one of them Remy: nipple to nipple, skin to skin. Silk tongues. Wet kisses.

Did she like girls best? Is that what she meant yesterday when she said she'd never kissed a man?

Christ on a stick. What a waste.

He'd never got that vibe from her. She'd kissed him like she liked it and afterwards, walking back, she'd let him hold her hand.

'*Last chance, sweetheart. I won't tell you again. Stand against the wall. Face it.*'

Suddenly, Seth wasn't stone anymore. He was all flesh and blood and he had to *know what was going on in there.*

Remy's porch was tiny. The only thing between him and the window was a near-empty woodbox, a collection of old teapots in a bucket, and a mess of Blundstones and rubber boots, plus yesterday's joggers. There was a crack at the edge of the curtain. If he leaned far enough...

'*This game is called Sixty Seconds. Here's how we play...*'

Seth snuck a quick peek at the street over his shoulder. That god-ugly hedge shielded him. The neighbours—those kids and the dog—weren't home. He put his palm to the rough weatherboard cladding and inched right. The window was open, curtain moving in the breeze. Damn big tear in the flyscreen, like someone shoved a rake handle through it.

'I stand here behind you, just like this. I can touch you, wherever I like. All over, if I want to. You get to turn that eggtimer over. See it there? Turn it over for me. When it runs out, I get to feel you. If I make you wet, I'll know you want me...'

Seth dug his thumb under the overhanging lip of timber, gripped hard for support, and leaned even further right. Then he saw her. Her face and shoulder were slightly turned away.

'Turn the eggtimer over.'

It wasn't hair her hand held at her ear, it was a phone. *She's on the fucking phone!* Seth jerked away.

A girlfriend then? A girlfriend who liked to play games.

Had Remy been laughing at him yesterday the entire time she kissed him, comparing his technique? Thinking about how much she preferred smooth feminine skin to his whiskers?

She lied to him. By omission. And this was a pretty fucking big omission.

He backed away from her door, leapt lightly off the porch. Thinking: *where's your fairy dust now, Tink?*

Chapter 5

Ten minutes after five o'clock most workdays, a girl could shoot a gun through the staff car park at Lasrey Estate and not be in danger of the bullet denting a fender. It was different during vintage. In autumn, when the grapes came off the vines, Lasrey was like a beehive on a summer day. Today, the car park was empty, except for Remy's mother's steel-grey Nissan Dual Cab and the rumble of an engine as the last staff car disappeared down the drive.

Remy sneezed. Sneezed again, and tried to ignore the scratch in her throat. She'd been fighting it off all day. Spending most of yesterday afternoon talking on the phone hadn't helped, but she had to catch up on her hours at White Knights after she'd ditched her roster to spend Sunday with Seth. She had five regular clients and they knew her schedule. Monday, Wednesday, and Sundays. Those days coincided with her mother's shifts at the supermarket, when Remy had the house to herself.

Sometimes a sneaky voice in her head would say: why not take on a few more regular clients, Remy? Think of the extra money.

Always she gave that little voice a mental whack with a bloody big hammer. If she took on more clients it would blur the line. She'd feel like a phone sex worker who had a second job in viticulture, rather than a viticulture worker making some extra cash to pay her father's debts. Plus it would get much harder to keep her little sideline from her mother.

Remy threw her work bag into the passenger seat and gave up trying to smooth her hair. She wiped her palms on her khaki work pants, breathed deep twice, and headed for the cellar door.

Come see me when you finish work. Seth had texted. *I'll be in the office.*

She'd never been in Seth's office. She'd only been in the administrative centre once, when Greg Trimble had interviewed her for the job.

She pushed into 'Old Joe's tasting room, with its lingering scent of polished jarrah, wine, and visitors perfume. The dishwasher hummed beneath the sink, washing lipstick from a load of glassware that would be pristine when cellar door opened for business next morning. She was completely alone, with no idea why she felt so jumpy.

She shivered. Since the Saturday at Vintage Festival, her life had been one big shiver. Now her uniform felt at once both too tight and too hot, and her skin felt hot all over.

The pale green corridor—some quarter-shade of the Lasrey corporate colour—seemed to shrink in and she had to stop herself checking over her shoulder to make sure her boots weren't tracking mud on the carpet.

She passed the boardroom on her left. Seth's door was further up on the right. It was open and she could hear him speaking.

About then she realised she couldn't understand a word Seth said, except that his conversation sounded French and important. Then she was at the threshold, shuffling her feet like a schoolgirl. He wasn't facing her, and it gave her the chance to study him in those seconds before he knew she was there.

His hand was on his hip. The flash of the watch on his wrist caught her eye. His other hand pressed the phone to his ear. He wore a white shirt, arms rolled to the elbow, waist tucked into his trousers with a black belt. The desk obstructed her view of his legs. He could have been barefoot for all she knew, like those newsreaders who wore posh jackets for the camera while their desk hid tracksuit pants.

Only she'd bet Seth wasn't barefoot. She'd bet his shoes were designer like his jacket, like his car. *Like him.* She hid another shiver and dragged her gaze away.

Built-in shelves lined the left-hand wall, most filled with textbooks or files. One held a copy of the globe, another, a series of framed certificates. Business degrees, Remy thought.

A huge triptych canvas covered most of the right-hand wall in thick textured blocks of colour. It looked like something a five-year-old might smush together, which probably meant it cost the GDP of a third world country.

The wall behind Seth was floor-to-ceiling glass. It overlooked the workings of the winery where stainless steel tanks and catwalks gleamed. The winery was well lit, daylight poured through high windows. In contrast, Seth's office was dark. None of the overhead halogens shone. Only a desk lamp added to the blue glow of a laptop screen.

The jacket that matched his trousers was slung over the arm of a black leather couch in the corner. On the cushions of that couch, papers spilled from an open briefcase.

No sound drifted from the winery. Not the beep of a forklift in reverse, nor the hum of a pump.

Remy stared at the damp patch on her knee where she'd knelt to repair a dripper tube earlier in the day, and at her dirt-capped Blundstone boots. This felt so far out of her league.

He felt so far out of her league.

Seth turned, locking his eyes with hers. There was a moment where that gaze was white-hot. Then it cooled.

'Excuse-moi, Helene.' Seth covered the receiver with his hand. 'Shut the door please, Remy. Sit there.' He indicated the couch. Then he turned his

back without waiting for a *yes* or a nod or anything and resumed his conversation, staring at something she couldn't see beyond the glass.

Remy stood rigid, halfway between his desk and the door, staring at the back of his head. If he'd been talking to the dirt crusting her boots he might have shown more warmth, and she didn't know what had suddenly changed. He'd been so open at Ellen Brook. He'd given her the best day of her life. The best weekend.

Hell and Tommy. She'd come here thinking bushwalks and kisses and dolmades, and Seth was all business.

She sat on the couch, then bounced up again, scattering some of his papers. Crossing to the door, she shut it behind her with a determined click. She didn't sit.

She remembered enough high school French to know an *adieu* when she heard one, and knew the conversation was coming to a close.

Finishing the call, he walked around his desk toward her, glancing at the papers scattered on the floor. He flicked two fingers toward the couch and settled with the back of his thighs against his desk. 'I'd appreciate if you could pick those up. I fly out tonight and I'll need them.'

Remy had forgotten all about the papers. Washing wineglasses for a week would be preferable right now to picking them up, but Seth was the boss. She needed this job.

Remy stepped to the couch. Kneeling felt more dignified than stooping. She scraped the pages together, tapped them against the briefcase to get a neat edge and left the stack on the leather seat.

'Okay then,' she patted the trousers of her Lasrey uniform, glanced at the door. 'What was it you wanted to see me about?'

Seth crossed his legs at the ankle. His eyes never left hers. Very, very softly he said: 'I want to see you stand against the wall, Remy.'

She forgot to breathe. When she remembered, the air leaked from her lungs. 'Pardon?'

'Stand against the wall. Face it.'

Remy took a shaky step backwards. Her insides were trying to hammer an escape through her skin. 'I don't think that's appropriate.'

'I didn't think it was particularly appropriate either when I heard you say it to your girlfriend yesterday. Don't let that stop you now.'

In the window behind him she could see their reflections: the back of Seth's head, shoulders broad and thick in a white shirt about nine hours shy of crisp; and her face, a blush running through it, lips popped open, eyes wide and wild.

'I don't know what you're talking about.'

Seth pushed off from the desk. His face was hard as the winery's concrete floor, his voice harder. The authority in it made her flinch. 'I heard you on the phone yesterday, Remy. Cut the act.'

'You heard me? That's—' *sick, crazy. I don't even think it's legal. Oh God. What did he hear? How much?* Her head spun. She wished her feet would spin, move, *anything,* but they were like lead. Lead buried in concrete.

'I couldn't last twenty-four hours without laying eyes on you, apparently. So I drove to your place to pay you a visit. I even bought you a coffee.' He laughed in a way that said he didn't give a shit about coffee. 'Maybe next time you play X-rated phone games with your girlfriend, you should shut the window.'

'You keep going on about a girlfriend ... I'm not,' she stumbled, 'not that there's anything wrong with it and each to their own and everything, but, I'm not gay.'

If it was possible for Seth's face to go even more rigid, it did. 'Then who were you talking to?'

Remy groaned inside. What was worse? For Seth to think she was a lesbian? Or for Seth to know she had a handful of female clients who paid her an exorbitant by-the-minute rate to make them come. Did she want Seth to know her family owed Doug Mulvraney so much money, that's what she had to do to pay it back?

Not in a million years. 'I was on my own time, in my own house. You were the one doing the eavesdropping. It's none of your business.'

'You lied to me.'

'I didn't lie. I don't have a girlfriend.'

'Then tell me who was on the other end of the phone?'

She opened her mouth, but no sound came out. Her throat felt like sandpaper and that wasn't because of the fledgling cold. 'No.'

He contemplated her for a beat longer.

'How did that game go again?' He was close enough now to reach for her hand and she was so stunned by the last three minutes, she didn't snatch hers away. 'I want to play. Stand against the wall, Remy.'

She couldn't move. She stood with her tummy fluttering like warm silk ribbons in a breeze.

'I'll make it easy for you. Come on. Here.' He turned her like they were partners in an old-style dance. Next second, the tip of her work boots nudged the skirting board and her nostrils filled with the faint scent of years-old paint.

***

Christ on a stick. What was he *thinking?* He'd never meant to go so far, but she'd been so damn *composed.* He'd just wanted to ... what exactly? Scare her? Punish her?

He'd wanted to make a fool of her, like she'd fooled him.

Only right now, Remy wasn't acting like any lesbian gold-digger he knew. Her scent was sunshine and cinnamon, she was warm and young and vibrant, and the longer he stood here—with her smell a sweet smoke in his head—the more he wanted to play this goddamn game for real. Play it with her. *Here.* Damn the consequences.

Seth liked women. He'd never needed props when he made love, never needed games, but if he touched Remy now, like he ached to, a line would be crossed. A huge great bloody black line and there'd be no going back. She was his employee. She was a goddamn lawsuit waiting to paper-plane through the door and land writ-side up on his desk. He was so close to being past the point where he could laugh the whole thing off as a joke.

Seth flexed his arm to take her weight, swing her back from the wall, but the apology he was preparing died in his throat because he heard, *thought he heard,* some indescribable sound.

He thought he heard Remy moan.

Her eyes were closed. She'd turned her head and her cheek rubbed gently against the paint. A small silver hoop he hadn't noticed before pierced her ear and Seth had time to admire the simple grace of silver curled against the smooth column of her neck. He wondered if he'd ever see anything so perfect again.

He wanted to take the elastic band out of her hair, tumble that blonde mane around her shoulders, and if one of his desk drawers had held a hairbrush he might have offered to spend an hour brushing out the day's knots. Then he'd like to tug it a little, see if he could get her to make that sound again.

There was a soft pop as her lips opened ... the rush of a shallow breath. Then she whispered, 'Don't stop now, Stud. It's just getting interesting.'

It shocked him so much he laughed, once he got over the minor earthquake her words caused at the base of his balls.

In answer, he picked up her right hand and moved it to her shoulder height, spreading her fingers and pinning them under his far larger hand. He was on the verge of leaning into her—wanted to put some pressure on her to let her know who was boss—when sanity clouted him across the head.

You are *the boss, goddammit. Let her go.*

'You're not very good at this are you?' She trembled, like her knees couldn't quite hold her up and the hand beneath his clenched, turning her fingernails dusky pink. 'Did you forget what comes next?'

'Of course I didn't forget what comes next. How the hell could I?'

'Well, go on then.' Her ridiculously long eyelashes fluttered open and Seth could have sworn he saw a smile curve her lips. 'Tell me to spread my legs.'

Either she was the best actress he'd ever seen, or his Snow White gold-digger in khaki was stark raving certifiable. Maybe both. Whatever was going on, she was too good at this game for him. Seth stepped back.

She clicked her tongue and sighed in what sounded like genuine disappointment and he almost felt sad for her until she added, 'Your problem is you're not nasty enough.'

'The hell I'm not.' *Certifiable.* She had to be.

'You're not,' she said, emphatically, turning slowly to face him. 'You ruined it when you said you'd brought coffee to my house. A nasty guy wouldn't bring coffee.'

He gripped her arm, gave it a shake. 'I am *not* nice. And you don't make a bluff like that based on whether or not I bought you *coffee.* What if I was some psycho?'

'I didn't say you were *nice.* I said you weren't nasty enough. Not nasty enough to do ... this.' She waggled her finger between their bodies, like a pheromone metronome. 'Not properly.'

'Go sit there, crazy girl. Let me think.' He pushed her gently toward the couch and watched her walk away, remembering how beautiful she was when she moved, forgetting whatever it was he needed to think about.

Lucky for him, Remy sat with her knees pressed together and her palms on her knees. The clutch and release of her fingers in the fabric of her trousers was the only sign that gave her tension away.

Where to start? He had so many questions. 'You're not gay?'

'I'm not.'

'You weren't spinning that story for a bloke, surely.'

'No. Not a bloke.'

This was like pulling teeth with a pair of tweezers. 'Then why do you do it?'

'Do what?'

'Make phone calls like that. What's that all about?'

She lifted her chin. 'I do it for the money, Seth. So I can pay the bills.'

'And you didn't want to tell me your mum stacked shelves.' He shook his head. Give him another few minutes and he might find this whole thing funny. Not quite yet. 'There's nothing wrong with working at a supermarket, Remy. Compared to—'

'Compared to what I do?' She cut him off.

'It's only one step from a prostitute, Remy. And a baby bloody step at that.' He didn't like it. He didn't like one bit of it, and there wasn't much use pretending otherwise. 'There are other ways to get money, like a loan from a bank. Did you ever think of doing that?'

'You find me the bank that will loan a twenty-three-year-old girl who hasn't held a job more than six months, and her unskilled mother, any money. We don't have any savings. We don't have any collateral except Mum's crapped out Nissan.'

'What bills are we talking about here exactly? I get the impression we're talking about more than a utilities bill, or the rent?'

She pinched the knee of her pants. 'It's not about paying bills, so much.'

'Are you in debt, Remy? You and your mum?' The urge to look after her gripped him. 'You could ask for an advance on salary. We've done that before when staff members have been experiencing hardship. It's no big deal.'

'I bet you have a policy for it.'

He did, but damned if he was confirming that right now. 'You need to ask your manager for an advance. I think we advance up to two weeks' pay. Greg Trimble brings the request to the board or to me. Depending on what the problem is, we might be able to do more than two weeks.'

Her shoulders did this little jump when he said two weeks', like she found it funny. 'Thanks for the offer, Seth. But we're fine.'

'What kind of debt are we talking about here, Remy?'

'It's nothing. Don't worry. I'm used to looking after myself.' She picked up the pages of the itinerary she'd knocked off the couch earlier and sneaked a peak. 'Charles de Gaulle?'

Changing the subject. 'That's in Paris.'

'I know where Charles de Gaulle airport is.'

'Sorry.' He kicked himself yet again, for being a patronising arse. Seth sucked in a breath. 'When I get back from Bordeaux—how about we go out and have that coffee for real. I'd like to get to know you properly. Start again.'

'There's still the workplace memo.' She pinched the seam of her work pants. 'I don't see how we can—'

'That memo is there to discourage personal relationships between staff where they might endanger a safe workplace. A few years ago one of the cellarhands crashed a forklift and knocked a stack of oak barrels. It just missed crushing another worker, and this was because he was flirting with a girl from cellar door and he wasn't paying attention.' Seth pinched the bridge of his nose. 'We know we can't tell our staff who they can and can't'—he'd been about to say *fall in love with,* but he changed it to: 'see.'

'*Hell and Tommy.* No wonder they call it the no bonking in the barrel hall policy.'

He laughed. 'Hell and Tommy. Where does that come from?'

'My father used to say it. It's about the only thing I kept of him.' She smiled, with her mouth but not with her eyes. A small, sad smile and seeing it, something inside him broke. He wasn't sure it was a part that could be fixed.

'Don't be sad, Rem.' If he kissed her again, could he kiss that sadness away?

Remy was on her feet, *moving,* stealing his heart. He didn't want to meet her halfway, because she was so very lovely to watch walk across the room, but her hands came out and he reached for them, and he was about to hug her tight to his chest when the handle of his office door rattled and they sprang apart.

'Seth? Are you there?'

'I didn't lock it,' Remy muttered, patting at her tangled hair.

'Seth?' The handle moved and the door was pushed open. His mother stepped into the room, twisting to her left to grope for the switch to the overhead lights.

'Don't switch the—' Light stung his eyes. 'Never mind.'

Ailsa's gaze flicked over Remy like she wasn't there. 'I thought you were driving to Perth tonight, Seth?'

Remy cleared her throat and said, 'I was just leaving. Thank you for that discussion, Mr Lasrey, it's very helpful. I feel a lot clearer about the policy now. Goodnight.' She turned to his mother: 'Goodnight, Mrs Lasrey.'

Remy ducked around his mother and fled.

Ailsa sat heavily on the cushions of his couch and wiggled her shoulders. 'She's left me a warm spot.'

'What did you want, Ailsa?'

'I *knew* that girl was trouble. What are you thinking? Have you lost your mind? What would your brother think?'

'She's not with Blake.'

'That doesn't mean I want her to switch her attention to you.' She recrossed her legs. 'Please will you invite Helene to visit for a few weeks after Bordeaux? That will stop tongues wagging. Or start them. Depending on how you want to look at it.'

'I'm not inviting Helene anywhere.'

He stonewalled her glare for a while and it was Ailsa who spoke first. 'Have you said anything else to Blake about this surfing thing?'

'Not since I saw him Sunday morning.'

'Well, he's just been up at the big house and he says it's definite. He's going to try out for the qualifying tour.'

'Did you wish him luck?'

'*Luck?*'

Seth shrugged. 'He's doing it whether you approve or not.'

'No I didn't wish him *luck.*' Ailsa had sat forward, now she relaxed into the cushions. 'At least, darling, I've still got you.'

'That's something else I'll be putting on the agenda for next board meeting.'

'What is?' She rocked forward again.

'I want to take some time off.'

'Excellent. I told you, you work too hard.'

'Extended time off. Four months maybe. The summer.'

'The summer? Are you serious? You're nearly thirty, not sixty. You're in the prime of your life. I can't believe this: first Blake throws it in, then you, all in the one night. Sometimes I wonder why I even bothered starting this business. When Joseph and I were thirty we—'

'—Planted the cabernet block by hand ... I know. You've told me.' He and Blake had heard the Joseph-and-Ailsa-plant-the-vineyard-all-by-themselves bedtime story like some kids got read *The Cat In The Hat.*

'It's that girl, isn't it? I can see it on your face. I wish Blake *had* slept with her and be done with it. He'd have her out of his system and *you* wouldn't want her if you knew Blake got there first.'

His voice cracked across the room. 'That's enough, Mother. I plan on seeing a whole lot more of Remy when I get back from Bordeaux. If she'll let me.'

'If she'll let you?' Ailsa swallowed a brittle laugh. 'Of course she'll let you.'

Seth rubbed his jaw. 'If, by some great stretch of the imagination, she doesn't run a mile from my family, get it through your head: I *like* the girl. I like her a lot.'

'You don't *like* girls like her, Seth. They're bed warmers at best. Underlay, not the quilt. She's not marriage material. Her father's a drunk.'

'Her father *was* a drunk. He's dead. And who said anything about *marriage?*'

'No one did. But I know you, darling.' She smiled at him without showing any teeth, and then she stood up to leave. 'Blake's not the marrying type, but you are and you can bet she knows it.'

'I'm going to pretend I didn't hear that, Mother.' He couldn't let her get away with saying something like that. 'But that's the last time you insult Remy in my hearing. She's important.'

'And I'm not? This company's not? You only just met her, Seth!'

'What's that got to do with anything? I've known you my whole life and all you're doing right now is pissing me off.'

'Seth!' Ailsa cried, as her knees crumpled. She sat back hard on the couch, on the verge of tears. 'How can you speak to me like that?'

'Look, Mum.' He softened his tone but he wasn't about to apologise. Ailsa's meddling had to stop. He and Blake weren't kids anymore. 'The last thing Dad said to me before he died wasn't about working longer, or working harder or earning more money. He said: do what makes me happy. Now if you'll excuse me, I've got a lot to do and I still haven't packed.'

He knew Ailsa wanted to have the last word—she was a master at that. Her mouth twisted. Her chest rose as she puffed herself up, but what came out was a whimper, not a roar. 'Well then, I guess there's nothing else for me to do but say goodnight. Have a safe trip.'

'I will. See you in a fortnight.'

Chapter 6

Remy drove home after fleeing Seth's office, detouring to the chemist for some cold and flu tablets on the way. The encounter with Seth had distracted her from her sore throat, but the chill evening air outside the winery freshened her cough and it was proving hard to stop.

Lexie was at work, but there was a plate of lasagne in the fridge and all Remy had to do was heat it up. Not that she felt like eating.

She was washing her dinner dishes when the phone rang in her work bag, and such was her rush to get to it before it flipped to message bank she bashed her hip on the table hard enough to send the packet of flu tablets skittering to the floor.

Then the screen lit with Seth's name and she forgot the pain. Remy picked up. 'Hi.'

'Hey. I rang to apologise for my mother.'

'A wise woman told me once you never should apologise for what someone else does,' she said.

'Who was that?'

'Meryl Streep in some movie.'

'Meryl is a very wise woman.'

They were quiet, just breathing, until Remy said, 'Where are you? What time is the flight?'

'I'm just the other side of Bunbury. It leaves Perth at 11.10 tonight.'

'When do you get back?'

'Two weeks. I'm back late on the Tuesday night.'

It felt like forever. Remy gripped the phone as if it might slip through her fingers. Like *he* might slip through her fingers.

'Remy?'

'Yes?'

'Whatever is going on with this money you owe, or your mum owes? Whatever it is that you think you can't tell me. I'd help you. I'd be there for you. You know that, right?'

It choked her up. It really, honestly, choked her up and it wasn't just that her throat was getting worse, or that her head felt thick and foggy. What did you say to that?

'Thank you.' It was trite. There were no words that could convey what she felt. In the last few days, Seth had made her feel less alone and Remy didn't feel like that often. She and her mother had been fighting an uphill battle for such a long time.

'I mean it, Rem.'

'I know you do. But we're fine. Mum and I ... we'll find our way through it. It helps though. Just the thought you care, that's enough.'

She couldn't tell him about Doug Mulvraney. Not on the phone. Mulvraney had eyes and ears everywhere and she wouldn't put it past him to know people who could trace such a call. If she was honest with herself—and she always tried to be—it was more than that. So far Seth didn't seem to care about her father's reputation, or her paltry finances, or the fact that she lived in a house that was falling down around her ears. But she'd seen his face when she admitted to the phone sex work: *a bloody baby step from prostitution.* Would knowing she owed money to scum like Doug Mulvraney be the final straw?

She wasn't ready to find that out. Not yet.

'Honestly, we'll be fine, Seth. It's just a short-term deficit kind of thing. A hitch in the cashflow. Another couple of months and we'll be through it.' She hoped that was true. She hoped she sounded convincing.

Maybe she did, because Seth said, 'When I get back, I'm going to prove to you that you can trust me, okay? But in the meantime, sweetheart, you sound like you should take it easy. That voice doesn't sound good.'

Sweetheart. 'I'm okay. It's just a sniffle. I think getting soaked on Saturday is catching up with me.'

'You should take tomorrow off.'

'Is that the boss speaking?'

'It's me, Remy. It's always me when I'm talking to you.'

***

It took a long time before Remy could fall asleep that night. She woke feeling lousy and she had to drag herself through the next morning, blowing her nose every five minutes.

Her mother said she should call in sick—even offered to phone in for her—but Remy didn't want to give anyone at Lasrey any reason to question her work ethic. Not after Ailsa burst in on them last night. Not with Seth away.

Greg Trimble rostered her to spray the cabernet for powdery mildew. It was a job she normally enjoyed, but today the noise of the quad-bike made her head ache, and time and again her mind turned to Seth—how he was, what he was thinking—and frustratingly, maddeningly, how amazing it had felt to be pinned by him to his office wall.

Seth wouldn't have needed Sixty Seconds to prove his point last night. If they'd played the game for real, he'd barely have needed six.

***

'Canasta.' Grinning, Allan Dale laid his cards on the lunchroom table. Remy and the other three players sitting with him groaned.

Remy was tallying the values of what she carried in her hand, when Rina Stein burst into the lunchroom like a boxer coming out at the bell. 'There you are, Greg! There's something wrong with the vines by the driveway.'

Greg put his cards on the table. He had a broad, leathery face and a sunglasses tan that made him look like a brown panda. He'd been at Lasrey for more than a decade and the staff who'd been there long enough, and dared, called him Pops. Remy hadn't been there long enough and Rina didn't dare.

'Whaddaya mean something's wrong?' Greg said.

'They're spotty-looking. They've got no vigour. They just don't look happy, dammit.'

Allan collected the cards and wrapped them in an elastic band. Allan, having been around Greg and Rina long enough to know when the shit was about to hit the fan, was first to check the clock on the wall, stretch, and mutter something about the bottling line not running all by itself. Remy would have gone then too, except Greg tipped his chin at her and said: 'How did the cabernet look to you this morning?'

'Fine.' Then she added, 'Sulphur coverage wouldn't make the vines spotty?'

'Shouldn't do,' he agreed.

Rina slapped her palm on the lunchroom table. 'I've been in town all morning and I only just got back. I can tell you right now, those vines aren't fine.

'Right-oh.' Greg heaved to his feet, sucked the last of his iced coffee and dumped the carton in the rubbish before he resettled his cap on his head. 'You come too, Remy.'

Rina trailed them.

Cabernet sauvignon was the first variety planted at Lasrey in the early seventies, in the original vineyard now bisected by the gravel driveway that took tourists to cellar door. It wasn't far to walk and it wasn't long before they could see Rina was right. Something was very wrong with the vines.

Greg put a hand on the timber fence bordering the staff car park, vaulting his legs over. Remy ducked through the fence and trotted behind him across the mown grass verge into the vineyard.

'See,' Rina said.

'Yeah, I see.'

Instead of sitting crisp and alert, some leaves had begun to curl. There were leaves with oily brown/black spots, now spreading in irregular shapes, like a mole or freckle turned cancerous by the sun.

Greg's attention narrowed on Remy, and through the flu ache and the fog in her head she did her best to answer his rapid-fire questions.

Yes, she'd sprayed here this morning. *Yes,* for powdery. *Yes,* she'd checked the concentrations and spray calculations against their spray charts.

'You're sure about that?' His watery-blue eyes held hers.

'Yes, I'm sure.'

But was she? Had she calculated the spray properly? Had she been paying attention? Her head had been so filled with Seth.

Sixty Seconds ... Stand against the wall.

She hugged herself hard, and the day seemed suddenly grey and cold.

'Where's the quad-bike now, Remy, and the spray gear? We need to check it all out.' Greg rubbed a leaf between his fingers and grimaced when he didn't like the feel.

'I told you—' Remy began, before the flare in Greg's nostrils told her to leave out the attitude. Lasrey's vineyards were his responsibility. *She* was his responsibility too. He had every right to grill her about what she'd done to his vines.

'Maybe you got a bad batch of copper sulphate. We can get it tested.' Greg headed back to the winery, his walk morphing into a jog.

Remy had to run to catch him. 'I don't know what there'll be to see, I washed the tank out when I finished the last pass.'

'Something must have got fucked up in the sprayer. It's all I can think of.'

'You mean *she* fucked up,' Rina shouted at them from further behind. 'Seth will hit the roof.'

Greg muttered something Remy was glad she didn't hear.

Lasrey had a full complement of sheds forming an industrial wedge at the winery's rear, separated from the polished veneer of the stone and timber façade the public saw when they visited cellar door.

The largest shed housed the tractor and the truck. Greg's work ute was in there too, plus the two quad-bikes and all the spraying gear. Chemicals and fertilisers were kept in a locked room accessed through the rear corner of the main shed. By the time Remy caught up with Greg, he was flicking through the pages of the spray diary and pages of stapled checklists Remy had signed off earlier that day.

'You filled this out properly, yeah?' he said, without looking up.

'I think so.'

Greg shot her a look, but it was Rina who pressed: 'What does "think so" mean? Did you? Or didn't you?'

'I'm sure I did.' But was she? Tick the same checklist one hundred times and you got to ticking on auto.

Greg sniffed the spray wand, checked for residue in the tank. 'All I can smell is water.'

'Don't ask me. My nose is so stuffed up, I can't smell a thing,' Remy said.

He snatched the key from the security board and unlocked the chemical room, snapping on the overhead lights. Remy followed him, moving further into the room, while Rina propped herself against the doorframe.

'Here's the copper sulphate,' Remy tapped the container.

It all looked normal.

Greg's eyes narrowed as he thought it through. 'What about adjuvant?'

'Alkylaryl,' Remy said. Mixing adjuvants or wetting agents was a standard part of the process at Lasrey. It improved how the sprays stuck to the leaves.

'So where's that?' Rina asked.

Remy waved her hand at the shelf, but she did it distractedly, thinking every bit as hard as Greg. What could have happened here? How had she got this wrong?

Rina moved toward where Remy pointed. 'This?' She laid her hand on a pack.

'That's oxfluorofen, Rina,' Greg said, like he was talking to a silly kid. 'Total opposite of what you're looking for. That stuff's a herbicide. Weedkiller.'

'Well I don't see anything here that says alky-whatsit,' Rina snapped back. 'Maybe someone didn't reorder it.'

That made Greg and Remy pay more attention. By now, both of them were in the corner with Rina, peering through the shelves. Greg examined the pack. Beside it there were telltale rings in the dust on the shelf that showed it had been recently moved. They all saw it.

'Oxfluorofen could do that to the vines, couldn't it,' Remy said, meeting Greg's unwavering gaze. 'I mean, if...' Her voice cracked just thinking about it and she couldn't get her mouth to close.

'My oath it could,' Greg said, rubbing at his chin like he might twist it clean off. 'But you wouldn't have mixed the two up, Rem? I mean, that's just not a mistake you'd make. I'd bet my left nut on it.'

Normally, Remy would bet Greg's left nut too, but she'd been so thickheaded this morning. Sick with the flu, lovesick. Try as she night, she couldn't rule it out, and she honestly couldn't see any other way.

'I'm so sorry.' She was. Desperately sorry. Cabernet was Lasrey's flagship and she might have killed the company's oldest vines. 'I'm the only one who's been in here. I can't think of any other possible explanation. I mean ... there's no other explanation? Is there?'

Rina snorted. 'You bloody *idiot*.'

'Rina, you're not helping,' Greg snarled back.

'Well, *someone* has to let the executive know what's happened. Seth won't be happy if I give him *half* the damn story. He'll want to know all the details. Maybe you'd like to be the one who tells him that *your* direct report poisoned his best vines?'

'Seth's in the air,' Remy said woodenly, cutting their argument short. 'He's on his way to France.' Greg's brow furrowed and Rina shot her a withering look. Neither of them asked how she knew the CEO's personal movements and Remy didn't care, she was beyond worrying about hiding things or saving face. This was too huge.

'Ailsa's at the winery. She'll want to know. One of us will have to fill Seth in when he lands. What a fucking balls-up.' Rina took off, boots churning through the gravel.

'I'm so sorry, Greg,' Remy said. The flu came with a crushing headache, but this new guilt made her want to throw up.

'Yeah, so am I. You didn't do it on purpose. Accidents happen, so let's see if we can fix this one up.' Greg started rifling through his pockets. Digging out his mobile phone, he dialled then spoke: 'Hey, Ed. Yeah. Good ... Hey, mate, we got a problem. My assistant sprayed oxfluorofen on the cabernet this mornin' ... Yeah. Dunno. Brain-fade I guess. Yeah.'

Remy watched Greg's face for any glimmer of good news, wishing more and more that she could rewind the day and start over. Finally, after a few more *yeahs* and *yeps,* he hung up the phone.

'Right, let's go. If the active agent hasn't sat on the leaves too long, we might come out of it okay.' He grabbed two nutrient packs from the shelves. 'You find the powdered kelp.'

Relief must have shown on her face because Greg quickly cautioned: 'Don't get your hopes up.'

'I won't.' Tonight she could bawl like a baby, not now. Not while there was a chance to try to make this right.

She followed Greg from the storage room with the kelp pack under her arm. Remy locked the door and slipped the key back on its peg. From the front shed they could see Rina striding up the hill toward them, elbows punching a path through the air like an Olympic walker.

As Greg measured product into the tank, Rina steamed up to them and without drawing breath, told Remy: 'Ailsa wants to see you.'

'Remy's gotta drive. We're doing a double foliar feed spray,' Greg said, adding out of the corner of his mouth for Remy's ears only, 'Mrs Lasrey can wait in line. I'm first to tear you a new arsehole.'

Remy knew Greg was making light of it, trying to make her feel better. It didn't work, she still felt like shit.

'*I'll* drive,' Rina snapped, crossing to the security board to pick out the keys. 'Ailsa said *now.* Given the way things are, I'd get a wriggle on if I were you. She's in the boardroom.'

Greg glanced at Rina, then at Remy. 'Go on, Rem. At the end of the day the buck stops with me. I'm your manager. I should have been supervising you better, obviously. I'll tell them that later.'

'It's not your fault,' she tried to assure him, but the sound of the quad-bike as Greg started the engine drowned her out. Rina climbed into the truck, reversed, and spun a turn that threatened to tear strips in the gravel before she gunned the truck after him.

As the engine noise faded, Remy trudged across the lot. It was the second time in twenty-four hours she'd had cause to enter the admin area at Lasrey, only this time it was via the back entrance and this time, there was no Seth.

***

Sally Deering, Seth's assistant, made her wait. Remy sat in the same green chairs where salespeople sweated before an appointment with Seth or Rina, or whichever decision-maker they'd come to schmooze.

Word of the morning's monumental stuff-up must have spread because the reception area had all the cheer of a funeral parlour. Even Sally, who had seen just about everything a wine business could toss at her, looked grim.

It felt like an age before Sally's phone buzzed and she picked it up, glanced across her desk at Remy and said: 'They're ready for you.'

Remy pushed to her feet, wishing her body didn't ache so much. The adrenalin that had driven her since lunch had faded with all the sitting still. She felt sharp as a sloth.

'Good luck, Remy.' Sally said it so low, anyone waiting in the boardroom would have needed bionic ears to hear. It wasn't a glowing endorsement of how she thought the interview might go.

Remy straightened her shoulders, knocked twice. A voice called her to come in.

Ailsa Lasrey sat on the long side of a timber table even more polished than she was. Diane Laurie, the HR manager, sat on Ailsa's right with her laptop cracked open. Both women glanced up as Remy closed the door, but only Diane's smile held any hint of warmth.

Remy had to stop herself from smoothing the creases in her khaki pants. She didn't own an iron on principle and these women wore clothes that screamed freshly pressed.

'Take a seat,' Ailsa waved her in.

Remy pulled out a chair and folded her legs into it. She'd picked a seat right by one of the ornate table supports and it took her a couple of tries to sit. First the chair legs, then her boots kept getting stuck.

'You know why you're here?' Ailsa said.

Remy nodded, drawing breath to launch into her version of the day's events.

Diane interrupted. 'Before you say anything, Remy, I should let you know I'm typing this up in an incident report because we may need to get insurers involved, and I'll print it for you when we're finished and get you to sign that you're happy it's all accurate. Do you want to have anyone here with you?'

'Do you think it's necessary?'

The HR manager shrugged. 'It's up to you. You can ask someone to come in with you if you like.'

Remy thought about that for a second. Greg was the obvious choice, but he had about six hectares of cabernet to save from weedkiller. Perhaps Blake—

'Blake isn't here,' Ailsa said, like she'd read her thoughts, lowering her chin to stare at Remy over her glasses. Thick, navy and black-rimmed, they were, with over-sized gold hinges that winked in the lights. With her almost white hair and eyes the colour of rain on ice, Ailsa looked like the fairy godmother in Shrek. The nasty one.

'It's fine. I don't need anyone,' Remy said. 'I take full responsibility for my actions today. I'm so sorry, Mrs Lasrey. I don't know what I was thinking this morning. I've done routine sprays almost every week since I started here. This is the first time anything like this has happened.'

'Why don't you tell us in your own words what you think went wrong, and we'll go from there,' Diane said, pulling the laptop closer.

So Remy did. She kept it direct and honest and tried to make sure Greg Trimble didn't cop any blame. When she'd finished, it took a lot of typing before Diane's fingers clicked their final clack.

Remy tried not to fidget. It was warm in the boardroom and stuffy with the door closed. Floral perfume permeated the air, adding its weight to the headache Remy had been fighting all day.

Ailsa scribbled notes in a personnel file on which Remy could see her name handwritten in black marker. Eventually, Ailsa put the pen down but it was Diane who spoke first. 'I don't like to be the one to say this, but I have to put it to you, Remy. Are you sure what happened today was really an accident?'

'Pardon?' Remy sat bolt upright and smothered her bark of nervous laughter. The suggestion was ridiculous. 'I would never deliberately set out to poison anything ... I mean, you can't think...'

Yet it was clear from the two expressions opposite, 'vineyard murderess' was what they'd like to scrawl across the pages of her personnel file, in ink dripping blood.

'You seemed ... upset when I saw you in the CEO's office last night,' Ailsa prompted. 'I overheard you say Mr Lasrey clarified a company policy to you, and I can only *assume* that policy was our workplace relationships memo.' She ran a nail on the margin of Remy's file, slowly, as if cutting it with a dull knife. 'There have been rumours about you and Blake. I see here a complaint was made. I had discussed that with Mr Lasrey previously and there's a note in your file. It's possible that you were feeling aggrieved with the suggestions Mr Lasrey put to you last night, Remy, and so you might have acted rashly this morning...'

'Even if you've since regretted it,' Diane finished, let the words hang over the table like sour mist.

That she would ever deliberately set out to poison the Lasrey vines was so far from the truth it took a good ten seconds before Remy could frame more than a stunned syllable in response. How did she defend herself without making things worse? How would Ailsa react if she told her the only dressing down the CEO had given her in his office last night had been with his eyes?

Placing both hands on the table, curling her fingernails to hide the dirt, she leaned forward. This was a witch-hunt and it had gone on long enough. 'I would never deliberately set out to kill a vineyard. Ever. I love nature. I love plants. Viticulture is my career.'

'Is it?' Ailsa said, bringing her hand to her cheek so the sparkle of rings vied for attention with the sparkle of gold hinge in her glasses. 'I'm not convinced.'

'I love my job, Mrs Lasrey.'

Ailsa's lips pursed. 'You've been with us, what now ... five months?'

'Six,' Diane interjected, shifting in her seat, not looking up.

'Six months. In that time you've poisoned my vineyard and complaints have been made regarding the nature of your relationship with my youngest son—it's hardly an auspicious start. Let me be very clear here, Remy. We can't afford to have employees with us who cannot give us one hundred per cent focus on the job. A winery is a dangerous workplace when people let themselves get distracted by workplace relationships that are anything other than professionally conducted. I think you've let yourself get distracted that way today, and this is the result.'

She's going to tell me not to bother coming in tomorrow. She's going to sack my stupid arse. It was there in the way Diane Laurie wouldn't lift her eyes from her keyboard, and how the keys clacking beneath her fingers sounded like they, too, didn't give a damn.

Remy gave a damn. She gave a bloody great big damn.

If she lost this job she'd have to front Doug Mulvraney and tell him she couldn't make a repayment for a few weeks. Mulvraney said he liked her. He said she had 'spunk'. She was pretty sure that wouldn't stop him cutting off her finger if he thought she was welching on what her father had owed him when he died.

'Rina says there are operating procedures in the storeroom for safe-handling of chemicals and a checklist to sign off, and that you signed against the checklist this morning,' Ailsa said.

'That's correct.'

'And would you say we've given you the training you need to complete a simple spraying task without supervision?'

'Yes,' she said miserably. It was true. Greg Trimble had been patient and thorough. As well as all the big stuff, he'd run her through the small: how you had to kick the bottom sliding door of the pump shed with your toe to get it to shut flush.

'I'm not trying to be horrible about all this, Remy. Truly I'm not. This is business and tough decisions have to be made.'

Yes. You. Are. Horrible. 'I understand.'

'You're a second-year university graduate, not a junior fresh out of school, and we pay you as such,' Ailsa said. 'Greg is a busy man. Your position is supposed to support him, not require his supervision of every basic task.'

'I know that, Mrs Lasrey. I'll do anything to make this right. If I could take the morning back and start again, I would. I'm asking you to give me another chance. Please.' *And I'll start looking for a new job tomorrow because if you think for a minute that I want to work here any longer than I absolutely have to, you've got another think coming. But I need a new job to go to first.*

Ailsa sighed as if she was being asked to give up a kidney. 'It's not a decision I can make on my own. Diane, can I see you outside for a minute?'

Diane Laurie finished typing and scanned the laptop screen. 'I'll send this out to the printer in reception, Remy. I'll get a copy for you to read and sign.'

'Okay.'

Although, as the two women left the room in a rustle of perfume and pressed shirts, Remy knew it wasn't okay at all.

***

Five minutes later, Ailsa re-entered the boardroom with a sheath of typewritten pages in her hand. These she passed to Remy. 'Have a read through. You can make any notes and discuss them with me. Sign on the last page that it's accurate.'

Ailsa sat again and stayed as Remy read. Occasionally the older woman shuffled a page in Remy's file or wrote a note in the margins, but for the most part she was spectacularly unobtrusive, except for her rings. One of those rocks caught in the lights and every time Ailsa twitched her fingers, the shine danced at the edge of Remy's vision.

Reading the report only reinforced Remy's view that she'd been a first-class ditz. *Hell and Tommy,* anyone would think she was a complete moron who couldn't find a bunch of grapes in a vineyard without a map. Ailsa Lasrey could have been nicer about it but Remy could understand the woman's frustration.

'Happy?' Ailsa said eventually, tapping the file with her pen, which translated to *hurry up and sign.*

'No. Not happy. I can't believe I was so careless. But I'll sign it. It's the truth.' So she did, and pushed the pages across the table.

'No questions?' Ailsa said, opening the three pages to check Remy's signature on the last.

'No. Can I just say again how sorry I am for all this? What I really want to do is get out there and help Greg fix my stuff-up.' *And get out of this room so I can blow my nose and breathe fresh air again.*

She was pushing up from her chair when Ailsa said: 'I'm not finished yet,' in a tone that glued Remy's backside to the seat.

Ailsa took a flimsy rectangle of paper from Remy's personnel file then folded the incident report inside the file. She closed it, lacing her hands over the smooth beige.

'Diane—' Ailsa waved a hand dismissively in the direction of the door '—says I have to give you two written warnings before I terminate your employment. I'm a bit more old-school. The way I see it someone is accountable and if it's not you, then it's Greg. You're his responsibility.'

'It's not Greg, Mrs Lasrey. This is all on me.'

Ailsa tipped her head in acknowledgement. 'Commendable. And I must say it's refreshing to come across an employee with that perspective. Most staff would have been covering their backsides from the moment Rina discovered there was a problem. They'd be telling me they haven't been trained properly or they haven't been *shown,* or they only did what their supervisor *told* them to do.'

'I've never had any problem with taking responsibility, Mrs Lasrey,' Remy said, fighting a mix of frustration, panic, and the growing urge to have a damn good cry. She didn't cry often, but it had been a shitty, shitty day—the queen of shitty days—and it wasn't getting any better.

'Good.' Ailsa smiled a smile so cold, it burned. 'You weren't concentrating on your job this morning and you mixed up the wrong chemical because you were a million miles away—caught up in some fool's dream involving my son. And this time, I don't mean Blake.'

The words were like a scalpel laying the truth bare, all Remy could do was blink.

Ailsa inhaled: long, deliberate. Then she exhaled, hard and fast. 'In my opinion you should never have been employed here in the first place, but I let Greg Trimble recommend you, and the board *chose* you against my better judgement. I want your resignation. I'll even say please.'

An image of Doug Mulvraney's weasel face filled Remy's mind. Her crappy rental house. That ugly hulking hedge. Lexie hefting supermarket boxes late on Sunday nights. Bills on the fridge.

Resigning wasn't an option. Not without something to go to. And what winery would employ her now, after this?

'I need this job. Please. I have financial obligations.' *Debts to a man who makes you look like a cuddly toy.*

'You think *you're* out of pocket,' Ailsa said, voice rising. 'You poison my flagship vines. Cost me a small fortune in man-hours trying to fix-up your error. If we can't fix it then my insurance excess and premiums all go up—not to mention the wine we can't make for years from the cabernet block.' Ailsa fingered the rectangle of paper she'd pulled from the file. It was upside-down on the table and she pushed it back and forth.

'The vines might not be that bad, Mrs Lasrey. Greg has a plan—'

'For a smart girl you're being very stupid.' Ailsa's finger stabbed the table once, diamonds flashing beneath the overhead lights. 'No winery in Margaret River will employ you after this. There's no happy ending here, Remy. I saw you in Seth's office last night. I saw the look on your face. I've seen it before. Girls have been throwing themselves at him since he was in high school. You do know he's about to get engaged, don't you?'

'I didn't throw myself at anyone...' and then the last word snagged in her head. *Engaged?*

Suddenly, Remy felt very, very tired and she just wanted this finished. All the emotions she'd weathered since Seth shielded her from the storm on Saturday imploded and fell flat, like fallout from a mushroom cloud. She'd been an idiot, quite obviously, in more ways than one.

'Everyone who works here knows about Helene, except you,' Ailsa said. 'That's why Seth's gone to France. Helene Bouchard is the daughter of our oak supplier. Bouchard is the most prestigious barrel manufacturer in France. She and Seth have been lovers for years. Helene understands him. Hers is a great wine legacy, too. Such a wonderful family...'

'He said he was going to an exhibition. Vinitech.'

'Oh, he is. That's first. He'll be finished with that in a few days. The rest of the time he'll be at the Bouchard Cooperage with Helene.'

Adieu, Helene. Remy remembered his farewell on the phone yesterday as clearly as if Seth had been in the room. She pushed up from her seat, not wanting Ailsa to see how much she hurt. This time, she made it to her feet. 'I won't waste any more of your time, Mrs Lasrey. I assume I shouldn't bother coming in for work tomorrow?'

'There's just one final matter.' Ailsa pushed the slip of paper across the table.

Remy hadn't been able to see it clearly before. Now she could see it was a cheque. 'Why did we bother with the charade about my job when you've already calculated my final pay?'

'Due process,' Ailsa said, tapping the cheque. 'Go on, take it. No hard feelings.'

Except Remy had plenty of hard feelings. Peer into her soul right now, she was iron.

She shimmied her thumbnail beneath the cheque, twisted it up, took a cursory glance, and stopped dead in her tracks. 'What the hell is this?'

Chapter 7

When he reached the hotel in Bordeaux, about thirty-six hours after getting on the plane in Perth on Tuesday night, Seth booked a wake-up call at reception for an hour's time and kicked off his shoes, sprawling fully clothed on the quilt. As flights went, the long haul from Singapore to Paris hadn't been bad but it was always madness at Charles de Gaulle. He'd had forty minutes to clear customs and make the regional flight to Bordeaux. About an hour in the air, half an hour to disembark, a taxi-ride and checkin later he'd finally been able to get horizontal.

Every time he'd tried to sleep on the plane, he'd thought about Remy, in his office. He'd hear himself telling her to stand against the wall, and she'd give that little moan.

None of which made getting any sleep particularly easy. Finally, his body succumbed to the long flight.

When the wake-up call came, he woke fast.

Throwing off the covers, he rubbed his hand through his hair, yawned, stretched, and was looking for a fresh shirt in his travel bag when the phone rang again, his mobile this time. He felt a jolt run through him, a hope that it might be Remy.

He tried not to feel disappointed at the name on the caller ID. 'Hey. I thought you gave up checking in on my flights years ago?'

'You never stop being a mother, darling. How was the flight?' The connection was perfect. Ailsa could have been next door, not half the world away.

'Fine. Long. I'm about to head downstairs for dinner. What's up?'

She laughed: a stretched, synthetic sound, like tearing one of those old vinyl Elvis records she loved. 'I think you could safely say we've seen better days, darling.'

'What's up?' Seth said again, sharper this time.

'That Hanley girl sprayed the cabernet block with something called,' Ailsa paused over the unfamiliar word, 'oxfluorofen this morning. It's some kind of herbicide—'

'I know what it is,' Seth interrupted. 'But *how?*'

'From what we've been able to gather she mixed the wrong chemical in the spray tank. She said she had a brain-fade. I'm not so sure about that but anyway, it hardly matters after the event.'

'Shit.' The back of his thighs hit the mattress with a whump. 'Greg discovered it in time?'

'Rina was coming back from Margaret River about lunchtime, our time, *thank God.* She saw there was something wrong and she raised the alarm.'

'Shit,' he said again, struggling through the fog of jet lag. 'She wasn't feeling well when I left. If she wasn't concentrating, that might explain it.'

Ailsa made a sound in her throat. 'She's the only one who knows what happened. She's saying it was an error—I hope so, Seth. I hope it was human error because I'd hate to think she'd done it on purpose.'

'Well that makes zero bloody sense. She'd never *mean* to do it.' He thought about Remy's love of growing things; the way she could spot orchids from twenty paces in the bush; and how she'd eyeballed him when his big feet had come too close to squashing one of those lady donkey cowslips.

'She was upset last night in your office ... I thought—'

'She wasn't well and she probably should have stayed home. Remy must feel terrible.' He wished he was there to tell her it would all be okay. 'What's Greg doing about the vines? Did he call the WA Ag Department? There'll be a precedent for this sort of thing. They could tell him what to do.'

'Greg seems confident he has it under control. Only time will tell.'

Seth grunted. 'I'll email Pops Trimble, but can you get Rina to tell him I want a report every day on how the vines are responding. I want to be kept in the loop.'

It was a fuck-up, and as employee fuck-ups went it was up there, but it sounded like they'd found it early enough, sounded like Pops had it under control. 'Lucky vines are tough. It might set them back a few weeks but it shouldn't kill them, if Rina saw it fast enough. I'll call Remy.'

'There's not much point doing that.'

'Why not?'

'She doesn't have her phone anymore.'

He was getting damn tired of asking all the questions. 'Why not?'

'I took it off her.'

'Mother?' A question and a warning. He'd been in planes and airports for almost forty hours. His patience was thin.

'I asked for her resignation, Seth. She gave it to me.'

'You shouldn't do that without referring it to me.'

'I'm a director of this company—'

He cut her off. 'I want to speak with Remy, Mum. I'll talk to her. Bring her back.'

'Don't you dare,' Ailsa spat, getting so worked up, Seth thought she might have a stroke on the other end of the line. 'You can't see it, can you? She's a disruptive influence and after today Rina and I shouldn't have to tell you she's also damn well incompetent. What type of message does that send to the other staff if you bring her back?'

'If she's incompetent, Pops would have told me. This is an accident. Shit happens.' He stared around the room. He'd drawn the heavy drape earlier. He opened it now, looking out the window at the Bordeaux lights. 'I'll get the first flight home.'

'Don't do that.' Ailsa let out a sigh. 'Look, darling. That's not all.'

'What do you mean that's not all? What the hell else can go wrong?'

'I didn't want to have to tell you this over the phone, but there's more. Darling, I hope you're sitting down.'

'Spit it out.'

'Seth, Remy accused you of sexual harassment.'

Seth dropped the drape. The Bordeaux lights winked out. 'She *what?*'

***

Ailsa Lasrey hung up the phone on her eldest son and permitted herself a tight smile. She'd done the best she could. She'd bought herself a few weeks.

She'd convinced Seth that if he came home now, he'd look guilty. *'Finish your trip, darling. Stick to your schedule. She's not going anywhere. We can thrash it all out when you get home.'*

Seth might try to phone Remy sooner, Ailsa didn't doubt that. Her son would want answers and he'd want those from the source. That's just the way Seth was.

Ailsa knew Seth didn't believe her. Not quite—amazing how hard he'd fallen for Remy, and so fast. But when he got home and Remy was gone, and Ailsa told him about the cheque she'd taken ... *Cheques.* That would change things. She was banking on it.

Money talked.

Remy wouldn't be easy to find. Ailsa had taken her work phone and the Hanley's didn't have a home number. Not one Ailsa had been able to trace. With luck, in a week Remy and her mother would be interstate and out of reach.

Blake had been the immediate problem. Blake would never believe Remy deliberately poisoned those vines.

Blake would want Remy given the benefit of the doubt.

Ailsa had called Blake before she'd spoken with Seth. She told him to take some time off to think about his surfing plans and work out what it was he really wanted. She'd even transferred $500 into his account. 'Petrol money, darling,' she'd told him.

By six o'clock the next morning, she knew Blake would be cruising past Perth with his surfboards strapped on the roof-rack and his music up loud, on his way north to the Bluff. The telephone reception up there was third world at best and Blake would be incommunicado for a fortnight. When he heard what had happened, it would be too late. Remy would be gone.

The girl had been an unfortunate blip. An expensive one as it turned out, but Ailsa could afford it. Seth had made her more money in his four years at the helm of Lasrey than Joseph had cobbled together in two decades. Seth would take the Lasrey name and brand far, she could feel it in her bones.

Without Remy around to distract him, everything would be fine.

Then her sense of elation cooled. Just because she'd got out of it easy this time, it didn't mean another girl might not try to trap Seth in the future. He was like his father; that hot-blooded Italian heritage turned him into a fool for a pretty face. She'd have to think of a way to protect him, protect herself, from gold-digging females who might try to split the family, split the business.

Ailsa mused. Rina had proven herself a loyal employee, possibly even director material. With just Seth, Blake and herself, it was too easy for the boys to vote her down. A fourth director would even things up. A vote Ailsa could control on the board would be useful.

Plus Rina was in love with Seth. If she played her cards right, that was knowledge Ailsa could use.

She sat in her office for a long time that night, permitting herself a brandy in the small hours, slowly allowing herself to gloat over what she'd achieved.

Now she and Seth would have years to build the Lasrey Estate brand together.

Starting tomorrow. And the next week. And the month after that.

Book 2

Chapter 8

Five years later

Remy Roberts paused to tip back her hat and take a long drink from the plastic bottle in her pack. When she'd had her fill, she let the liquid waterfall over her chin and throat to soak into her shirt. It was warm, but it was wet and it took some of the scorch out of the sun.

Tucking the water bottle in the pack at her hip, she paused for a moment to check where she was in the vine row before she started the steepest part of the climb for the eighth time in the last hour.

She liked the exercise. Liked the peace and quiet of walking amongst the vines.

She even liked the heat. Western Australia had its fair share of sun, but nothing prepared a girl for the eyeball-searing, scorching dry of a South

Australian summer. Especially now the drought had stretched into its third year.

Reaching into the vine canopy, Remy twisted a berry from the ripening bunch of sauvignon blanc. It stuck to the stem and she had to tug hard before she put the fruit on her tongue. The flavours were there, flitting in and out of the sourness like wind through the vine leaves.

She didn't expect sweetness. Harvest was six weeks away. Middle to late February, the local growers reckoned.

There was a thrashing in the vines out to her right and the sound of it made Remy smile. Seconds later her dog burst into the middle of the row in a mini-tornado of dust and dry grass. Breeze stopped at Remy's feet, mouth open wide, pink tongue hanging.

She scratched the concrete block of her dog's head. Breeze's tail batted up a new cloud of dust. 'Come on, then.'

She finished the last hundred metres to the top of the hill with Breeze at her heels, feeling the stretch in her calves as well as in her lungs.

Once there, she paused again, one hand on the roughened top of the trellis end-post. Breeze slumped in the shade of the vines at her feet and the sound of the dog's puffing drowned everything else.

Remy never tired of this view. First time she'd walked up on the hill five years ago, with the red-faced and wheezy real estate agent, and gazed across the valley, she'd known she had to buy the patch of land locals called Old Menzel's Farm.

Below, the vineyard sloped to the valley where the creek cut through. That creek had been running the first few years, but it was dry now, parched and cracked. The dam that fed from it was little more than a puddle for ducks. Ivy Lodge, Remy's cottage, stood there too. Iron roof shining in the sun.

According to her neighbour Zac Williams, whose family knew everything and everyone in this part of the Hills, Old Menzel's kids hadn't wanted to follow their father into grapegrowing. They'd chosen different paths. As Mr Menzel got older, Zac said he'd *let the farm go*.

Remy could remember the exact tone of Zac's voice. It was Christmas morning, the first one after she bought the farm. Seventeen-year-old Zac had been helping her dig a hole.

Breeze—a puppy then—had dodged a bullet that day. She'd chased the Williams' sheep. Remy had paid Zac's dad for a ewe that couldn't be saved, helped Zac bury it, and promised Bryce and Sheila Williams it would never happen again. If it did, Remy said, she'd put Breeze down herself.

Old Menzel let the place go, Zac had said, as they'd leaned on their spades looking over the valley, in much the same way Remy leaned on the trellis post now.

She was damn glad the old owner had let it go. It was the only way she'd been able to afford it.

Remy slapped her palm on her thigh and Breeze leapt up. The bitch was four now and in her prime: a tan and white ball of mischief with a chest like a front-rower and thighs to match.

'Come on lazy,' Remy said to the panting dog. 'This isn't getting our work done.'

***

An hour or so later in the cottage, Remy had made her second cup of tea for the day and was about to take it out into the shade of the big trees near the old stable, when Breeze growled in the yard. At the front of the house, Remy heard tyres crunching gravel.

She put her cup on the sink and crossed to the fridge, pulling out a bag of tomatoes, two zucchinis and a handful of basil with the ends tied into a bundle of damp cottonwool. Seconds later she heard the metallic clank of the lock at the side gate and paws scrabbling.

She pushed out the patio doors.

Zac Williams' leg came through the gate first, blocking Breeze who'd been trying to get her head past his knee. Zac had a carton of eggs in one hand and Remy's mail in the other.

Breeze growled at him. A low staffy growl that was like a vintage car engine cranking on a cold day, tail wagging hard enough to wiggle her entire body.

'One of these days I'll come in here and she'll take me bloody arm orf,' Zac grumbled.

'Nah. She *likes* you,' Remy said. 'People she gets along with fine. It's just anything on four legs, or if it has wings.'

'No wonder you don't keep chickens.' Zac shut the gate. In the next breath he shoved his sunglasses to the top of his mop of brown hair and held out the eggs and envelopes.

He was pushing twenty-three now, and no longer lanky. Like his dad, Zac had shoulders honed on years of tossing full-grown sheep like they were woolly pillows.

'Great, you've brought me bills.' Remy swapped the eggs and mail for her homegrown vegetables.

'Great, you're giving me tomatoes. Mum must be down to her last six dozen.'

'Well, if she would take any money for the eggs, I wouldn't have to give you fruit and...' It wasn't the first time they'd had this argument. It wouldn't be the last. Remy didn't want people's charity. Never had.

Zac's gaze travelled to her feet, where the big toe of her right foot emerged from her sock like a fat pink worm. 'Air conditioning?'

'Yep. Natural ventilation.' Who had money for inconsequential things like socks?

He laughed, dragging his gaze north, up her bare legs to worn denim shorts, before jumping quickly to her face. 'So,' he began, clearing his throat. 'Have you heard the news?'

'I never go anywhere to hear any news, you know that. What's up? You knocked up someone's daughter and you're leaving town?'

'You know you're the only girl for me, Rem.'

He almost carried it off too, Remy thought, but the bob in his Adam's apple gave him away. Zac had had an almighty crush on her for years. Starting, probably, the day they'd dug that hole for the dead sheep. Not wanting to embarrass him she said again, with a smile: 'Go on then, tell me. What news?'

'Max Montgomery sold Montgomery Wines. Walk-in, walk-out. Some West

Australian company brought it. Lasley or Laxley. Somethin' like that.'

And winter's ghost stole summer from the sun. The egg carton slipped. The mail slid from Remy's hand, fanning across her outdoor table until the envelopes rustled into the stone wall.

'Lasrey.'

'Ah!' Zac slapped the verandah post. 'Lasrey, that's it. Dad said you'd know 'em. They're big in the West, 'parently, and growin'. Not many wineries doing that right now so we knew they were a player.'

'They're a player,' Remy confirmed, then clicked her fingers to call Breeze so she could cover the shake in her fingers by stroking her dog's head.

Why was Seth Lasrey buying a winery here in the Adelaide Hills? Why did it have to be *Max Montgomery's* damn winery? He'd bought most of Margaret River and the Swan Valley in the last few years. *Hell and Tommy.* Wasn't that enough?

Zac chattered on. 'Dad reckons Max got over three million for it. The property, the restaurant, cellar door, the brand and the wines. Sue Mont is already in Sydney. It'd be a helluva shoppin' trip, Mum says, only Dad reckons the bank's probably gonna get most of the cash.'

'Banks usually do,' Remy said. She ducked her head, bending low over Breeze so the messy swirl of hair that escaped her plait fell over her shoulder and covered her eyes.

Zac had three older sisters and a knack for knowing when a girl was about to cry and Remy—trying desperately to keep her shit together and contain the scream that wanted to escape her throat—could sense him watching. Scratching at the paving with the toe of his boot, he said, 'Remy?'

'Yep?'

'You look like you might faint on me or somethin'. Not that I mind,' he added hastily. 'Like, I'll catch you. I promise.'

'I'm not going to faint.'

'You always said the Monts were like fairy godparents. Is that what you're worried about? That the new owner won't take your fruit? You've got a contract with Montgomery, haven't you?'

'Not in writing.' Remy shook her head. 'Max did everything on a handshake.'

Zac kicked the pavers again. 'Maybe that's why he had to sell.'

Remy knew what he meant. The locals said Max Montgomery was too soft. He'd kept paying top prices to his grapegrowers when other winemakers were slashing rates. These last few years of drought had coincided with a worldwide glut of wine. So many wine companies had gone to the wall and when the wineries started pinching pennies, first to get squeezed were the growers who sold them fruit.

In all that, Lasrey Estate had got bigger and bigger.

Pity Seth had earned a reputation in the industry for being ruthless in the process, but then ... you only had to look at his mother.

'You'll be right, Rem,' Zac said, when he couldn't handle her silence anymore. 'You've got the best sauvignon blanc vineyard in the Adelaide Hills. Everyone around here says so. Max Montgomery has all those gold medals to prove it. These new guys will want it and if they don't, they're dickheads.' He shook the bag of tomatoes as he said it, like that made it final.

'I wish I had your faith.'

'Well, if all else fails, you could always pull out that vineyard and run sheep,' Zac winked. 'Long as you can keep that dog from eating 'em.'

Breeze yawned, rolling out her long pink tongue. It was almost like she poked it out at him.

Zac pulled his sunglasses over his eyes. 'I gotta go, Rem. Me and Dad are going across to Murray Bridge this arvo to look at a new ram. Catch you later. Thanks for the tommies.'

She might have said 'no worries' before Zac opened the gate. She might have said 'seeya' or 'tell your folks I said hi', or any of those myriad meaningless things neighbours said to neighbours all the time. She hoped she did. She didn't want to be rude.

Truth was: Zac was there one minute and pretty much gone the next and when she thought about it later she couldn't remember saying a word of goodbye, because right after that her head filled with visions of Ailsa Lasrey's finger sliding that cheque across the boardroom table, and the day that changed her life forever.

'*What the hell is this?*' she'd said to Ailsa.

'*It's an incentive,*' the older woman said.

Remy recounted the zeros. 'It's for $100 000, Mrs Lasrey. That's not an incentive. That's half a house.'

Ailsa shrugged. 'You quit and it saves me a lot of paperwork. If there's one thing I don't like, it's hassle.'

If there was one thing being Wayne Hanley's daughter had taught Remy, it was there was no such thing as a free lunch. Whoever picked up the tab, you owed them something. There were always strings.

'*What's the catch?*'

'*I want you to stay away from my boys. Like right away. Like out of the state away.*'

Remy glanced at the neat swirls of Ailsa's handwriting. She had loopy, elegant handwriting. Little tails at the tip of the zeros. All those zeros. More zeros than she had ever expected to see written on a thin black line alongside her name. It wasn't a business cheque. It was from Ailsa's personal account. Perhaps it was easier to hide that way.

She'd be Ailsa's dirty little secret.

Remy sucked in a breath and wished the boardroom would stop swaying.

It was a brand new life for herself and her mother, $100 000. She could pay off Mulvraney and start again in a place where no one knew them. Lexie wouldn't be that drunk's wife. She wouldn't be that drunk's daughter. Nor would she be the girl left heartbroken when Seth married Helene Bouchard.

Still Remy hesitated. She waited so long, Ailsa sighed and leaned across the table and said, 'Do I have to take my money back?'

'There is someone in WA who I can't walk away from without paying.'

Ailsa fixed her with a hard stare, waited, as if measuring her up. Then she reached out and yanked the cheque from Remy's grasp. The thought of watching it be torn in shreds proved to Remy how much she wanted the money.

The older woman reached beneath the table, to her handbag Remy presumed, and emerged with her chequebook. Flipping to a new page, she started writing.

'Will 10 000 cover it?'

'No,' Remy said, feeling like the whole thing was a dream. A nightmare...

'Fifteen?'

Remy shook her head. Mulvraney's debt was eighteen grand.

'I'll give you $20 000 now.' Ailsa wrote the new cheque. Then she flipped to a new page and wrote another. Pointing at it, she said to Remy, 'This is the balance, but it's forward dated for two weeks. This $80 000, you call me before that date so I know you're gone. Otherwise I call my bank and cancel it. And you never contact my sons. Ever. You got that?'

Remy did. 'I'll pay it back, Mrs Lasrey.'

Ailsa actually laughed. 'If it helps you to think that way, dear. You do that. I won't hold you to it.'

'Will you make sure they ... Seth and Blake ... know it was an accident?

You'll explain to them ... I'd never try to poison their vines on purpose?'

'Of course.'

'Okay,' Remy said, and she held out her hand for the cheques.

Chapter 9

'Jennie Grey from Channel 7, Mr Lasrey. Can you tell us what it was about Montgomery Wines that first caught your interest, in terms of your latest merger?'

Seth turned his attention to the journalist sitting in the second row of restaurant chairs. She had straight blonde hair parted fiercely on top of her head, and bright pink lipstick on a mouth that seemed to frown, ever so slightly.

Merger sounded so much better on a journalist's lips than *buyout,* or *takeover,* or *acquisition,* Seth thought. That's why he instructed his communications team to use 'merger' in their press releases about Lasrey's buyouts, takeovers and acquisitions.

'We thought it was a good match for us right now, Jennie,' he said, waiting a beat: 'Max was ready to sell and the price was right.'

'Dammit, I knew I should have held out for more,' Max Montgomery, standing by Seth's side during the press conference, said. The journalists huffed with laughter and Max's ruddy cheeks reddened.

Seth laughed with them.

They were almost finished and the media had lapped the story up. South Australia needed a good news story. There'd been lay-offs in the local car manufacturing industry, plus the wine industry was in freefall.

'On a serious note, if you like: Montgomery Wines is a jewel in the Adelaide Hills. I couldn't ask for a better introduction for Lasrey into South Australia. We think there's a lot of upside for us here and we can't wait to roll our sleeves up and get to work.'

'So this year's vintage? Will we see a Lasrey style of wines, or Montgomery's?' Jennie Grey followed her first question.

'Max's people and ours will work hand in hand through this vintage so we can get a good feel for how they do things. Then, if we don't stuff everything up, they'll let us go it alone.'

'I'm sure you won't stuff it up.' Max smiled again, but the sweat had begun to glint on the bald patch on top of his head. The old guy was feeling it and fair enough, Seth thought, Max wasn't used to fronting a camera.

Not like me.

Whenever Blake rang from Brazil, or Hawaii, or Jervis Bay, or wherever the latest surf competition was being held—as long as it was a place with internet—he'd say: *'Saw you made the news again, bro. You make such a great talking head.'*

'What about local grapegrowers, Seth? Are their contracts with Montgomery safe for this year?'

Seth turned toward the new voice. It was a woman who asked the question. He recognised her as an editor of one of the wine trade publications based in Adelaide. He'd spoken with her before and like most of the questions he'd been asked so far, he'd anticipated this one. Fruit pricing and grower contracts were the hottest topic in the industry.

'We're still working through all the fine print,' Seth said. 'Max has been very strong throughout the negotiation process that his growers get looked after, and we're certainly amenable to that. At the same time, it's tough in this industry. Everywhere we can, we have to tighten our belts. That's just the way it is.'

The woman nodded, and added seriously: 'The latest price estimates coming out of the Riverland are down on last year...'

'That's the Riverland. That's different to here,' he said.

Beside him, Max shuffled his feet. He'd put shoes on in honour of the press conference, tan lace-up ones that had probably never been out of the box.

'I'm sure you've done your due diligence, Seth,' another journalist, male this time, spoke. 'But I wouldn't be the first to suggest you might be overextending. How many acquisitions is that in the last three years?'

'We have done our sums and as I said before, we obviously see a lot of upside to this new *merger,*' Seth said, ignoring the second part of the question. 'Sauvignon blanc is going to be the wine of the next decade—now there's a tip for you.' He laughed and clapped Max on the back as a camera clicked. 'The Adelaide Hills makes great sauvignon blanc. We can give the New Zealanders a run for their money.'

That was about it. He fielded a few more questions as the sweaty patch on Max's crown expanded, and when the questions dried he thanked the journos for coming. Maggie Castle from Montgomery's admin team, along with Seth's PR manager, handed each journalist a two-pack of Shiraz. The show was over.

'Thank God for that,' Max said, pulling at the tie cutting into his neck. 'Thought I was gonna expire. Now I know why these news things make me nervous. Guess you're used to them?'

'Pretty much,' Seth said. 'Most of the time journalists don't know anywhere near as much as they'd like you to think they do. The trick is only to answer the questions with stuff you want them to know.'

'I'll take your word for it.' Max wiped his hand over his head. 'Shit. I need a drink. Is it beer o'clock yet?'

'Must be near enough.'

Seth let Max lead him out on the balcony toward a table beautifully laid for the lunchtime trade.

'Can't quite believe it's the end of all this, you know?' Max indicated the landscape that fell away beneath them. White-puffed pampas grass bordered the edge of an enormous dam where a jetty had been built out into the middle. A young couple was out there, slowly making their way back to the shore. The guy had his arm around the girl and cuddled her close.

'Think of it this way, Max. No more call outs in the middle of vintage when the bloody filter clogs or the press breaks or some idiot driver's bogged a tractor up to the axle because he went too close to the bloody dam...'

'Yeah, I won't miss that.'

'Yeah,' Seth agreed ... and waited, because he could tell Max was working up to something. He'd spent enough time with Max Montgomery in the last few months to read the man's signs.

'Jeez. I don't know, Seth. I just hope I've done the right thing. Wine's a young man's game. It was easier twenty years ago. Now it's all about the branding and marketing as much as what's in the bottle. What do I know about that? I thought I did it right. Got good advice ... Every man and his dog planted grapes as a tax dodge in the nineties and now look at it. No one's making a dollar.' Max squinted at Seth. 'Well, except for blokes like you. You must be doing something right.'

The waiter arrived carrying a bottle of Montgomery's sparkling white and Max sat heavily in his chair. 'Thank God for that, my feet are killing me.'

'You and me both,' Seth said, although his feet felt fine.

The waiter poured two bubbling glasses.

'Your health, Max,' Seth said, tipping the glass in a toast. 'And a happy retirement.'

'To you and your team, Seth. I hope this venture brings you every success.'

They drank.

Seth could see Max tasting the liquid on his tongue, testing for flaws. It was a winemaker thing; Rina always did the same.

'So now we've done the three-ring media circus, where do you want to start?' Max said.

'Rina's meeting with your winemaking team today. They're showing her around.'

'Lewis Carney is a good bloke. You won't have any trouble with him.'

'Good,' Seth said. *If I do have trouble, Carney will be out on his arse.*

'And what about you, Seth?' Max said, putting his glass on the table. 'I have to admit you're not what I expected.'

'How's that?' Seth said.

'When I told people I was thinking about selling out to you, they told me I had rocks in my head. They said you were hard as they come.'

Seth shrugged. 'Not sure what I should say to that, except maybe I'm getting soft in my old age.'

'You've got a few years left yet, mate.' Max sucked down the rest of his glass and refilled it. Then he shifted his weight to the side and dug into the pocket of his pants, pulling out a sheet of typewritten paper. 'Here's the grower list I promised you. All up to date.'

Seth reached for the pages but Max resisted, and their eyes met. 'You will look after them, won't you? There are people on this list who are like family to me.'

'I'll do the best I can by them, Max. That's a promise. As long as no one on there is unreasonable about anything, we should be right.'

Max released the pages. Seth tucked them in the inside pocket of his jacket without looking. He didn't need to look. There was only one name on the list he cared about. One name he knew.

Remy Roberts, Red Gum Valley Road, via Oakbank.

Four months ago when he'd first started discussions with Max Montgomery's business broker, after word came through the industry grapevine that Max was ready to sell, he'd seen the name Remy Roberts on this same list. 'Remy' was unusual enough that he had to ask the question.

Max told him Remy had been in the Adelaide Hills for five years and had come from over West. 'Great grapegrower—there's never any problems with her fruit. She's pretty easy on the eye too,' Max had said. 'You wait till you see how all the blokes at work find stuff needs doing at the winery whenever Remy comes around.'

Roberts, he'd discovered, was her mother's maiden name.

So he'd found her. Accidentally, after all these years.

Seth took a sip of his drink. He didn't drink before noon as a rule, but hell, it was five o'clock somewhere and if Max was in a mood to celebrate, so was he. It was that kind of day.

'You look pleased with yourself,' Max said.

'I could say the same.'

'Yeah. I guess so. It'll take a while to sink in.'

'It'll help when the money hits your account,' Seth said.

'Only if the wife hasn't spent it yet.' Max laughed.

Seth laughed with him, but privately his mind skipped to Remy.

He'd thought about her less over the years, of course. Life moved on and he'd been busy building an empire. But it didn't take much to remind him. He stayed away in the wildflower season because he didn't want the memories of the picnic they'd shared at Ellen Brook. He hadn't been to Vintage Festival in four years, either. Left it to Ailsa or Rina to present his father's trophy.

Did Remy know he'd bought Montgomery Wines?

He would love to be a fly on the wall when she found out.

She wasn't there when he got back from France. He'd told her he'd help her deal with her debts. He'd begged her to trust him, and she'd gone without a word. Worse, she'd gone with a hundred grand of Lasrey money in her pocket.

He didn't even know if those debts were real: a story to put him off his guard. Make him feel sorry for her. Make him want to help her.

He'd been such a fool.

Remy Hanley/Roberts—whoever she was—she'd never needed help. She knew exactly what she was doing, and she'd used him to get her there.

'What's up?' Max asked. 'You've gone quiet.'

Seth sat back in his chair, swirled the liquid in his glass. 'You got me thinking about first impressions, Max. That's all.'

Through the glass windows of the restaurant, Seth saw Rina near the serving counter. Lewis Carney beside her.

'I'll ask them to join us, shall I?' Max said, gesturing to the restaurant.

'Sure,' Seth agreed, then as Max made to get up he said, 'you stay here, mate. I'll go.'

Max sat, muttering about his blisters. Seth strode along the balcony, feeling the resilience of the boards under his feet. The sun was shining, it was a beautiful day.

All in all, an auspicious start to Lasrey Estate's new venture into South Australian wine.

Chapter 10

For a week after Zac told her about the Montgomery buyout (that Seth insisted in interviews was actually a *merger),* Seth was all over the newspapers and TV. The media blitz tailed off as journalists ran out of angles to cover and now their interest in Seth had turned social.

You'd think Adelaide had never seen a handsome rich bachelor before, Remy grumped, snapping the Wednesday paper shut.

So far, she'd seen Seth photographed with the daughter of an Adelaide real estate stalwart at the National Wine Centre; in a corporate box at the Australia Day cricket match with someone called Paula; and at a basketball game with the team sponsor's niece and her friend.

It seemed the women and the events were interchangeable. Not that she cared. She didn't. But just let the bean-counters from Lasrey Estate try to tell her how tough times were, or that everyone in the wine industry had to tighten their belts. Every grower who sold grapes to Montgomery Wines knew those fruit negotiations were brewing. It was highly unlikely Seth would be as generous as Max.

She took her coffee out into the early afternoon heat, grabbing her hat from its hook on the wall and secateurs and gloves from where she'd left them on the outdoor table.

Breeze trotted in front, paws puffing up the sawdust paths, tail bashing a lacework of fronds and flowers that tumbled from the beds. Each whack of her tail released scents of lavender or the salvias fresh pineapple, or the sharp tang of rosemary. All of it helped cover the smell of the sheep manure she'd scraped from the Williams' shearing shed and dumped on the garden beds. It would decompose all winter and give the plants that perfect boost leading into spring.

Spring. Her mother's wedding. Lexie would be back from her round Australia trip with Bernie by October, and the two planned to tie the knot.

As Remy walked, she snipped, deadheaded, drank coffee, and tried not to think about how much she still had to get done to make everything perfect for the wedding. Paving. Fixing the outdoor barbecue. Fixing the brickwork where the old red quoins had cracked. She didn't want to think about what it would cost; and not about Seth Lasrey or kisses, or bushwalks, or dolmades. Not thinking about that at all. She didn't want to think about Seth Lasrey either, or bushwalks, or ... any of that.

Breeze huffed back and forth chasing a scent or a sound. Every tiny scuttle in the undergrowth made the dog freeze, then she'd pounce on stiff front paws to where whatever made the sound had either hunkered down for dear life, or vanished.

Each time Breeze was thwarted Remy laughed because her dog looked so damn *puzzled.* It felt good to laugh. She'd been living in a time warp since news of the Montgomery buyout broke, caught between past and present until she felt like an elastic band.

Ailsa. Seth.

The day she grabbed the money and ran.

She'd lost count of the times in the last five years she wished she'd never taken Ailsa's money, and double-wished she'd paid back the old harridan when she'd had the chance.

The secateurs snagged on a rose and Remy yanked the blades from the thorns, leaving a gouge in the stem, ripping her glove.

Pulling both gloves off in frustration, Remy whistled for Breeze. This half-arsed gardening wasn't helping anyone and when half-arsed gardening didn't do the trick, there was only one thing for it. Whole-arsed gardening.

Entering the stable, Remy left her coffee cup on the garden bench and hefted her best pair of shears from their place on the wall.

First victim was the thug of a wisteria that ruled the sunny side of the stable.

With the handles near chest-height, she thought about Ailsa Lasrey and her sparkly rings and her neat little zeros, extended her arms and started hacking at the thick shoots tangled over her head, making tentacles of wisteria whip to the ground.

Dust sloughed off the leaves and she coughed. Sweat dripped in a vee between her breasts, darkening her purple tank top. She kept cutting, shearing the canes until her arms ached and her heart raced and there was no room in her brain for worrying about the future or regretting the past.

A thick clump of green loosened from the stable gutter and fell at the same time as Remy dropped her arms to ease the muscle burn. Legs apart, shear tips low, she stood amid the carnage breathing hard.

***

Two days later official notice from Lasrey Estate came in the handful of mail Zac delivered. It was one of two letters. The other was from the bank. She ignored the latter. Bank statements never held good news.

Remy tore open the other heavy cream envelope and scanned the page.

Dear Ms Roberts

I write to confirm recent news regarding the Lasrey Estate merger (Remy nearly choked on the word) *with Montgomery Wines.*

For those of you who aren't familiar with our company, Lasrey is the largest winery by value of wine produced in Western Australia and we're committed to growing our business both within Australia, and abroad.

You should feel confident that we value your contribution toward making Montgomery Wines a favourite with wine lovers everywhere. Lasrey has always believed great wines begin in the vineyard, and with the assistance and expertise of existing and new grape suppliers, we are sure this relationship will continue.

It is my pleasure to invite you to a grower meeting at Montgomery Wines on Monday, February 2 at 8.30am. We look forward to providing you more information about our harvest procedures at that point, and answering any questions you might have.

It was Seth's signature at the bottom of the page but the letter wasn't personally signed. Instead, his scanned electronic scrawl was positioned in a perfectly sized gap between the lines *With Sincere Regards* and *Seth Lasrey, CEO.*

Hell and Tommy. That was it. After two weeks of nailbiting and soul-searching, four measly paragraphs were all she got.

Remy stuffed the letter back into its envelope.

So what did she expect? A smiley face near his signature? A note on scented paper: 'Hi, Remy, Seth here. Let's do lunch.'

She'd been making this buyout personal and yet Seth's letter was all business. Was it possible he hadn't connected the dots? Could he truly not know who Ms R Roberts was? Or if he knew, maybe he didn't care. It was all so long ago, everything that happened in Margaret River: mountains in her life, molehills in his.

He would have tried to contact her otherwise, wouldn't he? At some stage over the years he would have tried to find her?

He hadn't. Neither had Blake, and for Remy's part she'd kept her side of Ailsa's bargain.

For the first month, not calling Seth or Blake had been the hardest thing. She'd pick up the phone then slam it in the cradle before the dial tone could go through. Then when she banked the second of Ailsa's cheques, the whole thing seemed so final.

In the second month, she dreamed she'd wake and find Seth outside the Adelaide Hostel where she was staying. That he'd ignored whatever his mother said and found her, and she could explain everything.

After the third month it got too painful to hope.

Not long after that, she'd opened her copy of *Grapegrower & Winemaker* magazine to find a small item in the *Grapevine* section announcing Seth's engagement to Helene Bouchard.

Chapter 11

The drive into Montgomery Wines wound around the side of a camel-hump shaped hill. In winter, the hill was green. This time of year like everywhere else, it was sun-baked brown. Cars had to leave the safety of the bitumen to drive the two kilometres into the winery and Remy always had the feeling that the Mercedes and BMW drivers braving the gravel path enjoyed the thought they were officially off-road. Gleaming, expensive cars wore the shimmer of dust like a suit of honour. The owners probably didn't get them washed for a week.

On the Monday of the growers' meeting, it was too early to have to slow for tourists and she was too preoccupied to pay attention to the view. Parking under some river gums, she left her car without bothering to lock it. No one would steal the car. No one would steal any of its contents either, unless they had a hankering for old Fleetwood Mac CDs, a pair of well-worn Blundstone boots or the big box of vegetable seedlings tucked in the passenger footrest.

Remy had dressed to blend in. Her hair was in a sloppy bun at her neck, cap pulled low over her forehead, big sunglasses. Her usual denim shorts had been replaced by faded denim jeans. Add flat shoes instead of boots and an over-sized blue long-sleeved shirt and she had a look Zac would have called *incognito.*

She wished she felt incognito. Unfortunately, she felt more like a high-kicking chorus line of neon fairies sat on the brim of her cap, chanting her name. *Remy. Remy. Remy.*

A sign at the bottom of the stairs directed growers up stone steps to the balcony. From there the timber decking led into the back of Montgomery's restaurant. Remy had been there plenty of times with Max and Sue, celebrating their big wine show wins, celebrating the Christmas party Max threw every year.

It wasn't like that now. The atmosphere was subdued. Normally, get a bunch of blokes together they'd be talking football, ribbing each other over teams, talking about what they'd got up to the last weekend, or what might be planned for the weekend ahead.

Quite a few growers had brought wives or partners, which made sense, Remy thought, because these were business decisions that affected the livelihoods of entire Hills families. The wives would want to hear from Seth Lasrey too. Get it straight from the horse's mouth.

'Come to see what the new boss has to say, hey, Rem?' Dave Hackett slotted himself beside her shoulder and they joined the bottleneck at the base of the stairs.

'Thought I'd better, Dave,' she said.

The Hackett property was a few kilometres further along Red Gum Valley Road. Dave and Nance had sold grapes to Max Montgomery for years.

'Heard this Lasrey guy's a tough operator.' Dave placed his foot on the bottom step and moved up. 'Dunno why he had to come sniffing around here anyway.'

'He smelled blood in the water, I'd say Dave.'

'Yeah. Maybe. That's why the big keep getting bigger. Way of the world these days.'

Once he'd crossed the threshold, Dave headed straight for a trestle table laden with white coffee cups and saucers, two big freshly brewed glass coffee jugs, and a stack of sugar in those dainty packets blokes like Dave opened by ripping in half.

Remy ignored the coffee and the trays of mini-muffins. Her stomach was twitchy enough.

It was almost impossible not to surreptitiously hunt the restaurant for Seth, but she didn't want to risk eye contact. She had no idea what reception she'd get. So here she was—hiding in a group of blokes gathered around the morning tea, trying to work out the safest place to sit.

Carefully, she raised her chin. *There.* That row of vacant seats behind Matt and Melissa Gilmore. Matt was built like a bus and his wife was even wider. Together, they presented a united front the size of the People's Republic of China. Aiming for that spot, Remy crossed the polished concrete floor, tucked herself behind the Gilmores, and sank into her chair.

Only then did she push her sunglasses to the top of her cap, and dare to look around.

At the front of the restaurant near the cashier's counter, two tables had been laid end to end with four chairs behind them, only one of which was currently filled. The person seated wasn't in a Lasrey uniform, and he wasn't Seth. Remy let out a slow breath.

Leaning to her right, she peered around Melissa Gilmore's neck and saw the back of Rina Stein. The woman was in deep conversation with a man near the dessert counter.

Rina's dark hair was shorter than when Remy had last seen it, cut in layers that shaped her neck. She wore the Lasrey khaki pants and a short-sleeved shirt. Her elbows and hips were every bit as pointy as Remy remembered.

It was the man Rina was talking to who gave Remy her first real shock of the morning. She hadn't recognised Montgomery's winemaker, Lewis Carney, in his Lasrey uniform. Lewis *never* wore uniform. She didn't think Montgomery Wines had ever even *had* a uniform. Certainly Max never wore one.

Matt Gilmore bent his head to the right to listen to his wife. Remy leaned with him, pretending to knock a stone out of her shoe. That was when the peal of metal on glass quietened the room like a headmaster's visit to a classroom of kids.

Remy slumped low in her chair.

'Can I start by thanking you all for coming? I'm Seth Lasrey. I've met some of you already, and it's great to see so many of Montgomery's grapegrowers here. I know it's a busy time of year for you and I appreciate your interest.'

At the sound of Seth's voice, Remy's heart moved from jog to sprint, and when Melissa Gilmore tilted her head sharply to the left, Remy was sure Melissa was about to alert the crowd to an animal stampede or an earthquake, so loud was the thumping in her chest.

Melissa beckoned down the aisle and whispered: 'We saved you a seat.'

'Yes. Please, sit down,' Seth broke his speech to encourage a tall man now crab-walking down the Gilmore's aisle. 'Make yourself comfortable. There looks like some room in the middle there.'

Melissa shuffled her bulk into the vacant seat on her right, Matt moved too, and through the gap presented by Matt's now-vacant chair, Remy got a perfect view of Seth at the front of the room, as relaxed in the spotlight as any career politician.

His gaze connected with hers and her heart did a lava lamp somersault through her stomach. Why her heart bothered with the calisthenics Remy didn't know, because Seth continued his speech without a hitch.

He didn't even have the decency to blink.

***

The second Remy stepped from her truck, tugging that cap like she'd pull it all the way over her nose if she could, Seth knew she was there. Remy Hanley might try to hide under a new name or a baggy cotton shirt or those sunglasses that hid half her face, but nothing short of a wheelchair could disguise the way she moved.

Watching her walk across the driveway, rubbing shoulders with a big guy with a beard when she got to the steps; laughing with him like they were old friends, she still moved like a goddamned angel.

Goddammit.

He knew from what Max had said that she hadn't let herself go, but that didn't stop him wishing his first sighting of her in five years didn't kick him quite so squarely in the balls.

There wasn't a silver earring in the world that he could see against a woman's neck without Remy crashing through his thoughts like a fireball.

Silver suited her. There was a time he would have bought her all the silver or gold in the world.

More fool him.

Standing a few steps back from the window on the first floor of the winery building, Seth watched until the angle became too great and he lost her.

'They've all got their cup of tea,' Rina's voice dragged his attention from the window. 'Some are on their second muffin. I'd say it's as good a time as any to get the show on the road.'

Funny how the mood of a grower meeting could turn based on a free scone. Give a bunch of grapegrowers morning tea and they were happy enough. Skimp on the muffins and you had a mutiny on your hands.

Seth was about to follow Rina into the restaurant when his phone rang. Glancing at the screen, he told her: 'It's Bainbridge.'

'Again?' Rina made a face. 'That guy is *such* an old woman.'

Seth accepted the call and waved Rina on, holding up two fingers. *Two minutes.* He'd had a gutful of Dan Bainbridge and his whining: a raindrop fell on the guy's head and he called for Noah and the fucking Ark.

By the time Seth dealt with Dan and entered the restaurant, there were only a couple stragglers hovering around the coffee pot. Most seats were filled.

Conversation dipped then buzzed anew as the growers worked out who he was. Remy, at least for the moment, must have found herself some dark corner. He couldn't see her anywhere.

Rina, who'd been in conversation with Lewis Carney, caught his eye. 'All okay?'

Seth spoke out the side of his mouth, still scanning the room for Remy. 'Yeah. Bainbridge can't organise getting his own arse out of bed in the morning.'

'That's why you've got me,' Rina said and she laughed. Carney did too, even though it was obvious the winemaker wasn't sure what they were laughing about.

Seth cut him some slack. He needed him. One thing that helped smooth any acquisition was keeping a key player from the old firm onside. With Sue and Max gone, the Montgomery's winemaker was last man standing.

Seth picked up a glass tumbler and tapped it with a restaurant spoon. Rina and Lewis pulled out the chairs behind the trestle table at the front of the room, but Seth ignored the seats. He couldn't remember the last CEO he'd seen give a welcome-to-the-new-order speech while sitting behind a trestle table covered in white tablecloth.

The room hushed.

A beanpole of a latecomer was trying to find a seat. Seth waited for the guy to come through. A lady shuffled sideways to make room. The bloke beside her moved too, and in the beat of shuffling chairs, while the beanpole apologised for stepping on toes, Seth came face to face with a pair of grey eyes staring out beneath a navy blue cap.

In a sea of faces that were a mix of expectant or heard-it-all-before resigned, Remy's stunned-rabbit expression was worth every cent of the $3.12 million it cost him to buy Montgomery Wines.

He was glad he'd given this exact speech so many times. Easy now to switch to autopilot while his brain registered all the little details: the hair escaping her cap was blonder than his memory, probably due to summer sun. Her throat was bare and her skin flushed, but was it with sunburn or a guilty conscience?

He tugged his hungry gaze away and kept talking, and after he wound up the spiel he asked for questions.

'What are my grapes worth?' That was first cab off the rank. It always was.

'I understand that's the question everyone wants me to answer, but it's simply too soon to talk about individual price per tonne. What I can say is that all of you will have a place for your fruit this vintage. Max was very strong on that point.'

'Who'll be making the wines?' A bloke in the second row wanted to know.

Seth opened his arm to indicate Rina and Lewis. 'I'm really pleased that Lewis Carney has chosen to stay on with us through the merger. Help us learn the ropes.'

Lewis smiled. Like Max, he wasn't a great fan of all the attention.

Seth continued: 'You will also get to know Rina Stein in time. Rina is our senior winemaker for Lasrey Estate. She oversees our entire winemaking technical operations. She's also part of our senior management committee, and, with my mother, brother and myself, a company director.'

That was Rina's cue to smile at the room, but Rina—who loved the spotlight—looked like someone had squirted too much lemon in her tea. It puzzled him, until he realised where she was staring.

Rina had just found Remy.

Perhaps he should have warned her? But if he'd disclosed that his plan to purchase Montgomery Wines came with that sort of string attached, the board would never have backed his bid.

Seth returned his attention to the room, and couldn't stop his gaze revisiting Remy. He could see the crescent bones of her collarbone outlined through her shirt. Remembered how they'd looked under that pink dress in the park when the wind and rain had lashed them in that storm—

The same guy who asked the question about contracts had his hand in the air again. Seth nodded at him, grateful for the distraction, but annoyed that he needed one. 'Yeah, mate?'

'My bank manager is breathing down my neck. I gotta be able to tell him something. When will we have some idea of what price you're offering?'

Offering. Seth admired the man's optimism. *You think of it as a negotiation if it helps, mate.* 'Over the next week, Rina and I will personally visit your vineyards. We'll talk with you about our expectations for the fruit and we should have a better idea then, about price.' He spread his hands wide, palms up. 'Give us a chance, mate. We've only been here five minutes.'

It got him a laugh. Part of him wondered if Remy had chuckled with the others. He refused to look.

'Any more questions?'

There were none and he turned to Lewis and Rina and asked if they had anything further to add. They didn't.

'I'd like to thank you again for coming this morning. We've put a schedule of our grower visits up on that whiteboard over there, so check it on your way out. Rina is doing the vineyard visits for the growers with surnames alphabetically from A to M and that means the Ns to Zs are stuck with me.'

Some of the growers got to their feet. The older ones had stiffened after half an hour sitting in the restaurant chairs. They had to spend a few seconds stretching before they moved. In ones and twos, people wandered toward the whiteboard, checking the lists. Some nodded. Some shook their heads.

'If that time or day doesn't suit, give us a call and we will do our best to reschedule.' Seth's gaze scuttled toward the centre rear of the room, where Remy had yet to move, then back to the whiteboard. He watched as a grower stole a last handful of mini-muffins. 'Jeez ... Rina, I can still see a few plates of morning tea that hasn't been eaten. I hope our chef's scones were up to scratch?'

That got him a rumble of laughter, too. It always did.

He checked the centre of the room again because he couldn't help it. *Nope.* No laugh from Remy.

***

Feet, get up and move, Remy ordered.

She had no good reason to stay seated. More than half the people had already checked for their appointment time and gone. If she stayed any longer she'd be last to leave.

She'd felt Seth's gaze touch her during his speech. Felt it sweep past her like a winter breeze. She hadn't wanted to look at him. Couldn't bear the thought of being caught staring because there were so many emotions in her head she was a whirlpool. He would see that confusion, and he'd know.

The last time she'd seen Seth Lasrey, she'd been ready to sink to her knees on the carpet with him, lie on his office floor and stare at him in wonder until she worked out whether his eyes were charcoal or black; and whether if he kissed her and smiled, she'd taste that smile on her lips.

He'd been smiling two minutes ago—cracking jokes about the bloody morning tea—then his winter gaze whistled across her skin again and she knew those smiles weren't meant for her.

To think, she'd once accused him of not smiling enough.

If you don't get up now, feet...

Carefully, she braced her flat shoes on the polished concrete floor and rocked forward. The restaurant chairs were solid timber, and the seats now vacated by the Gilmore family gave her something to anchor against and pull herself up. But the aisle of chairs didn't last forever. She had five football-field metres to traverse to reach the whiteboard, and nothing to hold her straight except her pride.

It felt so darn open out there.

'Remy Hanley? It is you. I thought so. I didn't see you on my list?'

Hell and Tommy. Remy's eyelids fluttered closed before they sprang open. 'Small world, Rina, isn't it? And you're a director now? Congratulations. It's Remy Roberts these days. How are you?' Remy turned to greet Lasrey's winemaker as the growers at the whiteboard glanced their way. Remy could see them thinking: *Hanley? Remy Hanley? Dumb Sandgropers. Can't even get our names right.*

'You got married?' Rina asked, with what might have been hope.

'Um, no. Not married. Roberts was my mother's maiden name. I changed it.'

'Oh.' Rina waved Lewis Carney into the conversation with one hand. 'Last time we saw each other, Remy had just sprayed our Margaret River cabernet vines with oxfluorofen.' She gave a tinny-sounding laugh.

Lewis's eyebrows took off like twin rockets.

'I didn't mean to, Lewis,' Remy said, as more of the growers near the whiteboard turned for a proper look. 'It was a dumb accident. I wasn't paying attention and I lost my job over it.'

'You're not poisoning vines now, I hope. Right?' Rina said. There was a flush in the woman's face that Remy attributed to the awkwardness of the situation. It *was* awkward. Remy would have done anything to find a gateway to another universe about now and throw herself through it.

'Remy has a sauvignon blanc vineyard at Red Gum Valley, Rina. We use her fruit in Chameleon wines. It's our top-end label,' Lewis Carney said.

'She's one of our most consistent growers.'

Remy could have kissed him. Rina looked like she might kill him.

There was a buzz in the crowd and growers shuffled away from the whiteboard like a flock of disturbed birds.

'Hey, Seth? Look who the cat dragged in,' Rina said, crossing her arms over her chest so her elbows made triangles either side. 'She's Remy Roberts now.'

'How are you, Seth?' Remy said, amazed she could hear herself over the whoosh in her heart.

'I'm well, Remy, thanks. And yourself? It's been a while.'

So we're going to be polite. Remy stared at a spot on the bridge of his nose. 'It has.'

'If you're Remy Roberts now, you'll be on my list.' Seth leaned forward, causing her pulse a moment's panic. 'Roberts. Red Gum Valley Road.' His finger traced the whiteboard. 'There you are. Ten-thirty Wednesday out at your place. I'll look forward to it.'

'Me too,' Remy muttered, pulling out her phone. She tried to give herself time to breathe by entering the time and date in her electronic diary. At least, she hoped that's what it looked like to anyone watching. The truth was her fingers wouldn't work, she couldn't remember the sequence of key instructions, and nothing came up except a useless toggle between her calendar and her email inbox.

Why hadn't he ever tried to find her? Why hadn't he called her? What happened to him and Helene? So many questions and this wasn't the time to ask them. There might never be a time to ask them.

'Bet you're the only one out of this lot with a gadget like that,' Rina said.

Lewis Carney took half a step forward. 'Actually, most of Max's growers are pretty good with technology. It was Max who didn't know his BCC from his CC.'

'The Remy I remember never had trouble working a phone,' Seth said.

Remy's gaze flew to his face, and this time not to the bridge of his nose.

Rina and Lewis chattered in the background.

Of course they were oblivious. Seth's words had meaning only to her. They told her faster than any neon sign that the past wasn't forgotten, that her mistake wasn't forgiven, and that a hundred grand was a hundred grand, in anyone's language. Whether it was a loan, or a gift, or a bribe. *Whatever.*

She couldn't change the past, but she could get rid of the loan. This year's grape cheque would have to cover what she owed Ailsa. If that meant no paving or no wood oven, and no perfect spring garden wedding for her mother, so be it. She'd cross that bridge when she came to it.

'Ten-thirty it is. Goodbye, Lewis, Rina...' she couldn't look at Seth again, so she said: 'Seth,' over her shoulder and kept walking.

***

Rina Stein had spent years perfecting her technique of tracking Seth wherever he went. It was so second nature these days she hardly knew she did it. Out of the corner of her eye, she watched Seth watch Remy's back as the woman walked away.

Her observation skills were a useful talent. Many times she'd cautioned Seth about a person he'd been dealing with: something about their posture, or the way she'd felt they were holding something back ... her ability to read people genuinely amazed him.

She played along with it, joking that all she did was pay attention.

Rina knew Seth's surprise at seeing Remy was feigned—she could see it in the set of his shoulders as he pointed at *Roberts* on the whiteboard. He'd known Remy would be on his list.

What Rina couldn't yet tell was how Seth felt about the girl. He'd kept his face turned away, and while he'd been standing at the whiteboard, nothing about his body softened in Remy's direction. He'd been like stone.

This, Rina decided, was a good thing. Stone she could deal with. Stone was okay. Stone was a long way from the frailty of flesh and blood.

Rina didn't know what the comment about working a phone meant. Remy hadn't liked that.

Did Ailsa know Remy was back on the scene? *No.* She dismissed it. Ailsa would have said.

Some people (Seth included) might consider it an obsession, were they to know how closely Rina watched everything he did. These days, she considered it part of her job. Seth was a bigger target for women now than he'd ever been. She owed it to him and she'd promised Ailsa she'd help keep the gold-diggers and hangers-on away.

A month or so after Remy left Margaret River, Ailsa had sought Rina out. Over a bottle of Joe Lasrey's famous 1992 Back Paddock Cabernet, Ailsa shared what Remy had done: that she'd tried to cash in on Seth's wealth by accusing him of sexual harassment, and that Ailsa had to pay her a considerable sum to keep it out of court. Rina never asked how much money. It wasn't her business, and if Ailsa used the word 'considerable', that told her enough.

The accusations Remy made against Seth horrified Rina. Disgusted her. More than anything, it justified all she'd done to get Remy sacked.

'Seth and Blake are such easy targets,' Ailsa had said, over that late-evening wine. 'I won't let the company Joseph and I built be destroyed because some woman sees herself as the next Mrs Seth Lasrey. You watch them a few years later when they're bored with the country life. Divorce and get half. Well, that's not going to happen. You understand, Rina, don't you?'

Rina said she did.

'If you'd keep an eye on Seth for me. Discreetly, you understand—he can't know that you're watching. If you could let me know if anyone gets close. I'd be grateful. In fact, I'd be so grateful, I'm sure I could convince Seth and Blake to find you a spot on the board.'

Ailsa had smiled and it made Rina feel good to be trusted, to be part of the inner sanctum. To be rewarded for her loyalty. She took the responsibility seriously.

When Seth brought Helene Bouchard to Australian shores, Rina had been so jealous, she'd made herself sick. She drank to cover the hurt. She couldn't sleep. Worse, it had impacted her work and that was something her professional pride wouldn't allow. She'd been smuggling hip flasks into the office, throwing fresh-mints into her mouth to cover the smell, and she knew if she'd kept it up, it would have been only a matter of time before a colleague smelled alcohol on her breath or she made the type of mistake that would get her dismissed.

So she'd pulled herself together. Cut down on the drinking through a mix of sheer bloody willpower and the knowledge that Ailsa and Seth had faith in her. They believed in her, and she wouldn't—*couldn't* —let them down.

Her thoughts about Seth weren't romantic any more. Too many years had gone by and Rina wasn't stupid. Seth didn't care for her that way, but she was the woman who had Seth's back professionally and personally. It was Rina who Seth shared coffee with most mornings, turning over events for the day, and it was Rina with whom he confided his business plans.

That had been enough.

Until Seth sprang this Montgomery Wines acquisition on them, with Remy hiding in the fine print like a cleverly hidden clause.

Chapter 12

The Wednesday of Seth's scheduled vineyard inspection dawned skittish and cloudy as Remy's mood. The day threatened humidity and every now and then the clouds would part and let a fickle blue sky poke through.

It had been the hottest start to February in five years, yet Remy couldn't get her hands or feet warm.

She'd roast if she wore jeans. Shorts were out of the question. She didn't own a suitable work skirt. In the end she chose a pair of long fawn-coloured cotton pants that tied with a drawstring around her waist and a long-sleeved shirt over a tank top to cover her skin. Put all that with a pair of Blundstone boots and she felt country without being try-hard. The last thing she wanted Seth to think was that she'd tried hard.

Why would she want to look good for him anyway? What was the point? The photos she'd seen of Helene Bouchard—when the French wine heiress came out to Australia and all the wine sites on the internet had carried photographs of the pair together—were enough to make any girl keen on Seth weep. Their so-called engagement hadn't lasted long. It was a rumour the Lasrey PR machine quashed almost as fast as it arrived. If elegant Helene hadn't been enough to hold Seth's interest, what chance did Remy have?

The longer she dicked about over whether to wear her hair loose or tied, or in a headband, or under a hat, the more pissed off with the world she got. *Hell and Tommy.* Who cared? Seth was coming to inspect her grapes. Not *her.*

She didn't know where to put herself. She didn't know what to do with herself. Wait inside for his knock? Wait in the vineyard, leaning on a post like a model in a fashion shoot? Loiter on the front steps with Breeze at her feet, like he'd surprised her on a tea break?

She wished he was here already. She wished It was over with already. Anything would be better than this bloody anticipation squeezing her from the inside, out.

At 10.30am, she sat on the front steps of the cottage with Breeze at her feet.

At 10.35am she locked Breeze in the backyard, before resettling on the front steps.

At 10.40am, she raced into her ensuite and slapped lipstick on: a new muted colour called dusky-rose that was so barely-there it couldn't be called a colour at all. She pulled a hairbrush across her scalp and on impulse changed her headband from green to cornflower blue with pretty white squiggles. She made a face at her reflection, at over-bright eyes and the flush in her cheeks that put dusky-rose lipstick to shame. Then she went back outside to wait.

And wait.

Maybe she had the date wrong.

Perhaps he wasn't coming.

Maybe he didn't want to buy her grapes at all.

At 10.50am, after racing inside to rub dusky-rose lipstick from her lips and plait her hair, she heard a vehicle change gears on the bitumen road. Flicking out the unfinished plait, she tugged the headband back over her crown then scuttled through her bedroom and out the front door, jumping as it clanked closed behind her.

A shiny new black utility sharked into her driveway, nosing its way into the shade of the Redwood Pine. The pine dropped sap and usually Remy told her guests to give it a wide berth. Seth, however, wasn't exactly a *guest.* So he didn't count. Let him park there at his peril.

The engine shut off, and in the quiet it was as if her garden and everything in it held its breath. Then the dog in the back of Seth's ute whined and from the rear of the cottage Breeze let out the kind of high-pitched bark that could break windows.

Thank goodness she'd locked Breeze away. Imagine kicking off this strange new relationship with Seth with a massive dogfight at Ivy Lodge.

I'd like $3000 per tonne for my sauvignon blanc, and you can pick up the vet bills, Seth, thank you.

The driver's side door opened and Seth buried his boots in her gravel and straightened. He turned a slow circle, taking in her cottage and her farm, a bit like Neil Armstrong might have looked before he planted that American flag on the moon.

Adjusting her headband, Remy realised she was sweating beneath it.

'Morning,' she called.

'Remy,' he acknowledged. 'Sorry I'm running late.'

The dog in the utility whined.

'No problem.' *I hang out on my front steps worrying about lipstick and headbands every day.* She could look at Seth now, as she hadn't been able to during the growers' meeting. There wasn't much point hiding anymore, not now he knew she was here. Or had he always known?

He lifted his sunglasses to the top of his head and stared out from eyes dark as ever.

'So how are you finding things at Montgomery?' she asked.

'Fine. Busy.'

Remy ran a quick scan as he cleared the bonnet of his car: hair short as she'd ever seen it and no grey, or not from this distance; short-sleeved black shirt with a bold L emblazoned on the pocket; dark hair where the shirt opened at his throat. Khaki pants. His uniform clung to his body in a way that really wasn't fair to single women everywhere.

'Nice place.' He extended his arm and waved a red clipboard at the dam and the vineyard beyond it.

The two dogs whined again. Much more of this and they'd have a canine version of duelling banjos.

'Occhy. Shut up,' Seth growled.

The dog shut like an obedient clam and Remy didn't blame it. Seth's voice startled her off the step and she stumbled as the ground leapt up at her boots. When the earth stopped trying to trip her, she said: 'Don't tell me that's Occhilupo?'

The big brindle male couldn't resist a whine as Remy said his name, stretching his bowling ball head over the rim of the ute's tray, putting one massive paw on the ledge like he'd give anything to be allowed to jump.

'*Stay* there,' Seth said, and Occhy retracted his paw as if to say the whole paw-on-the-rim thing was a mistake. 'I'm dog-sitting for Blake.'

'I'm surprised you're over here long enough to make it worth bringing him?'

'I'm here for a while.' He didn't smile. Nor did he elaborate.

He's got so hard, Remy thought. *When did that happen?*

'Can I pat him?' She moved toward the ute, then stopped. 'I don't want to get him in trouble.'

'Pat him if you want.'

Remy held out her hand for Occhy to sniff then scratched behind his ears where the short, dark fur was so soft. His coat had a faint light stripe through the darker brindle. He was all muscle, an American Staffordshire male in his prime. Breed-perfect.

'I know some people in Adelaide who'd love to see him in the show ring.'

'Yeah?' Seth said, politely enough, but with no real interest.

Remy took hold of the fur on either side of the dog's jaw and tugged it, like she used to do when Occhy was a puppy; like she did all the time with Breeze.

'He's beautiful,' she said to Seth.

She's beautiful, Seth said to himself, and he had to tamp it and tamp it hard and remind himself about who was really under that gorgeous skin. This woman was a gold-digger. Blackmailer. Liar. Thief.

Her attention slid from the dog and she fixed her gaze on him. 'You didn't seem surprised to see me the other day at the grower meeting?'

He thought about it for a beat, thought about lying, and decided it didn't matter. 'Your mother's maiden name wasn't much of an alias. I've known where you've been for a while.'

She let Occhy's face go. Her hands curled to fists at her side. 'For a while?'

'Yeah.'

'How long is a *while?*'

'We should look at your fruit, Remy.' He heard her suck a big angry breath, and enjoyed it. 'So how about we do that so I can tick you off my list and call you done.'

'Fine.' Head down, she turned on her heel.

'Stay there, Occh.' Seth leaned into the back of the tray and checked the clip on Occhy's chain. He didn't want the dog getting off and eating whatever mutt was barking at the back of the house. If Remy was into dog shows these days, it was probably a poodle with a pretty haircut. Occhy would toss it like a rat.

Remy didn't wait and Seth didn't hurry. He walked behind her, watching her shirt tails flap in the breeze, listening to her boots slap dirt. Last time he'd seen this woman, shirt tails and boots had been flapping too. That was the night she'd run from his office. The last night he'd seen her before she tried to fleece him. *Tried to?* Make that *did* fleece him.

She paused for a few seconds at a pump shed beside a puddle masquerading as a dam. There she washed the smell of dog from her hands under a tap. Then she was off again, climbing the slope toward the vines, walking fast enough and far enough to make sweat dampen Seth's back.

Remy opened the gate into the vineyard, held it for him while he caught up. It swung easily on oiled hinges.

'Vineyard looks good,' he said, as she shut the gate behind him, hands expertly finding the perfect angle to slot the pin mechanism into place. 'Why don't you tell me what I'm looking at here?'

Remy nodded toward the green vines striping the north-facing slope. 'It's all sauvignon blanc. That's all I grow. I'm sure that's in your notes. I have an integrated pest management program. I don't spray for pests unless I have to. I don't irrigate unless I *really* have to.'

'Lewis Carney says you got these old vines back from the brink. He sings your praises.' *Christ on a stick did the man sing her praises.* Everybody did. Max Montgomery never shut up about Remy Roberts and how good her sauvignon blanc fruit was.

'It's been a lot of work.' She set off purposefully, like she wanted to get this over, angling for the nearest entry to the vines. He stayed with her this time, a pace off her left shoulder, close enough to hear her breathing.

When did she start wearing headbands? They suited her. Caught all that wheat-gold hair up from her face and let it flow down her shoulders as she walked.

'About four months,' he said.

She glanced sharply sideways, slowed a little. 'Pardon?'

'That's how long I've known you were here. I saw your name on Max's grower lists during due diligence on the sale.'

'Oh.' The word dropped like an iron curtain between them.

They walked some more. Seth could almost hear the way her thoughts churned in her head. His churned too. Then he heard the faint pop beside him as her lips opened to speak. 'Did you ever ... I mean, you or Blake—did you ever try to find me?'

'You didn't make it easy, Remy. You were gone by the time I came back from France. You changed your name. Trust me, I wanted to find you. There was a helluva lot I wanted to say. I can't speak for Blake.'

All that seemed to confuse her. Why, he had no idea. She must have known the day would come when every lie she'd told would catch up with her.

'I rang Greg Trimble once,' she said.

'You talked to Pops?' She rang *Greg Trimble* after she left, but she couldn't bring herself to call *him?* 'When?'

'A few weeks after. I wanted to know if the vines made it,' she said. 'Greg was really nervous. He said he wasn't supposed to talk to me, but he told me he thought the vines would make it. He said all the staff had been banned from speaking to me because it was an ongoing investigation with the insurance company. I didn't want to get him in trouble. He'd already gone out on a limb for me.'

Pops kept that fucking quiet. Or, it never happened. It was hard to know when it came to Remy. She'd told so many lies.

Now it was her turn to press him: 'So did the vines make it, Seth?'

He wondered what answer would please her most? Yes or no? 'Yields were down that year and it put the vines back a bit, but all in all, they were fine. Pops did the right thing to treat it. He and Rina did a good job.'

'Thank God for that.' Her hand fluttered to her throat. 'I'm so glad.'

Don't get too glad, Pollyanna. 'It doesn't change anything, Remy. Whether you called us or I called you. Or Blake called you, or whatever.' Something else hadn't changed, he discovered. He still didn't like putting his brother's name and Remy's in a sentence together. 'It doesn't stop what happened. It doesn't change that you ran away.'

'You're right. It doesn't change anything. I know.' She dug her hands in the pockets of her pants, making the fabric pull tighter across her curves, making the air squeeze tight through his lungs. 'I just want to say this, okay, so that you know I said it. I'm really, really, sorry for what happened. I felt terrible that day. It was the worst day of my life.'

'It wasn't a great day for me either,' he said.

'I can imagine.'

He stared hard at her face, saw only sincerity there. Didn't trust it. 'You could have told me that before. You could have apologised to me years ago.'

'No I couldn't. Your mother said I couldn't.'

'What's that supposed to mean?'

Remy crossed her arms over her tummy, glared at the vines for a moment, then muttered more to herself than to him: 'Fuck it. It wasn't me who broke my promise.' She lifted her chin and locked her gaze to his. 'Ailsa said if I stayed in Margaret River she'd make sure I never got work in the wine industry again. She offered me the money on the condition that I'd resign so she didn't have to go through the process to sack me. I had to get out of Margaret River and promise never to contact you, or Blake, again. She didn't want me to tempt her precious boys to go slumming. So she offered the money to me and I took it. I'm not proud of that decision, but it's the one I made at the time.'

It took every year of standing up in boardrooms and making wine deals across the world to keep his face straight. What she said was ludicrous. He didn't believe her. He didn't. Yet 'slumming' was a word Ailsa would use. It sounded right.

'Why—Nah, forget it...' Everything between them couldn't be sorted on one morning's walk in the vines. Ten minutes he'd been here, and he'd let her get to him. Already he'd let himself think about burying his face in her hair. Seth adjusted his grip on the clipboard. The fingers on his left hand had held it so tight, they'd gone numb. 'I don't have time to go into it properly now.'

Get it back to business. Flicking the clipboard open, he stopped walking. 'These vines, Remy—they look thirsty to me.'

'You're seeing them with Margaret River eyes,' she said, coming to a standstill a few steps further uphill. 'Rainfall patterns are different here. My fruit style is different too. I don't irrigate unless they'd die otherwise, and I haven't had a full dam to start the summer in three years. These only drink what falls from the sky.'

Seth reached for a bunch of grapes, testing the weight in his hand. The berries plucked free when he pulled them, but not without a firm tug. He put three sun-warmed berries on his tongue and slowly crushed the mass.

Remy's cough caught his attention. Her eyes were wide and the heat or exertion had tainted her cheeks. She covered her mouth with her hand, burying another series of jerky coughs in her palm.

Seth felt a kick of alarm. Spitting the fruit pulp to the ground, he took a step toward her: 'Are you okay?'

'No. Yes.' She batted at him one-handed, took a hasty step back. Her face coloured to crimson.

Damned if he didn't suddenly think he might have to perform mouth-to-mouth right out here in the vineyard. His eyes snuck to her lips. A jolt of pure lust came out of nowhere and he almost had to cough himself to cover how much it rocked him.

One of her hands kept batting at him, a clear signal to stay away.

'I ... just need a drink of water. You don't need me here anyway, do you?' She dove past him, down hill—gone before he could say Heimlich, leaving him in the middle of the vineyard with the view and a hint of air scented with flowers and fresh hay.

He chose to focus on the view, rather than what remained of the scent he'd forever know as Remy's.

It was easy to see why she chose this farm. He'd seen some of the most spectacular vineyard regions of the world in his day, but this view was right up there.

His family's money had helped buy it. In a way, he even owned it. Part of it at least.

Seth tasted another couple of berries and decided he'd seen enough. He couldn't fault her fruit. He'd wanted to fault her fruit. Wanted to a whole damn lot.

On a whim, he dug his phone out of his pocket and thumbed through it for Pops Trimble's number. It was still early in Western Australia, but Pops was an early riser.

His vineyard manager answered fast. 'Hi, Seth. What's happening?'

'I know it's going back a while, but do you remember when Remy Hanley left Lasrey?'

'Yeah. That was all pretty hard to forget.'

'Did she ever ring you after she left? Did you talk to her?'

Greg hesitated. Seth could almost picture him slowly taking off his cap, putting it back on his head. 'Yeah. She rang. We weren't supposed to talk to her. Ailsa was pretty hard on that—a memo came round.'

'What did Remy want? Can you remember?'

'Yeah. She wanted to know about the vines. She asked if they were going to be okay.'

'What did you tell her?'

'Well ... it was still pretty early days then, but I remember right off the bat we lost a lot of leaves, but within two or three weeks secondary buds started swelling. So I told her I thought they were going to be okay.'

'Okay. Thanks Pops.'

'We good?'

'Yeah. No worries. Look after things, hey?'

Pops assured Seth he would, and they hung up. Seth shoved the phone in his pocket.

It confused him. If he believed his mother—and he'd struggled with believing her for a long time after France—Remy had purposely tried to kill the vines. Why she'd call Greg Trimble to check on them, why she'd be so happy they'd survived, didn't make sense.

And where did sexual harassment and the $100 000 fit with what Remy just said?

It didn't. She said Ailsa offered her the money to get out of town.

Nothing fit at all.

Chapter 13

Hell and Tommy.

Remy hadn't been kidding when she told Seth she needed a drink of water, but her dry-as-a-desert mouth wasn't due to any cough.

Surely fruit-testing was never that sexy when Lewis Carney did it?

She'd watched Seth's big hands cup a bunch of her grapes, squeezing each individual berry like a blind man learning its shape. He'd plucked the berries from the bunch and put them to his lips and she couldn't help but think about how those hands would feel caressing the warm, weighty, dangly parts of her own anatomy. The second the sneaky thought entered her head, she had as much hope of stopping the thrum in her pulse and the tingles that sparked all over as she had of stopping sunset tonight.

She fled toward her cottage, kicking dirt clods into dust, wishing she could kick the drought, Seth, and his fruit contract into next week.

It so wasn't fair.

Occhy whined from Seth's ute and Remy let herself be drawn into the shade of the pine. The dog leaned his huge head into Remy's hands as she rubbed and they stayed like that while Remy collected her thoughts. It took a while.

Eventually, she convinced herself her reaction to Seth was perfectly normal. All the history between them was bound to leave her unsettled. And as far as her body's response to him was concerned ... she attributed that to a drought of a different kind. On the sex front, it had been a *very* long time between drinks. And he looked good enough to drink, or eat, or whatever.

See. Normal. Perfectly.

'He remembers you.' Seth's voice spun her around, Occhy's chain rattled on the metal tray and her nerves took off like ducks in hunting season.

He opened the clipboard, took out an A4 sheet and handed it to her, all business. 'This is a spec sheet outlining our fruit requirements. You'll need to liaise with me nearer harvest so we time the fruit delivery right.'

She scanned the page. 'When will I know what rate you pay? Does this tell me?'

'Always interested in the money, aren't you, Rem?'

She ignored the sarcasm. 'I have commitments, Seth. You heard what they said at the meeting. Most grapegrowers have bank managers on their case. I know I do.'

'Okay. I should know more about tonnage rates in another week. We've just about finished all the initial vineyard visits.'

'So you'll let me know?'

He nodded. 'I'll let you know.'

She gave Occhilupo a final pat and stepped back from Seth's vehicle, noting with a certain satisfaction that there were at least two sap stains on his paintwork. *Good on you, Redwood Pine.*

'I'll be in touch,' he said, climbing into his car.

***

After her meeting with Seth, Remy changed into her gardening gear then drove straight to Dottie Howlett's place, feeling like she was fighting the car the entire way. She turned corners too sharp, braked too hard, drove too fast and she made the journey in record time, not that it was a record she'd ever want to repeat.

Dottie lived in Woodside in a small group of single-storey units built in reddish-brown brick with cream window trims. She sat in a chair on her front porch with a scruff-ball of white dog in her lap, near a doormat that said welcome and meant it.

'Lovely day for gardening, Rem dear. Not too hot. The side gate's open,' she called, as Remy climbed out of her car.

'Don't wish summer away on me just yet, Dot, winter is long enough up here, thanks very much.'

'I've had the most lovely tomatoes this year,' the old lady prattled, following Remy as she dragged a shovel from her ute, and carried them into Dottie's back yard. 'I've had to give some to the lady in number 6, I had so many. So much flavour. So much better than what you can buy in the shops. Taste like cardboard.'

Remy took a few minutes to check the vegie patch she'd built Dottie last spring. The plot wasn't big. Dottie didn't have the space, but no-dig gardens were good like that. It was amazing what could be done with twelve square feet of earth, newspaper, compost and a few bales of pea straw.

Dottie's tomato bushes were still going strong but the spinach had bolted to seed, along with the coriander. The zucchinis had mildewed leaves and Remy pulled them out first, throwing the plants to one side.

'I'm going to leave the tomatoes a bit longer, Dot, but the rest can all come out. I've brought broccoli, new spinach, climbing beans, and a pot of parsley for your window box.'

By the time Remy had re-layered the no-dig garden, planted and watered everything in—Dottie filling her ears the entire time—she felt far more relaxed. Gardening did that for her. She loved making these nodig gardens for the older people around the Hills. It was her way of contributing to their quality of life.

Sometimes she accepted payment for the gardens, if they could afford it or if their families wanted to foot the bill, like Dottie's daughter did. Often she did it freely. She had a pantry stocked with wonderful jams and preserves that the oldies offered her in return, and she was rarely short of sides of meat in her freezer, or firewood in the winter, or all those things that people who didn't always have money could find to trade.

Every third Sunday she held a stall at the Williamstown market where she sold her cacti teapots and containers of fresh herbs. A lot of her commissioned vegetable patch work came from that stall.

No matter how desperate she got for money, one thing Remy had sworn she'd never do was phone sex, ever again. That, she'd put to bed the day Seth overheard her on the phone.

White Knights had caused her nothing but trouble.

Chapter 14

'The problem with owning an old house,' Remy said to Breeze the next day, 'is that nothing's ever bloody straight.'

She was trying to re-lay the front steps to fix broken, rickety bricks, because her mother was very likely to want photographs stepping up or down those bricks, or sitting there with Bernie. She didn't want her mother to trip in her wedding dress, and she didn't want to spend years contemplating wedding photos where all she'd see would be the steps she should have fixed.

She'd mixed cement, chiselled out the dodgy bricks, and had the replacements all ready to go. Like most things, a simple job in theory was never quite as simple in practice. It was hot, and the cement kept going off that little bit too fast, adding to her pressure to try to get everything done too quickly. To compensate, she'd added too much water to the cement mix, which made it too squishy, and it was hard to get a good depth of mortar to match the other steps.

So she'd chiselled the entire row of bricks out, painstakingly chipped off the old mortar, and tried relaying the entire step again with a new batch of cement.

The good news was: she was nearly finished.

The bad news was: she probably should have bitten the bullet and paid someone who knew what they were doing.

'I make a lousy brickie,' she said to Breeze, who yawned in response and sat on the grey bag of dry cement, making it puff like a sleeping dragon.

That's when Remy glanced toward Red Gum Valley Road and saw the black ute winding its way up the driveway, coming fast, dust flying from the wheels.

Occhilupo had his head hanging out the side of the ute, so Remy's first instinct was to drop her trowel, grab Breeze by the collar and haul the dog safely behind the garden gate.

Then she tried patting her shorts and wiping her face to get the cement dust off. Then she gave up. He could take her as he found her, or not at bloody all.

Once again, he parked under the Redwood Pines. Once again, Remy didn't bother mentioning the sap.

'Hi,' he said. 'I'm glad I caught you at home.'

'I don't go very far this time of year,' she said. 'There's always too much to do leading into vintage. What's up?'

He was in uniform again, but khaki shorts today instead of trousers. He wore a cap, and sunglasses, and he hadn't lost that red clipboard. It was tucked between his arm and his ribs. He hadn't shaved.

Straight off the bat, the dogs started their two-way whine-fest between Occhilupo in the back of the ute and Breeze in Remy's garden.

Seth ignored them. 'I had a few more questions to ask you.'

'Fine. Go for it. I hope you don't mind if I keep doing what I'm doing here, though. I'm at a critical point.'

'Please.'

Remy slathered mortar on her trowel and transferred that to the brick.

Scraped it bottom, back, and two sides, then slotted it in place.

It fit first time. 'Well whaddaya know,' she said to herself, to Seth, and to anyone else listening. 'It's about time something went right.'

She tapped the brick with the rubber mallet she'd borrowed from Zac. Satisfied she had it level, she stood, stepped back, and admired her work from a distance.

'Not bad.'

'Looks good,' Seth said, waving his clipboard at her bricks.

Remy wiped her palms on her thighs. 'So what questions did you have, Seth?'

'What row spacing is your vineyard, Remy? What row width?'

She looked at him. 'You came out here to ask me that? I'm sure it's in Max's file.'

'Hate to break it to you, but Max doesn't have much by way of files.'

'Oh.' She released the elastic band on her hair, shook cement dust out, and scooped her hair into a tidier mess at the base of her neck. 'You could have texted me or something.'

'It's fine. I had to get out to the Hackett's place again too.' He opened the clipboard, found his pen. She got stuck looking at his hands. He'd always had nice hands. Big. Strong. Capable. She bet he'd lay a mean set of bricks.

'Remy?'

Stop ogling his hands. 'Pardon?'

'What's the row spacing and width?'

'Three-metre row spacing. Two point four-metre row width.'

'And what clone of sauvignon blanc is it?'

'*Hell and Tommy,* Seth. I don't know. Do I need to get an ampelographer out here?'

'Nah. It's all good info to know if we can. Don't worry about it.'

'Okay. Anything else? Do you have any news for me on price?'

His gaze skipped away and returned. 'I'd say, depending on quality and our production needs, absolute max would be $3000. It could be anywhere from $1500.'

'Max paid $3300 last year.'

'That was last year. I'm not certain we'll be making Chameleon this year.

Rina and I have been discussing it with Lewis Carney.'

'Not making it?' Remy's heart missed a beat. 'You can't not make it. That wine is Max's flagship.'

'Yes. And Max doesn't own Montgomery anymore.'

Remy fell silent. There wasn't much that could be argued on that.

Seth closed the clipboard, but Remy had the sense he wasn't finished. He took a moment to grope for the words, and whatever she'd expected him to say, it wasn't this: 'Why did my mother write you two cheques?'

Remy tapped the mallet a couple of times, wishing conversations about his mother didn't make her so nervous. 'What did Ailsa say?'

'I'm not asking her. I'm asking you.'

She'd bet her last dollar Ailsa had told Seth something entirely different, but for her, it was time for the truth. She had nothing left to hide, and no reason to hide it.

'Do you remember how you offered me an advance on my pay that night in your office? I told you I owed some money and you said Lasrey had a policy that might assist staff in financial hardship?'

'I remember. You didn't take me up on it. I also told you to trust me, and that I'd do whatever I could to help you. You didn't take me up on that.'

Remy ignored the latter part. 'When your mother offered me the $100 000 to resign and to leave, I told her there was someone I couldn't leave Margaret River without paying.'

He started to speak, changed his mind. 'Who did you owe $20 000 too?'

'When he died, my father had debts to a loan shark called Doug Mulvraney. Dad was into Doug for $18 000. Mulvraney made me and my mother responsible for those debts.'

Seth let out a long, slow, breath. He bounced the clipboard on his thigh, like he'd seen a mosquito there to squash, then tucked It beneath his arm.

'Ailsa wrote me that first cheque so I could pay Mulvraney and pack up the house. The second cheque she dated two weeks later. I had to call her and prove that I was out of West Australia or she said she would cancel it.'

'*Christ on a stick.* What was your father into, Remy, that he owed $18 000?'

'Greyhounds. Shares. Horses. You name it. When he died, Mum and I had bills coming from all over the place. Liquor store bills. He had fuel accounts set up at service stations from Augusta to Capel. He was drunk when he crashed the car, so the insurance wouldn't pay up. He and Mum were already mortgaged to the eyeballs when Mum had to sell the house.'

'This is why you were doing the phone sex?'

'That's why. It's the only thing that kept us afloat. It's the only way we could pay Mulvraney's interest, and bring the loan down.'

'Did your mother know?'

Remy bristled. 'Of course not. That's not the kind of thing you tell your only parent. I used to log in for phone times when she was at work, when she was out of the house. I was very careful about that.'

'Didn't she ever ask where the extra money was coming from?'

Remy hesitated before she met Seth's eye. 'I kind of, um, elaborated, when I told her what my wage was with you.'

'Ah,' he said.

Breeze let out another of her glass-breaking squeals.

'What the heck sort of hellhound have you got around there anyway?' Seth glared at the front of her cottage like he expected to see claw marks in the stone. 'Occhy. Shut up.'

Occhy cut his barks to whines, then whimpers. He shifted on his front paws, alternating between one paw on the rim, then two, then back to one again.

Seth scratched the side of his head, and even through the sunglasses Remy could see him squinting at her, trying to work it all out. Then he tossed the clipboard on to the bonnet of his ute. It didn't land flush. It skidded across the polished metal before it dropped to the ground.

'I have to wash out my wheelbarrow, Seth, or it'll set.'

He was nearer the hose and he turned the tap on for her, kinking the hose to save water when he passed it to her.

'Thanks,' Remy said, tipping the wheelbarrow and washing it so the dirty water flowed into the agapanthus. They were tough. They could handle it. When she finished, he turned off the tap and coiled her hose into a neat figure eight near the new steps.

'I bet you hang all your shirts beautifully, Seth. Not a crease to be seen.' It popped out before she thought about it, and she regretted it straight up. It felt intimate and she couldn't afford to get intimate with Seth. 'Sorry.'

'What are you sorry for?'

'It's none of my business what you do with your shirts.' Then she thought: maybe he isn't staying at a hotel at all. Maybe he's staying with one of those girls from the social pages. Maybe *she* irons his shirts.

The thought hit her so hard and so heavy, she almost dropped the wheelbarrow. He didn't seem to notice how she had to wrestle to keep it straight.

'My mother said the first 20 000 was to stop you taking allegations to the police that I'd sexually harassed you, that night in my office.'

This time, Remy, did drop the wheelbarrow. It knocked the trowel to the concrete path, making a metallic scrape that hurt her ears. 'Ailsa said *what?*'

'She said two weeks' later you called and said you wanted more money. That if she paid you another eighty, you'd be gone for good and we'd never hear from you again.'

'Wow,' Remy muttered, standing the barrow straight, kind of slumping against it to cover her shock. 'No wonder you think I'm the lowest of the low. I told Ailsa I'd pay her the money back. I've been saving to pay her back.'

The muscle in his jaw twitched. 'And how's that savings plan going?'

She swapped her weight to the other foot. 'I have $78 000 sitting In a high-interest account. I had more. I had most of it at one stage but then—' she took a deep, noisy breath and let it go with a whoosh: 'look, I had trouble with a tradesman working on my renovation and my roof started leaking, okay? And the Nissan blew a head gasket. I had to trade it in on the Rodeo. All anybody was talking about was drought and grape prices went down the gurgler. I had a perfect storm of crap.'

'So you spent the money on your house and a new car?'

'You make it sound like I bought a palace and a Porsche. Every spare dollar I make goes into that account so I can pay Ailsa back.'

He frowned, and she knew immediately what he was thinking—that it was phone sex paying those extra dollars. She would have told him then that she didn't work for White Knights anymore—that she hadn't in years—but before she could get out the words, Occhy's chain grated across the tray. The scream of the chain on the rim ripped the air, and the dog launched himself from the back of Seth's ute.

Remy shouted, and both she and Seth lunged forward. Neither made it before the leather collar pulled tight and Occhy fetched back with a jerk, paws scrabbling thin air. Then mercifully, the dog slipped the collar and thudded to the ground. He sat there for a few seconds like a boxer trying to work out if he had it in him to stand up.

Breeze's next squeal cleared Occhy's wits fast. The dog scrambled for the verandah and they watched his tail disappear as he raced for Breeze and the gate.

'That bloody dog,' Seth muttered. He didn't climb her newly-repaired steps. He made a running leap through the agapanthus clumps and landed on the verandah.

Remy was a step behind him all the way and that's why when Seth stopped at the timber gate like he'd smacked into the side of a barn, she almost collided with his broad back.

She expected him to grab Occhilupo by the scruff of the neck and drag the dog away. At the very least she thought he'd give both dogs such a telling-off, they'd stop their whining and yelping for a week. But he did nothing like that. He stood stock-still, staring over the gate at her garden.

Slowly, he shunted his sunglasses to the top of his head then snuck his hands into his pockets. 'I guess that answers my question.'

'What does?'

As best she could tell, he was mesmerised by the silver birch grove in the far corner, where white trunks gleamed against leaves coloured mustard yellow. If it wasn't the birches, then maybe the rustic timber bench in the foreground where her mother had liked to sit and read; or perhaps he was a closet salvia nut—she had about twenty varieties growing.

'No one who could grow a garden like that could try to kill a vineyard. I can see that now.'

Remy's heartbeat skipped, and it took a few seconds to kick properly again. 'I'm glad you think that, finally.'

For the first time in a long time, he turned directly toward her. 'My mother said you heard a rumour I was visiting Helene Bouchard in France, and you were jealous. You told her you had a "brain-fade" that day. Ailsa didn't believe it.'

Remy laughed.

Seth got right up in her face. 'It's not funny.' He didn't shout it. He didn't need to.

'Sorry, I know it's not funny.' She wiped the smile from her face but held her ground. 'I didn't even know Helene existed until Ailsa told me about her, and that happened after the whole spraying thing.'

'Blake never believed you'd poisoned the vines on purpose. You never fell off his pedestal.'

'Like I fell off yours, you mean?'

There was a flat spot on the stone windowsill. She sat there, rubbing her hands on the fabric of the shortest pair of shorts Seth had ever seen. The gesture tugged at a memory he couldn't quite place.

Eventually, she lifted her gaze to meet his. 'I wanted to give the money back to Ailsa, but I wanted to give it to her in one go. Pride, I guess. I wanted to see her face when I handed her all those zeros and she'd know she didn't have anything to hold over me anymore. Then I was going to come find you and Blake, and explain everything.'

Seth ran a hand through his hair. What with those two idiot dogs and all their snapping and snarling, and Remy being gorgeous, beautiful, independent Remy—turning everything he thought he knew as fact into fiction—he couldn't think. She made it impossible for an honest-to-God thought to actually hit his brain and transmit a sensible message. Nothing about Remy made him sensible and he could trace that right back to the day he'd put his hand up to plank-walk with her in the park.

Plus she kept talking with her hands. She'd take one from where it pinched at the material on her thigh and she'd wave it at him as she made each new point. Her arm would jerk and weave and the tank top scrunched higher up her waist. He could see milky skin peeping beneath the bottom of her shirt and the top of those shorts.

And she'd gone and put Blake's name in a sentence. *Again.*

So he took two steps forward, bent low, and kissed her.

Chapter 15

It wasn't the same kiss as they'd shared at Ellen Brook years ago. There was nothing questing or careful about it. It was filled with yearning, desperation, confusion, and he had nothing to give. It was a kiss that tried to take.

Remy put her hand on his chest and shoved. Two fingers caught inside the vee of his shirt, touching crisp hair and warm skin over a fast-beating heart, and it sent a zap through her fingers like static off steel.

'Remy,' he said on a groan, before he returned to her lips, and the kiss changed. Got tender real fast. She could have coped with his frustration, even anger, because it mirrored how she felt, but tenderness was something else. Tenderness played and plucked on her heart, made her mind and her body dream. It meant she'd start hoping again, and she'd wished her last wish for Seth.

So she kicked him, because her hand on his chest had given up pushing. All it wanted to do was wrap itself in a fistful of his shirt and tug him closer.

From the windowsill her leverage was off. She miscalculated, kicked the concrete before she got to his shin and her howl of pain was loud enough to snare the dogs attention.

'The least you could do is hop about a bit. I think I broke my bloody toe.' She rubbed her toe through the cap of her boot.

He let her go.

Her toe was going numb but her lips felt sweet and tingly, kind of like they did when she ate fresh pineapple. She took a tiny taste of her top lip, checking if it really *did* taste of pineapple. It didn't. It might have tasted of grapes, though, and sunshine.

She tried to slide away. The problem was, sitting on the windowsill with Seth's leg between hers made sliding difficult if she didn't want to look like she was humping his thigh.

Hell and Tommy, did I just think about humping his thigh?

At the edge of her vision Occhy crouched low on his front legs, wagging his tail. Breeze snapped and snarled at him.

'Tell her she should make love, not war,' Seth said.

Remy smiled, but only for a second. This was serious. The kiss, the aftermath—something in Seth had softened today, she could feel it. If she could only work out how to get through to him, maybe they'd end up okay. Maybe she could find the way to put the past behind them. If she was brave.

Remy dragged her courage all the way from her throbbing toe. She looked up, met dark eyes staring down and said: 'We never had any time to get to know each other, Seth. We only had two days. I mean ... you never did take me for that cup of coffee. I think if you knew me, you'd know I'm honest. I try to be a good person. A good friend. I don't lie.'

The warm pressure of his hand on her neck stilled. 'I don't think I know how to be friends with you, Rem.'

Slowly, he leaned closer and as gravity opened the vee of his shirt, she could see the springy mat of dark hair on his chest. She wondered how it would feel if she tangled her fingers in it and the part of her thinking about *humping* and *tangling* and *kissing* woke like a slumbering daisy in the morning sun.

'Remy?' A voice shouted.

Footsteps pounded the verandah.

Zac Williams burst around the corner, skidding on the concrete. He took one look at Seth and the dog near the gate, dropped the carton of eggs and cast about for something more lethal to use as a weapon. Fleetingly, his eyes settled on the solid handle of an old hoe propped near the shed door.

Seth dropped his hand from Remy's throat. Both dogs barked. Occhilupo growled.

'Occhy! Down!' Seth ordered. Occhy dropped his hindquarters to the concrete and sat there like a lit gunpowder barrel on paws.

'It's okay, Zac. *Don't.'* Remy sprang from the window at the same time as Seth stepped lightly back, clearing a space for himself.

'Thought there was a pack of dogs trying to kill each other up here ... and I get round here and this guy's got his hand 'round your throat,' Zac said, eyes darting everywhere.

'*On* her throat, mate,' Seth responded. His confident tone didn't help Zac's face brighten from thundercloud.

Zac advanced. He looked alert, but not scared. Between the dog and the men, Remy had more testosterone under her verandah than an all-boy dorm.

'Zac, it's okay. He's a—' *friend* didn't quite cut it so she took a slightly hysterical, steadying breath and started again. 'Seth, this is my neighbour, Zac Williams. Zac, this is Seth Lasrey. He bought Montgomery Wines, remember?'

They were close enough now to shake hands. Seth held his palm out first and Zac hesitated before he shook it. 'I didn't realise you two knew each other ... like that.' The hand not shaking Seth's motioned between Seth and Remy.

'We don't! Not like that,' Remy said. 'Seth's here to assess my grapes.'

Zac's eyebrows quirked. 'Is that what you call it, hey? Well, sorry to interrupt.' He glanced over his shoulder, where twelve eggs had smashed themselves on Remy's concrete. 'Shit. Sorry about those eggs, Rem. False alarm I guess.'

'Never mind, mate. It's good to know Remy has friends who look out for her,' Seth said.

'It's okay,' Remy said, feeling for Zac. 'I didn't hear your ute. I would have come out.'

'I'm driving Mum's car. Mine's getting new tyres.' He kept a wary eye on Seth, and Occhilupo.

'I've got to go anyway, Rem,' Seth said. 'I'm seeing Dave and Nance Hackett at noon.'

'They grow for Chameleon too,' Remy said.

Seth nodded in a way that told Remy he already knew. 'I'll be in touch. Good to meet you, Zac.'

He called Occhilupo. It took a few seconds, and a sharper, 'Occhy, get here,' to break through, but eventually the man and his dog were both in the ute, and gone.

'So that's Seth Lasrey, hey?' Zac said, leaning his backside on the same stone window ledge where Remy had been thinking about *humping* exactly three minutes ago.

'The one and the same,' she said, listening to the sound of Seth's ute engine grow fainter.

'You two looked pretty cosy, Rem. You never said you knew him.'

'I used to work for Lasrey Estate in Margaret River, before I moved here. I had some trouble there and he sacked me. Well, his mother sacked me. It's a long story, and if I tell you, I'd have to kill you.'

'Hey! My lips would be sealed.' He made a zipping motion.

'You're a bigger gossip than any of your sisters, Zac Williams, and don't think I don't know it.'

'Harsh, Rem. That's harsh.'

***

By the time Seth reached the end of Remy's driveway, he was planning when he might see her again. He slowed, checking for traffic before pulling out to the bitumen, picking up speed.

Occhilupo plunged his head out the side of the ute. Tongue hanging out, mouth open into the wind, rocking and rolling with every bounce of the tyres. He seemed none the worse for wear for his dive off the chain.

Pity he couldn't keep Occhy with him all the time. Days like this when he was out and about, Occhy could come along. The days when Seth was at the winery, or in back-to-back meetings in the city, Occhy had to stay on a very short chain at the dog-friendly motel. It was the only pet-friendly accommodation close enough to Montgomery to make the travel time feasible.

'Nothing like what your girlfriend's got to run around in, hey, buddy?' Seth said to the big mug head that was so close to his driver's side window, he could have reached back and given it a pat.

Whoa. There's an idea. Maybe he could talk Remy into keeping Occhilupo at her place?

He tossed that idea around all the way to his next appointment and when he was almost there, he had the plan together.

Seth used the blue-tooth connection in his car to dial Maggie at Montgomery Wines.

'Welcome to Montgomery Wines, this is Margaret speaking,' she said.

'Maggie. I'm on my way to the Hackett's. Then I have to go back to Remy Roberts' place. I'm a couple of hours away if anyone's looking for me. I'm about to lose the battery on my mobile though. Anything urgent, you can get me at Remy's.'

'Okay, Seth. No problem, I'll pass that message on.'

'Thanks, Maggie,' Seth said, and there was a grin on his face as he broke the connection. A plan always made him feel better.

Buzzing down the window, he hung his arm out the opening and let the warm wind buffet his hand. Thinking about the dogs. Thinking about Remy.

He felt good. For the first time in a long time, he felt good.

Then he thought of all the things he had to discuss with his mother, and his mood dimmed.

Chapter 16

Remy made coffee and escaped to the garden after lunch, past Breeze who lay slumped on the pavers, head toward the gate, like a waiting sphinx.

She walked across the lawn, feeling its soft give beneath her bare toes. She'd washed the dust out of her hair and changed into a long loose skirt and white shirt after her brick-laying stint, and now she sat on the garden bench with her coffee, tipped her hat over her face and let the sun dry her hair as she tried to think things through.

Carefully, she put her fingers to her lips and pressed, as if she might trace Seth's kiss. Then she took her hand away.

Since she moved to South Australia, she'd had a few opportunities to date some of the local men. She'd only taken one guy up on the offer and that had turned out to be a disaster.

She remembered it clearly. Andrew Straw was the tradesman she contracted to repair her roof. He was charming in a roguish way and she'd thought he might be fun. He'd taken her to dinner then to see a play at the Stirling Theatre.

Unfortunately, he'd thought paying for her meal earned him the night in her bed. When Remy knocked him back, he said he understood and no hard feelings. The next day, he left a tarpaulin off her roof. A thunderstorm ruined half her insulation, not to mention part of the ceiling, and in the insurance claim nightmare that followed communicating with Straw became impossible.

He denied any negligence. He blamed the freak storm.

After that men stopped asking. Remy was sure Straw had warned them off. It didn't matter. She had enough to keep her busy with her house and the vineyard and her gardens, and in the earlier days doing puppy school with Breeze.

Seth coming back into her life had proved one thing to her. She was drifting. Her life had no colour. Sure there were pinks and whites and lilacs and every shade of green, but there was no screaming yellow or red or orange or purple. All she had was washed-out colours and faded hues. No patterns, no squiggles, no swirls. Nothing that clashed, and it was so long since she'd done anything imaginative or bold.

No wonder Seth's return had her heart beating faster. She was alone, and lonely, and it didn't take Einstein to know how vulnerable that made her to the romance of a reunion of sorts with Seth.

At least if she recognised the attraction with Seth she could fight it. Five years ago he'd snuck up on her with a daring rescue and a bushwalk, and a picnic and that kiss ... but she wasn't that girl now. She wasn't going to be pushed around—not one shove more—by Seth Lasrey or his family. Five years dancing to that tune was long enough.

Breeze whined, and got to her feet.

It was then Remy caught the engine hum Breeze's keen ears had already heard. The dog wagged her tail and whimpered as the engine noise neared, then cut off. A car door opened and closed.

Hell and Tommy. This place was like Grand Central Station today.

***

Occhilupo launched himself off the ute the second Seth unclicked his chain. Seth was a little slower. By the time he'd rounded the verandah and could see into Remy's backyard, she'd come floating out of the jungle like some barefoot wood nymph: apple-green coffee cup in her hand, white shirt flowing, floppy straw hat shading her face.

He thought if she'd smiled at him then and promised to spirit him away to the deep dark forest ... he would have followed her siren call and never thought about phone sex, or poisoned vineyards, or blackmail, ever again.

Only she didn't smile.

Remy stepped from the circle of lawn to the pavers. 'Twice in one day, Seth? That's some kind of record.'

'Yeah, must seem that way.'

'Did you forget to tell me something?' She was cold, like a statue, and any progress Seth thought they'd made that morning faded.

'No. Not really. There's a favour I want to ask you. I thought of it when I was driving to the Hackett's. It's a long shot though. I'll understand if you say no.'

The mug in her hand twitched. 'Asking is free.'

'Can I come in?'

'If you want.'

Seth blocked Occhilupo at the gate, letting himself in before the dog could charge through, and latched it shut behind him.

'It's a bit out of left field, but what I'd like to know is: would you be prepared to take Occhilupo for me, while I'm here?'

'Take him?'

'Keep him here. I brought him with me because I promised Blake I'd look after him, and because I knew I'd be here a while, but it's not much of a life for him on a chain all day. I was thinking: he knows you, and you know Am Staffs. It's obvious Breeze is happy and healthy. She's in great nick.'

Like any pet owner the world over, Remy puffed in pride when he complimented her dog. The puff didn't last long. 'What about at Max and Sue's old house? Couldn't he stay there?'

'I offered the house to Rina—'

'I'm sure she'd share.'

'She doesn't like dogs, and Lewis Carney has the cottage as part of his package. He doesn't want a dog around. He's got young kids. Occhy freaks his wife out and besides, she's got a cat.'

Remy looked at Breeze, then back at him. 'She isn't much good with other dogs. I don't know how she'd go ... Haven't you met anyone *else* since you've been here who could look after him? Any special friend?' Her voice tailed off and Seth realised by the blush in her face exactly what she was asking. *Was he seeing anyone? And why couldn't that person look after the dog?*

'There's no one I'd feel comfortable leaving Occhy with,' Seth said, turning to where Breeze had her neck arched at the gate, while Occhy pranced on the other side. 'If you don't want to do it, that's okay. He'll just have to stay at the motel if I can't take him with me.'

'You're in a motel?'

'I am.'

'That's not much of a life for him, and you're coming into vintage. You'll have even less time to spend with him.'

'She doesn't look too unhappy about him being here, Rem. Should we just see how they go if I let him in?'

'He's on the other side of the gate, Seth.'

'Occhy can look after himself.'

'Okay. Let him in. Let's see the damage. I'll say one thing right now, any injuries, you foot the vet bill.'

'That's fair. Are you ready?' Seth put his hand on the latch of the gate.

'Ready.' Remy got out of the way.

He opened the gate and Occhilupo barrelled past his knees. The two dogs stood muzzle to muzzle. They were close to the same height, but Breeze was prettier, still a bundle of muscle but finer somehow. Beside her, Occhilupo looked the canine equivalent of a mafia thug.

Then she yapped and licked at Occhy's jaws. She jumped backwards, nimble as a twenty-kilo flea. He jumped backwards too, rump in the air, tail waving. Then they raced into the garden—Breeze fastest—and two sets of pounding paws and huffing breath faded into the afternoon.

'See. She's just an over-muscled pussy cat.'

'She's never done that before,' Remy said, gazing at the spot where the dogs had disappeared, listening for any sound of a fight. 'She hates other dogs. Every time I took her to the dog shows, she was a royal pain in the arse. I got so many foul looks from other dog owners, you wouldn't believe it.'

'I never pictured you as the dog show sort.'

'At puppy school they told me to socialise her with other dogs every chance I got. I figured outside of puppy school, a dog show was the best place to start. There were breeders there with an eye for what makes a good Am Staff, and they liked the way she looked. I got a bit bedazzled for a while because you can sell a puppy for around a $1000 ... but they were worried about her temperament, and to be honest after the whole sheep incident, I was worried about her temperament. I didn't persevere with the dog breeding idea for long. She's beautiful with children, but hopeless with animals and it all sounded a bit too ... hard.'

'Sheep incident?' Seth asked.

'She got through the fence when she was a puppy. She chased Zac's dad's sheep. One of them died in the paddock. This all happened Christmas morning.'

'How's that for Christmas spirit?'

'The Williams were very good about it, all things considered.'

'So what do you think, Rem? Is it okay to leave him with you? I promise Occhy's never chased a sheep.'

She squinted at him, weighing it all up: 'How long for?'

'Until vintage is over, or until I'm sure everything at Montgomery is running right,' he said. 'Then I'll take him back to Margaret River with me.'

'I'm not scooping his poop.'

Seth laughed, he couldn't help it.

'I'm serious,' Remy said, severely. 'Breeze always goes in the same place, by the back fence. Anything else will be his. I'm not scooping it.'

'Fine.' Seth straightened, watched her for a moment longer. 'I'll come here after work each day and I'll poop scoop. Do I need to BYO spade?'

'I have heaps of shovels. Have you got a bowl for him? And what about food? Breeze gets dry food and chicken carcass. Raw chicken.'

'That's fine. I'll go to the motel after work and get his bowl and whatever food he's got left and I'll bring it back. Okay? I'll pay for him while he's here too. I don't want you to be out of pocket.'

'Don't worry about it.'

'We'll talk about it later. I'll be back when I'm finished up at the winery. Thanks, Remy. You've helped me out.'

For the second time that day, Seth said goodbye.

***

Maggie Castle phoned as he was driving back to the winery.

'Hi Seth, it's Margaret.'

'Hey, Maggie. What's up?'

'Lewis wants a word with you this afternoon. How far away are you?'

'About five minutes. Do you know what he wants?'

'Not really.' She hesitated, and Seth could picture her looking around to see if anyone was listening. 'He had an argument with Rina.'

Another one. There'd been a few. 'Okay. You'd better get Rina to sit in then. Earliest I can do is three-thirty.'

'I'll send them an email. Thanks, Seth.'

'Hey, one thing before you go...'

'Yes.'

'You introduce yourself as Margaret on the phone, but everyone calls you Maggie. Do you have a preference?'

She laughed; a pleasant sound, low in his ear. 'I prefer Margaret to Maggie. Maggie sounds like a magpie.'

'Okay. Sorry about that, Margaret. Thanks for letting me know.'

'Thanks for asking. I've been Maggie around here for a long time. It doesn't really bother me.'

'It's Margaret from now, from me at least. If I stuff up, call me out on it. Okay?'

She said okay, and Seth said: 'See you soon.'

As he cancelled the hands-free, he frowned. He didn't think of his father that much anymore. Joe was coming up to ten years in the ground, and most of the pictures of his father at his mother's house had been put away. Part of him knew his old man would never have missed something like getting Margaret's name right. His father had been Joseph to Ailsa, and Joe to everyone else.

Joe Lasrey would have asked Margaret what she preferred the day they met, and he'd have remembered. He was just that type of guy.

Seth used to pay that kind of attention. Somewhere in the last five years he'd stopped noticing the little things. Why was that? And what had changed today that made him notice again?

Chapter 17

Lewis Carney had gingerish hair that was thinning on top and a gingerish moustache that clung to his upper lip like the mess from a kid's toffee ice-cream. He was a tall guy, slender, and up until the buyout he'd worn jeans to work every day. Max Montgomery had described him to Seth as a good worker. A winemaker who never groaned about the night shift during vintage or got so high on the whole 'winemaker' status he forgot how to clean an oak barrel. He was in this game for the long haul, and Max had seen him well rewarded. On that count, Max had seen all his staff well rewarded, which compounded his eventual financial shit-storm. One thing was sure, Carney was a talented winemaker. Otherwise Seth wouldn't have been so keen to keep him on the payroll.

Carney got to Seth's office first, with Rina less than a minute behind. The door wasn't shut and she didn't knock. Seth took one look at his senior winemaker, marching in with a notepad in her hand, and thought: here's trouble.

When she was pissed off, Rina carried it in her mouth and chin. Her lips would tighten like she'd downed a shot of vinegar when she'd asked for lemonade.

Carney took the seat nearest the window, crossed his legs, uncrossed them. The new uniform khakis rode up his hairy shin. Rina took the other chair, near a cabinet that used to hold Max's treasures but now had nothing in it. Seth wasn't a hoarder, nor he did he keep treasures, and this wouldn't be his office for long. When vintage was over and he and Rina let go of the day-to-day, he'd appoint a general manager or operations manager to look after the Montgomery profit centre and he'd visit once a month to keep the lot of them honest. That's how it usually worked.

This latest acquisition was a bit different. This was Lasrey's first interstate expansion and Seth wanted it to go smoothly. It would pave the way for other negotiations he had in the pipeline for South Australia and Victoria come spring.

Yeah, and Montgomery Wines came with a package deal called Remy Roberts. That made this acquisition a bit different, too.

'Okay. What are we looking at here, Lewis?' Seth began when Carney stopped with the leg crossing, and Rina flipped her notepad open. 'You look like you need to get a few things off your chest.'

'I didn't think there was any need to take notes,' Carney said, eyeing Rina's poised pen.

'I'm not taking notes,' Seth said. 'Don't worry about it. What's up?'

'Rina says you won't be making Chameleon this vintage. I know you've been out Red Gum Valley Road this week. Max and I used to earmark the fruit from Remy's farm and the Hackett's block every year for Chameleon. What did you think? Did you taste it?'

'Yeah. It's good. They're both good blocks,' and he thought about it some more. 'Really good.'

'So she hasn't poisoned all her grapes this time then?' Rina muttered.

Both men ignored her.

Carney said: 'Rina said the two of you think you can't make a dollar from high-end Adelaide Hills sauvignon blanc. You can't compete with what the Kiwis are pumping out.'

'Rina and I usually are on the same page, but that doesn't mean we don't disagree now and then on how best to write the book. New Zealand sauvignon blanc outsells Australian two, pushing three, bottles to one, and that share's growing. There's a restaurant market though.'

Rina made a note in her pad. Carney saw it and didn't like it. Seth could tell by the way the tall man looked at her pen like he wanted to rip it from her and ditch it across the room. Seth didn't blame him. Rina's note-taking made *him* want to throw her pen across the room all the time.

'You told me part of your deal with Max was that I guaranteed you at least a year in the job 'cause you wanted continuity, and to be a bridge between the new guard and the old. I think I've been doing that okay, under the circumstances.' He glanced at Rina's pen.

'You have, Lewis. I won't bullshit you. You're a valuable part of the team. You have a big part here moving forward. We see you in all of it.' What he'd seen of Carney so far had him thinking the guy might just be that general manager material he'd be looking for.

Carney took a big breath, sat forward, and everything rushed out fast. 'You guys are moving too quick. There's been too much change. If you ditch Chameleon you're dropping our flagship brand. We've got more workplace policies all of a sudden than you can poke a stick at—'

'That's because Max didn't have any policies *at all,* except the one about knocking-off early for Friday drinks,' Rina said.

Seth flicked his finger at her and she shut up.

'I told you I won't bullshit you, Lewis. I meant it. I had thought we couldn't justify the input costs on Chameleon. Not this year. But that was before I assessed those blocks. Both those vineyards are premium. I'd hate to lose that by mixing it in with the middle-tier stuff. Rina's not spinning you a line. She and I did talk about pulling Chameleon from production. I'm not thinking that way anymore.'

Rina stabbed the tip of her pen at the page. Her lips were like prunes.

'Thank God,' Carney said, putting both feet flat on the floor, hands on his thighs. 'Honestly. This will mean a heap to the guys. They've all been thinking you're just trying to turn us into another mid-size winery, churning out cheap and cheerful wine for the masses.'

'I'm not saying that long-term Chameleon is the best use of resources,' Seth qualified. 'But for this year I agree with you. There's more upside in keeping it. I'd like to see what you do with it.' He glanced at Rina, sitting so straight-backed she could have been a chair, and added: 'what *both* of you do with it.'

The mention of working with Rina dimmed the smile on Carney's face but not by much, then he stood and leaned across Max Montgomery's old desk to shake Seth's hand.

'I'll get to it then,' Carney said.

***

It had taken a while for Rina to calm down after Carney left and it meant their afternoon meeting took longer than it should. On the fruit assessments, Rina had finished her list. Seth still had a couple of places to visit. Rina offered to do those for him because he had back-to-back meetings tomorrow.

After he finished with Rina there were reports to work through, budget figures to comb, expenditure to sign off. His email inbox was a nightmare and Sally wouldn't let him ignore it anymore. Sally Deering had gone back to the West after the merger excitement died, but that didn't stop her haranguing him twice-daily with colour-coded bullet-point lists of all the things he hadn't done.

It was after eight when he left the winery to drive the fifteen minutes into Mount Barker, pack up his room, and check-out. Without a dog, there was no point paying for a room at the only dog-friendly motel in town. So he'd decided to book into the motel units at the back of the Oakbank pub.

***

By nine o'clock that night, Remy was tired of jumping every time the dogs twitched at some mystery noise in the night and sick of flicking through television channels that couldn't hold her interest.

Then a growl from the dogs had Remy off the couch in a flash.

It was dark outside, but the house lights shone through the windows, throwing light into the patio. Occhy and Breeze were at the gate, heads up, on alert.

Remy clicked the television off. From the front, above the trill of cicadas, she heard the sound of a car engine and a few seconds later, headlights played across the garden.

She opened the patio doors, flung them harder than she wanted on a burst of adrenalin, and waited at the gate with her heart thumping.

The sensor light switched on and Seth came round the corner carrying a bulk bag of dog food under one arm. He had a shiny silver dog bowl in the other hand. She thought he looked tired.

'Hi,' he called. 'I hope reception isn't shut yet?'

She smiled even as she told herself not to. 'No. But I was getting close to putting the *no vacancies* sign out the front.'

The corner of his mouth twitched and Remy had the feeling they'd called a truce. At least for now.

She opened the gate. 'I made a bed up for Occhy just there. See?' She indicated a big cushion on the pavers near Breeze's kennel. 'Put his bowl so it's a bit separate from hers. I don't want them fighting over food.'

'Okay. Thanks, Rem. I appreciate this.'

'I'm not doing it for you, Seth. I always loved Occhy, he's a great dog. I don't like the idea of him being chained up all day where people might tease him.'

'No. I don't like it either. That's why he'll be so much happier here.' He passed her the bag of dog food. It was a bulk eighteen-kilo bag, but it must have been more than half empty. It wasn't heavy.

'So where are you staying?'

'I thought I'd try the Oakbank Pub.'

'Have you eaten? They might have shut for meals now.'

'I didn't think of that, but I'm okay, thanks. I had a late lunch.'

'Okay.' She looked him up and down, and made a decision. 'Hey, when you come here, don't park under that big tree at the front, okay? It drops sap. It's a bitch to get off.'

'Thanks for telling me.'

'Don't mention it.'

Occhilupo and Breeze crawled into Breeze's kennel, ignoring the cushion she'd put out. Occhy was a black burr in the dark. The white of Breeze's chest was a clearer target. She had her head over Occhy's back.

'Good to see he's made himself comfortable,' Seth said.

'He's a male and he's a dog. They're good at making themselves comfortable.'

Seth laughed and they stood looking at each other, with Remy holding the bag of dry food and wishing she could keep the same tight grip on her heart when Seth was near.

'I'll let you go,' he said. 'Have a good night.'

'See you for poop-scooping duty tomorrow.'

'Now there's an invitation I haven't heard before.'

She smiled sweetly at him. 'And here I was thinking you must have heard them all.'

Chapter 18

'Morning, Margaret,' Seth said the next day as he entered the admin area, where Margaret Castle was already behind her desk looking remarkably efficient.

'Morning, Seth,' she said, and she smiled, like they'd shared a private joke. Which in a way, they had. 'Rina's been looking for you. She asked that I let her know when you get in.'

'I've got two conference calls this morning first-up then I'll touch base with Rina,' he said. 'Can you hold any other calls till nine?'

He was in the middle of the first conference call when Rina knocked on his office door and entered. He waved her in, because she brought coffee.

Rina closed the door behind her. That in itself was unusual enough to make him notice. Rina liked other staff to know she was part of the inner sanctum and had his ear. She rarely closed the door when she came to see him.

She put the coffee on his desk, sat on the same chair as yesterday and crossed her legs, sipping at her coffee in silence. He couldn't see a notebook, but she had a pen behind her ear. When he finished the call, he said: 'I've got five minutes till the next one. Thanks for this. I needed it.'

'You might need something stronger in a minute,' she said, resting the coffee cup on his desk. 'The newspaper says it wasn't just grapes you were tasting out at Remy Roberts' place.'

'Yeah?'

'*The Advertiser* has a segment in today's Confidential—'

'Ahh. So that makes it true. Confidential...'

'What's going on, Seth?' Rina leaned forward, cutting to the chase.

'Remy's neighbour sprung me out there yesterday morning. I guess he must have blabbed.'

Rina went statue-still. 'Sprung you doing what?'

'Kissing Remy.'

'Kissing her!' She jerked hard enough to dislodge the pen from her ear. She caught it against her thigh before it hit the floor. 'Bloody hell.'

'It's not so strange. Remy and I ... had something together years ago.'

'What? Before or after that bit where she poisoned your vines? I gotta hand it to you, Seth. You're the *king* of moving on.'

'Remy tells a different story, Rina. She says she never did it on purpose.'

'She would. Ailsa always said she's a compulsive liar.'

'Keep it down, hey? The walls aren't that thick.' He had to add some heat to the words, almost growl it at her to cut through.

'When Ailsa hears about this, and she will,' she pointed her pen at him and stood up to leave: 'Just don't say I didn't warn you.'

'That's enough, Rina. Butt out. It has nothing to do with you.'

'She's one of our growers. That makes it business. I'm a board member these days and that makes it *my* business, and your mother's. Don't you remember what happened last time you got involved with this girl? Doesn't that mean anything?'

Margaret Castle buzzed his internal line then, and he knew she was calling to let him know the next conference call was waiting.

'Rina, there's a line you shouldn't cross, and you're right on it.'

'If I can't tell you when you're being a total dick, who can?' She left the room.

Seth snatched his phone up and had to force himself back to the topic at hand. Retail wine sales to supermarket chains. Beating the bastards into a better deal.

After the phone conversation finished, Seth googled the Adelaide online newspaper. He found the item in Confidential. It was a small headline link in the sidebar that said: 'The Hills Are Alive With The Sound Of Love'.

Seth clicked and waited for the story to load. It didn't take long.

Is it love in them there Hills for Aussie wine tycoon, Seth Lasrey? Confidential heard Seth's been paying vineyard visits to some of our local grapegrowers in the last week, and spent extra time at a property on Red

Gum Valley Road yesterday, rekindling auld acquaintance.

Long labelled one of Australia's most eligible bachelors, Seth's been on the Adelaide A-list in the month he's been in South Australia, since his wine company merged with Montgomery Wines in January.

Confidential's source said the lucky local lady grower is from the Margaret River wine region originally, and that she and Seth 'go way back'.

What we'd like to know ladies is: does this mean another bachelor bites the dust?

Seth finished his coffee in a disgusted gulp. *It must have been a bloody slow news day.*

He should phone Remy. Give her the heads up. She wasn't used to the media scrutiny and she might not know the mantra he used: deny, deny, deny.

Plus who was he kidding? He wanted to hear her voice. Last night when he'd watched Occhilupo cuddling up with Breeze, it occurred to him how much he'd like to be camping out at Remy's place too, and not in a kennel.

***

Rina walked out of Seth's office fuming, amazed she had enough control not to slam his door off its hinges. The mix of caffeine and adrenalin in her system had her buzzing like a wasp in the window.

She knew this would happen. She'd known when she'd seen Remy at the growers' meeting, popping up like a bloody weed that wouldn't die.

Shutting the door of her office, sinking into her chair, Rina put her hand to her temple and tried to massage away the headache threatening there. God she wanted a drink.

Leaning across her desk, Rina picked up her office phone and dialled Ailsa's number.

'Ailsa? This is Rina,' she said, as the Lasrey matriarch answered the phone.

'What's happened now?' Ailsa said without preamble.

'There's an article in the local paper today that links Seth with Remy. It doesn't name her, but I know that's who it's about. Someone saw him kissing her out at Remy's property. Seth is her vineyard liaison.' And because it felt like she should, she added: 'I'm sorry. I feel like I've let you down.'

'I would have thought you'd find a way to make sure *you* were Remy's liaison officer, Rina?'

'How could I? I had no idea she was even here,' Rina defended.

Ailsa stayed silent. Rina let her think.

'You said it was in the paper?' Ailsa asked.

'Yes. The gossip column. I'm sure it will all blow over.'

'It might help us if it doesn't blow over. Remy isn't used to the media pressure that comes with Seth. She has no idea how much attention he gets.'

'You think we can use that?'

'I do. She won't like it. It might make her reconsider whether she wants to get in too far with him. Especially if the press hears some of her dirty little secrets.'

'Secrets?' Rina said. 'Not the sexual harassment or the blackmail, Ailsa, Seth would be furious if the media got wind of that.'

'No. Not that,' Ailsa agreed. 'That looks as bad for us as it does for her.

There's plenty of other things. Her relationship with Blake for a start. We can suggest to the media she was involved with him first.'

'Blake will deny it.'

'Maybe, but it will make a good story anyway.'

They talked it over some more, and Rina's headache was gone when she hung up the phone.

***

After the third phone call before 10.00am from a news reporter trying to confirm whether she was the Hills grapegrower linked in the newspaper with Seth Lasrey, Remy stopped answering the phone.

One journo had even gone so far as to ask if she could come up to the farm that afternoon to take a few pictures. Remy told that caller she had a dog that would eat Cujo for breakfast and she wasn't afraid to use it. The reporter thought she was joking.

The phone rang again. Remy listened to her answer machine run through its message: 'Hi, this is Remy. I'll get back to you.'

'Remy, it's Seth. I'm calling because—'

She leapt for the phone and got there before his next words. 'Seth, it's me! What's going on? I've had three reporters call so far today.'

'We made the news. Well, I did. You didn't, which is a good thing.'

'How? What news? Why?'

'I'm not certain, but I think your friend Zac might have told someone what he saw yesterday at your place. Journos don't need much more than a rumour these days to publish.'

'But Zac didn't see anything. You'd already kissed me at that point. It was all over.'

His voice dropped a notch. 'I hope you're not complaining about the length of that kiss, Remy. You're the one who kicked me. I could make it longer next time.'

Hell and Tommy. 'I am most definitely not complaining about the length of that kiss.' *The intensity in it. The fire, maybe. The way I think it means so much more to me than to you. Not the length.*

'Good.'

'So what does it mean? Can I leave the house? Will there be photographers stalking me at the post office?'

'I just own a few wineries, Remy. I'm not a rock star.'

'There've been enough pictures of you in the paper in the last few weeks for a rock star,' she grumped.

'It will all blow over. Don't worry.'

'If my mother hears about it, she'll have a fit.'

'Your mother? What about what happens if my mother hears about it? She'll have a stroke.'

'Ailsa won't have a stroke. She's too mean to die.' Then: 'Oh bloody hell, I didn't mean that, Seth. Not really.'

'Yes you did,' but there was a smile in Seth's voice as he said it. 'Where is your mother anyway, Rem?'

'She's driving around Australia in a caravan with Bernie. He was my tiler. He was working on the splashback in the kitchen when my mum was visiting and they hit it off. That's great. He's a good guy, but the bummer was, he goes gallivanting off around the country with my mum and I was hoping I could rope him into helping me redo my bathrooms.'

Seth didn't ask, but she was on a roll, and she couldn't seem to stop talking, so she said: 'They're getting married in spring. They want to get married in the garden here. Bernie figured if they could travel for four months in a caravan, they could cope with married life. That's why I was trying to fix the step yesterday ... so it will look nice for them in the photos. I've got a lot of jobs to do before October.'

There was a pause, which Remy didn't know how to fill.

'So you're alright then, Rem? About the media? If any of them ask you anything, just deny it or say "no comment".'

'I'll tell them it's a really bad connection and I can't hear them. That's what I do with telemarketers. They hang up pretty quick.'

'As long as you're okay. I'm used to them coming after me, but you're not. I don't want anyone to scare you.'

'It's nice of you to care.' Remy drew a careful breath. 'I'm not about to fall to pieces. I'm okay. I will, however, be ringing Zac Williams to give him a piece of my mind.'

'Don't give him a piece you'll need.'

'Oh, ha, bloody, ha.'

Seth's internal line buzzed. 'I've got to go, Rem. I'll see you later. Have that poop scoop ready.'

'I will.'

He hung up.

Remy ended the call and glanced around her house. There were magazines everywhere, letters on the bench, remotes trying to fall off the couch; books, bills.

If she had company coming, she should tidy up. Shouldn't she?

Yes.

***

It was after seven by the time he got to Remy's. She met him at the side gate in a blue dress with a darker navy swirl through it, and no shoes. Her hair was in a high ponytail, and she'd missed a chunk at the back when she pinned it.

He said hello, or something equally enthralling, and she told him where to find the shovel. It felt a bit like the story of their lives.

'Where do you want me to throw it?' he asked.

'Over the back fence is fine.'

It took him two trips. When he finished he propped the shovel against the stable wall.

That stable was interesting. He could have spent longer inside. There were teapots with various cacti spilling out of spout and holes; seedlings and cuttings, pea straw bales and stacks and stacks of wooden pallets. Some of those were pulled apart, with timbers painted white, others blue. He had scores of the same pallets at the winery and had no idea why Remy would need so many, or why she'd paint them.

She came out into the yard to hang a load of washing while he was snooping and when he looked up and his eyes found her, the sight of her hit him like a punch. There was a gentle breeze that blew the dress into her body, outlining it for only his eyes to see. She had more curves than the Remy of his memories. She'd been a girl back then. She was all woman now.

She threw a ball for the dogs, which only Breeze was interested in chasing. Occhilupo chased Breeze.

Seth came out of the stable and joined her on the lawn. 'Did you get any more calls from the press?'

'Only one. They stopped after lunch.'

'Good. Did you read the riot act to your neighbour?'

'Yes. He said he told his mum and his sister, Clea, and he reckoned none of them would have said anything to the paper. Clea and I are the same age. We used to hang out a bit when I first got over here. Then she met a tuna fisherman and moved with him to Port Lincoln. Zac's mum doesn't mind a good old chinwag either. Sheila could have told anyone and not given it another thought.'

For a long time they played with the dogs. She'd pinned sheets on the line and he watched them billow and sway, brushing the lavender bushes planted around the base, imagining the sweet lavender scent in the cotton. He admired the bare curve of Remy's neck and her cheek, the grace of her shoulders, ponytail bouncing as she threw the ball.

Breeze brought the ball to Seth. He picked it up and launched it toward the silver birches and they listened as the dogs crashed after it. It was lucky Remy's garden wasn't delicate.

'I think they've given up,' he said, when the dogs didn't return.

'Breeze will look for it all night. When I wake up in the morning, she'll have put it on the mat.'

'Yeah?'

Remy shivered and hugged her arms with her hands. Seth didn't think it was cold. He was still getting used to daylight saving in South Australia. It stayed light so much later.

He dug in his pocket. 'Here,' he said. 'This is for you.'

She looked at it. 'I don't want any money. I'm happy to have Occhy here. It's fine.'

'I was paying to keep him at the motel. I'd have to pay if I put him in a kennel. Take it.' He waved the cash at her. 'It's $200. A hundred a week. Is that enough?'

'Hell and Tommy,' she muttered. 'Of course it's enough. This is hardly the Ritz. He's not at doggy day care. I don't have a dog spa, and you're scooping his poop.'

He picked up her hand and pressed the money into her palm, closing her fingers around the notes. 'Take it.'

'Okay, then. Fine.' She waited, arms wrapping her ribs then she looked at him and said: 'Do you have to be anywhere tonight? I made soup. It's nothing much, but if you're hungry, you're welcome to have some before you head off.'

'That would be great,' he said, and it was only as he said it, and they walked toward her house, he realised how much the simple invitation meant to him.

Remy opened the French doors and stepped through onto the floorboards. Seth followed.

'Sure smells good in here.'

'It's lentil and curried vegetable.'

No, it's you. Rich timbers and home-cooking and spices.

'You've got a nice place.' He looked at her and waited until her grey eyes met his. 'Thanks Remy. It's good of you to take Occhy like this. I really appreciate it.'

She waved the compliment away but it left her all flustered. She hadn't expected to be thanked for her dog-sitting, or her soup.

Remy ladled soup into bowls and made toast. Seth pulled out a chair at the kitchen table and sat. She joined him, sitting opposite, one chair along so he wouldn't feel like she was in his face.

The spoon seemed so small in his fingers. It felt so surreal having Seth here. But *man,* he looked good in her house.

'Tell me about this place,' he said, glancing around. He tore a piece of toast in half and dunked it through the soup.

'Well ... The front rooms, the bedrooms, and that nook there where the TV is, they are all part of the original 1890s cottage. My bedroom has an ensuite off it, going down the other side of the verandah.'

She pointed as she talked and when Seth's gaze wasn't on his soup or his spoon, it was on her face.

'The kitchen and this part we're sitting in are new. If you keep going round there,' she pointed to where the corridor disappeared behind a built-in pantry: 'there's the second bathroom and the laundry and a door to get outside.'

Seth mopped his bowl with the last of the toast before pushing the dish into the centre of the table. 'That was great. Thanks.' Then he shoved his chair back and relaxed, splaying his legs comfortably, while he watched her finish. Her foot bumped his beneath the table.

'I'm doing too much talking. I've got heaps to go.'

'Don't rush.'

Remy tucked her feet under her seat so he wouldn't think she was playing footsies. She took a couple hasty spoons of soup.

'Eventually I'll whack the bathrooms off too and rebuild that entire side. I was going to do that—' she hesitated.

'And?' He prompted, eyes on her face.

'I ran out of money.' Remy's skin grew warm and she hoped she'd dimmed the lights enough that he wouldn't notice the flush in her face. 'I told you I got ripped off by my carpenter? It cost me heaps.'

Seth rubbed toast crumbs off his chest, then cupped his hand at the edge of the table and swept up the specks.

She hoped he didn't ask about the carpenter because she sure didn't want to bring Andrew Straw into her living room.

Seth stood, flicked the crumbs from his hand to his bowl and took his crockery to the sink. He rinsed it and packed it in the dishwasher, along with the spoon. He asked her where she kept her glasses and she half-rose from her seat, thinking he was the guest and she should get it for him.

'I'll get it,' he said. She sat her butt back down.

He was the first man who'd ever helped himself to a glass of water in her kitchen. If she didn't count Ryan

Gosling, he was the only man she'd ever dreamed of in this house, too.

Seth poured a big glass of water and drank. A trickle overshot his mouth and when he'd finished, he wiped moisture from his chin. There were drops on the t-shirt. He wiped at those too.

They were quiet for a while and then Seth said: 'Can I ask you something? I don't want to wreck the mood.'

'It's okay.'

He put a hand on her kitchen bench, flexed his fingers on the wood. 'When you left Margaret River, you had our hundred grand—'

They'd been playing nice before, well, *she* had been, but those words were sandpaper across her spine.

Seth saw her stiffen, and quickly qualified: 'What I mean is: how did you do all this on that hundred, less what you had to pay that loan shark? I can see it might have been a deposit on the land, but you'd still have needed a loan to do up the house.'

Briefly, Remy debated whether that was any of his business. She didn't like the way he continued to talk of Ailsa's money as something she'd sought and taken. Ailsa had written her that bloody cheque. Till the day she died Remy would remember those lines of lilting zeros. Under the lights, they'd dazzled her almost as much as Ailsa's rings.

'You don't have to tell me,' he said softly.

His interest seemed genuine and Remy made her decision. 'My Grandma Roberts—mum's mum—died a few years back. She never had much money, but she owned her house. It's in Vic Park in Perth on one and three-quarter acres. You know how Perth property has been ... Mum was an only child, and the property sold to some developers for a good price. Mum and her parents were estranged because of my dad—they never liked him. Not long after I came here, Grandma Roberts had a fall and broke her hip and she couldn't live alone again after that. Mum moved to Perth to care for her. When Grandma died, Mum helped me out. It gave me enough equity that the bank would lend me some more. That's how I had money saved toward paying Ailsa back.'

'But the bank stopped lending?'

She nodded. 'Like every grapegrower in the country, I imagine. I'm right on my limit. I'm over my limit. That's why I had to dip into Ailsa's cash the last two years to keep things afloat. The bank sends me letters telling me they're drawing money from the account I have in credit to pay my overdraft monthly minimum. They're allowed to juggle their customers' money like that, apparently.'

'Banks do what they want,' Seth agreed. 'Okay, that makes sense. I thought you must have got a windfall or—' this time he was the one who baulked.

Remy was on it in a flash. 'Or what?'

'Ah, jeez.' Seth ran his hand through his hair and contemplated the empty water glass, shining in his hand under the lights. 'Buying a property needs money. Rejuvenating a vineyard takes money. Extending a 1890s cottage takes big money.'

She concentrated on the first of the wet spots on his t-shirt, a fifty-cent piece blob right beneath the Lasrey logo on his pocket. She didn't want to look at his face. Looking at him scrambled her wits. 'How else did you think I got the money?'

His gaze settled on her, eyes blacker than midnight. 'I figured either Max Montgomery was paying you better than I thought, or telephone sex pays better than I thought—'

Remy got out of her chair. 'So it couldn't be that I won *Lotto* or something. Oh no.'

He shook his head. 'You're being ridiculous.'

'No, *you're* being ridiculous. You're wrong about me, but you're too pig-headed to see it. You told me the other day you believed me about the vines, and then yesterday when we were talking about the blackmail, I thought you believed me then too. But they're just words to you, Seth and they're cheap. In your heart, you've spent so long thinking I'm the bad guy here, it doesn't take much to make you doubt yourself all over again.'

'Give me a break—'

'You don't know me at all.'

'Rem—'

'No. I can't do this now. I'm tired. It's been a big day. Please, Seth. I'd like you to leave.'

***

So that didn't go well.

Why did he push her so hard? He hadn't been thinking about money, not really. Not until she'd brought it up with the story about the carpenter who ripped her off. Before that he'd been enjoying the way her lips moved when she talked, and how there was a bit of hair she couldn't keep out of her eyes, and the way every now and then she'd realise she was talking with her hands and she'd sit on them to keep them still.

The last twenty minutes couldn't be undone so there wasn't much point dwelling on it.

The dogs huffed at him as he closed the French doors and stepped into the night, but they didn't bother to crawl from their kennel.

It felt like a long drive back to Oakbank, to a lonely hotel room and a lumpy pillow.

Chapter 19

Seth woke to his phone buzzing on the bedside table and flung his hand out for it, half asleep but waking fast.

'Yeah?'

'Seth, it's Remy. We made the headlines again and this time they've got my name.'

He sat up, pushing back against the headboard. 'Read it to me.'

'It's online. The headline says: *Love Me Tendril,*' and she started to read.

He snickered at the headline—how could you not—then he almost forgot what she was reading because he got lost in her voice.

'*Confidential can reveal the name of the mystery grapegrower spotted in a clinch with Seth Lasrey at her Adelaide Hills vineyard on Thursday. She is a former employee of Lasrey Estate in Margaret River, and she's now living near Oakbank. She is Eremia Roberts, better known as Remy.*

Confidential spoke to several people who knew Remy in Margaret River, who confirmed she quit her job as a vineyard technical assistant at Lasrey more than five years ago after an alleged incident involving a mix-up with vineyard chemical sprays.

"She was there one day, and gone the next. It happened fast as that," said the source, who continues to work for the company and didn't want to be named. "No one knew she had a soft spot for the boss. We all thought she was chasing the other brother, Blake."

Blake Lasrey, now a star on the international surfing circuit, was at Bells Beach in Victoria yesterday where he is in preparation for the famous Easter surfing tournament. He wouldn't comment, other than to say he wished his wine tycoon brother and Remy "all the luck in the world."

We give you the choice ladies. Which Lasrey brother would you pick?' And then there are two photos of you both.'

There was a pause.

'Seth?'

She really could read the phone book to him backwards. He'd listen. 'Sorry. Is that it?'

'Isn't that enough? Negligence. Blake. And they used my real name, *Eremia.*'

'I never knew Remy was short for Eremia. You never said a word.'

'I don't think you're concentrating properly, Seth. Did I wake you?'

'You did. What time is it?'

'Almost eight.'

'Shit. Tell you what. Let me get out of bed and have a shower and buy the Saturday paper so we know if that says the same thing. How about I meet you out at your place in an hour? Is that good for you?'

'Well, yes. I guess.' Her voice cooled.

'I want to talk about last night anyway. I'll bring croissants if you make coffee.'

She brightened. 'Okay. If you insist. There's a brilliant bakery at Balhannah.'

'See you soon.'

***

'It's a terrible bloody photo of me,' Seth said, as he opened the side gate, dodged the dogs' madly wagging tails, and found Remy sitting at the patio table.

'*Hell and Tommy.* That's the least of our worries.' She took the paper from him and spread it out, going quickly to the centre pages, stopping at Confidential. 'Oh, it's not the same photo of you as they've got online. You're right. I'd pick Blake.'

Blake was coming out of the surf in his photo, all naked chest and muscles, water dripping from his blond hair. Seth looked like he was in the middle of telling the cameraman to fuck off.

'That entire vote thing is rigged,' he said as he sat.

'Coffee's hot.'

She had a pot brewed, sugar bowl handy. The bag of croissants crackled as Seth split the paper in half.

'Butter? Jam?' Remy asked him.

'I'm good. You help yourself.'

She disappeared inside and came back with those two items and a carton of milk. 'I wasn't sure if you drank it black.'

'Sometimes. Milk's good today.' He stirred it in.

'So who do you think their source is? It can't be Zac. He didn't know any of the stuff about the oxfluorofen or about Blake.'

'It wouldn't be hard to find someone still at Lasrey who was there then. Pops. Rina. My mother. Allan Dale still works there. It's not that long ago. And if they dug further back they'd find Amanda Laurie too. Blake wouldn't have said anything, so I'll rule him out.'

'Can it do any permanent damage? This sort of writing?'

'Nah. It's just gossip. It's a pain in the arse but it doesn't mean anything. It'll stop when they run out of new stuff to say.'

Remy bit into the croissant. Buttery flakes crumbled into the hand she raised to catch them.

'About last night, Rem.'

'I don't really want to talk about it. You made yourself clear.'

'Look at it from my side for a minute, without getting huffy.'

She waved him to continue. Even that had attitude, the kind of wave you do when you're faking the Queen.

'We only ever had that one weekend together five years ago. We had the day at Vintage Festival and the picnic. I had to get past a lot of things in those two days: I had to work out whether or not you were seeing Blake. Then there was the whole employee/employer thing. That's not saying that weekend with you wasn't one of the best of my life ... but, then that Monday, I come to see you at your house and overhear you on the phone—'

'Eavesdropping,' she added.

'Whatever ... You're the only person I've ever heard put dripping wet pussy in a sentence, who wasn't talking about washing their cat.'

She giggled, covered her mouth. 'People wash their cats?'

'I made a judgement call that afternoon based on what I heard you say on the phone, and I got it wrong. I always thought I was such a good judge of character.' Looking up, he met her eyes, clouded grey with concentration. 'When everything happened later: there's my mother on the phone and I'm in France and Ailsa's saying Remy did this and Remy did that, and by the way, she says you sexually harassed her and she'll go to the police? I didn't believe it for a long time, but I kept coming back to that Monday when I heard you on the phone. It's the only day that I heard you myself, with *my* ears, rather than take someone else's word for it. I thought: if Remy could sell phone sex for money, she could do anything, right? So yes, that stuck. And yes, if someone told me tomorrow you had a bunch of sugar daddies visiting here every Sunday and you fucked them to help pay your rent—I can't promise I wouldn't think the worst.'

'Then we don't have anywhere to go, Seth. There's nothing else to say.' She hugged herself with her arms, hating how his words made her feel. 'If you think I could do that...'

'The point is, Rem, dammit, *listen* ... Even if those sugar daddies came up the road right now, I'd expect you to stay and talk to me, and not run away.'

'Talk is cheap, Seth. My father spent years telling my mother: I'll quit drinking. I'll quit gambling. I'll be a better father. I'll pick Remy up from school and I won't forget. I won't be late home. I'll be a better husband.' There were tears in her eyes and she swiped them away. 'They were just words. He never meant any of them. Just once if he'd followed through with something, it would have meant so much more: one day, where he actually did come and get me from school on time so I didn't have to sit on the bench outside the classroom, telling the teacher, *"Dad's coming to get me today,"* and see that pity in their eyes every time they walked past and I was still sitting there, clutching my schoolbag. Don't talk to me about words.'

'You chose action five years ago rather than words, Rem. You chose to take that money, and you chose to run. I'd already told you I would have helped you. I'd asked you to trust me.'

'You don't know how many times I've wished I never took Ailsa's money. That's why I'm going to pay her back.'

'She doesn't expect it back.'

'I know. But that's the only way I'll be free of her.'

He nodded, because he understood, and for the morning at least, they left the past right there.

***

Seth stayed most of the day. Remy had used his $200 to buy a four-litre tin of Indian-Red paint and a new set of wide-bristle brushes at the hardware store, and between them they'd painted the verandah posts, downpipes and fascias of the patio in a dark burgundy red: the colour of a rich wine sauce.

Between coats she fed him lunch and more coffee, and told him more about the Menzel family and the history of the farm as she knew it, and how she caught Bernie the tiler with his hand down her mother's shirt on the garden bench one afternoon when they thought she wasn't home.

'Mum was mortified. Bernie never knew what all the fuss was about. It's impossible to embarrass Bernie. He's one of a kind.'

It was easy. It felt natural. Having something to do eased the tension that usually wanted to escalate whenever they spent time together, and possibly, at least for the moment, they were all talked out.

Remy felt drained. In a good way. She was tired physically from yesterday's brick-laying and today's painting, and for the first time in a very long time, felt at peace emotionally.

'That looks good,' she said when they finished, stepping back to admire their handiwork.

'It does.'

'After we rinse these brushes, I think it's time for a beer.'

'I can't, Rem,' he said. 'I wish I could. There's a dinner at the restaurant. Lewis Carney hosts it. It costs $130 a head. I can't pull out. I want to see how Lewis handles himself in front of a crowd.'

'He'll be good. You'll see,' Remy said. 'He has a good way with people.'

'I think so too. He underestimates himself. I'm looking at him hard for a general manager role at Montgomery in the new financial year. Don't say anything to him.'

'I won't.'

Seth took the ladder to the stable. It was getting late and he needed to get back to the hotel, clean off the paint spots that he could feel in his hair and on his skin, and get himself in host mode for the evening.

'You don't look particularly enthused about tonight,' she said.

'I'm not particularly enthused about many things right now, if they don't include you.'

She patted his arm, leaned in close. 'You can always come back and poop scoop later.'

That was so Remy. He gave her something heartfelt and she came back at him with a joke. 'You could always come to this dinner with me.'

Remy let go of his arm, standing back so she could meet his eyes. 'Oh, no.' She drew out the two words. 'I'm gonna have a beer and a hot bath and I think I'll make pasta. Dessert will be ice-cream, straight out of the tub. I'm too tired to bother with anything else.'

'I'll think of you when I'm having crab, and poached scallops and whatever else is on the menu.'

'You do that. I'll think of you when I'm in the bath.'

He grinned at her and she blushed beet-red and looked at her feet. 'Hold on. That didn't come out right.'

'No, Rem. That came out perfect.'

Chapter 20

Remy did have that beer after Seth had gone. She drank it with the dogs, watching the cockatoos fly through the big gum trees on the other side of her back fence; watching the dogs chase the last patches of sun to lie in, as the shadows advanced across the pavers.

When the sun disappeared and it cooled to the point where she had to go inside, she swapped the beer for a glass of Chameleon sauvignon blanc and started chopping parsley and basil, garlic, spinach and fresh tomatoes into a sauce for her pasta, toasting pine nuts and adding them late.

After she'd eaten and packed the dishwasher, she fed the dogs, poured a second glass of wine, and took that to the bath.

As Remy saw it, there was one good thing about living through a drought. It made a girl very appreciative of a bath when she treated herself to one. Most of the time Remy existed on three-minute showers. She brushed her teeth in the shower and kept a bucket under the shower-rose to catch the water until it ran hot. Those three minutes included the time it took the old pipes to get hot water from A to B. Sometimes that took a minute all on its own.

When she had the money, bathrooms were next on the agenda. Blue tiles for the floor in her ensuite. White tiles on the walls. The blue would be that deepest hue of a late afternoon spring sky. The white would be, well, shiny bright white. She'd have a claw-foot bath with brass feet, a big pedestal vanity basin under the window and one of those old-fashioned hallstands with a big mirror and pretty silver hooks. She'd paint that hallstand white. The bath she'd get enamelled the same blue as the floor.

Remy sank under the water and closed her eyes on the patchwork of chipped beige and pink tiles with stained murky grout that no amount of scrubbing with bleach and a toothbrush had ever been able to clean. In her dreams, the bathroom was bright singing blue and crisp, clear white. A lace curtain billowed gently in the breeze, and everything smelled fresh as lemons.

It was nine-thirty when the bath water cooled to the point of not being fun anymore. Plus she was out of wine.

The third glass is always the sneaky glass, she told herself as she poured. Two glasses of wine were relaxing, almost therapeutic. The third glass turned a good girl bad.

Remy took the wine to the couch, messed around with the television stations and gave up. She wondered if Seth was enjoying himself. She thought about calling him twice before she actually did it: just to wish him good night and say thanks for helping her paint.

It was after ten o'clock. He answered, and she could tell from the background hum he wasn't alone.

'Hey, Remy. What's up?'

'You haven't poop-scooped yet.'

'Ah, there's a thought that goes beautifully with chef's dessert. Can't I do it in the morning?'

A giggle bubbled from her lips. 'It's Sunday. I like a sleep-in.'

'Remy, are you drunk?'

'Noooo. Tipsy maybe, but not drunk. It's that sneaky third glass.'

'That sneaky what?'

'Never mind.'

'I think I should take the phone outside. Hold on a minute, Rem.' There was a pause, and then he said: 'You really want me to come over tonight?'

Did she imagine it, or was his voice pitched lower? Did she really hear that husky note in it? 'You promised. You said you'd come once a day.'

'Yeah ... but I have already spent most of the day there. Aren't you sick of me?'

'Not schick of you.' *Hell and Tommy, I'm slurring my words.*

'You sure you only had three glasses of wine, sweetheart?'

Sweetheart. Something melted inside and she wondered if she could blame the wine. She sat straighter on the brown couch. 'And a beer, if we're counting.'

She felt echoes of his chuckle all the way through the phone.

'I thought of you in the bath. I mean ... I thought of you, when I was in the bath.' She giggled.

'I think that's the nicest thing you ever said to me.'

In the background she heard someone call his name.

'I've got to go, Rem.'

'Goodnight, Seth.'

'Sleep well. I'll bring you headache tablets and more croissants when I come poop-scooping in the morning.'

'Seth?'

'Yes, Rem?'

'I think that's about the nicest thing you ever said to me.'

'Go to sleep, crazy lady.'

***

Until Remy's phone call Seth had been enjoying himself, relatively speaking. After the phone call he couldn't remember much except how he'd got hot all over when Remy said *thought of you in the bath.*

There were forty guests in the restaurant. It wasn't only Lewis Carney who Seth had been keen to see perform. He'd wanted an idea of how the entire restaurant handled itself under pressure.

They'd passed with flying colours.

Along with the paying guests, he'd invited a few industry heavyweights. The head of the Winemakers' Federation had accepted, plus a couple of guys from the Wine & Brandy Corp. They'd been talking about research levies when Remy called.

Research levies. The fee per tonne all wineries got slugged for industry R&D. Conversation had moved on now and Seth had a struggle trying to get back up to speed. In the end, he didn't bother. Coffee pots were circulating and some of the guests had begun to leave.

Half an hour later, as he was shaking hands around the room, thanking his staff and wishing his last guests goodnight, a woman at a table held his gaze and mentioned Remy by name. 'I saw that story about you and Remy in the paper today. Remy Roberts is a gem. She does a lot for the community here, so you'd better look after her or there'll be a whole heap of old people chasing you with a dirty great spade. My mother will be one of them. Her name is Dottie Howlett.'

He had no idea what it was Remy did for the community, or why Dottie

Howlett or anyone else might chase him with a spade, but before he could ask about it the Winemakers' Federation chief caught his eye and the woman moved on.

Later her words played on his mind as he reversed the ute out of its parking spot. That lady had been fierce, like a lioness protecting its cub. He knew that was important but he couldn't put his finger on why. He was almost all the way back to the pub at Oakbank when he worked it out. By then, it was eleven o'clock.

He didn't care about the time.

Seth turned the ute and headed for Red Gum Valley Road.

When he got there, the cottage was in darkness. He dimmed the headlights so they wouldn't glare, nosed into the driveway and parked where he wouldn't get spat at by the sappy pine.

The dogs huffed at him sleepily as he opened the gate. Breeze was one big wiggle; Occhy's tail slapped Seth's knees. He spent time with them, rubbed and patted and listened for any hint of movement from inside. Nothing.

He pulled at the patio doors, turned the handle on the cedar French doors to get inside, but they stuck.

Locked. Of all the—

Seth tried it again. Then he walked around the back of the cottage and tried the laundry door. *Locked.*

Remy would be sheet-warm, soap-smelling and beautiful, and now he couldn't get to her, short of knocking on her front window and possibly scaring her out of her wits.

***

Remy hadn't been in bed long when she heard a vehicle on her driveway. Her first thought was *Seth.*

When she pulled the curtain aside on her bedroom window, the headlights on the oncoming car blinded her before they winked out. The car finished the last part of her driveway in the dark.

A second thought crawled behind the first.

Why would that car turn out the lights? What if it wasn't Seth?

Her heart spiked in her chest. She had two dogs to protect her, but she was a hell of a long way from help if she needed it.

She swung her legs out of bed, keeping it dark because she didn't want to turn on any lights inside.

The dogs won't let anyone in. She said it like a mantra.

Remy heard the side gate latch. The dogs weren't worried. They'd stirred, but they weren't upset.

Even knowing all that, nothing could account for the feeling that flooded through her when she heard Seth tell the huffing, sleepy dogs to 'get back in your house' and 'be quiet' and she knew without doubt it was him coming through the dark.

Her legs went all rubbery. She had to put her hand on the wall to stop sliding down it.

He was right there trying the locked doors, but she couldn't make her legs move and she didn't get there before Seth gave up. He moved around to the laundry.

That handle rattled too, but Remy was there this time, pushing the door open in the dark.

'I...' She couldn't speak. She couldn't hear herself think, her blood was singing too loud.

He stepped up, inside, and reached for her. Wrapped his arms around her: toe to toe, hip to hip. He stood with his chin on the crown of her hair, holding her so tight it was as if he could stop her breaking apart.

'You're cold.' It was the only time his hand wandered, so he could feel her skin. 'Remy, you're shivering.'

'I'm happy here.' She didn't ever want to move.

'Come on,' he said, walking her inside, closing the laundry door. He led her through the house to her bedroom, crab-walking her sideways until the back of her thighs hit the bed and she crumpled.

He folded her into the warm dent she'd left in the mattress and closed the quilt like she was stuffing in a crepe. Then he knelt on the bed and eased himself across so that he was lying on top of the quilt beside her, elbow cocked and one hand propped under his ear.

His hand touched her face, traced the line of her cheek. His fingers played in her fringe, smoothing her hair. It was tender. Incredibly sweet.

'I didn't think you were coming,' she said.

'I couldn't stay away.'

Remy rolled on to her side, facing him. The quilt and sheets were tight across her body where Seth's weight pulled them, but she worked an arm free. Slowly, she laid her fingers on the side of his jaw. When she'd finished exploring there, she touched his lips with the pad of her thumb.

'I met someone tonight who knew you.' He caught her hand in his free one, kissed her thumb, then let go.

'Who?'

'I don't know her name but she said a lady called Dottie was her mother. She said you were a "gem" and if I didn't look after you there'd be old people chasing me with spades.'

Remy huffed a laugh.

'She *knew* you, Rem. Does that make sense? She's the first person I've ever met who had no vested interest in you or me, or money, or family.

None of it. She had nothing to lose, nothing to gain, and no agenda. She *knew* you, and she spoke up for you. And I almost missed what made that so important.'

He rested his forehead against hers in the dark and she could feel the perfect clean heat of him, like its own scent, coming off his skin.

'Why was it important?'

'When I found you—when I found out you sold grapes to Max Montgomery—I thought of all the ways I could make life difficult for you. I could have dropped your contract or I could have strung you along till the last minute then reneged on a deal. I thought about doing that.' That sentence took all his breath. Midway through it, Remy pulled her hand away but Seth held on. 'I thought about trying to buy you out. I already felt like I owned part of this place because it was my family's money that bought it. I knew how much it would hurt you if you had to give this place up. I thought you deserved to hurt like that.'

'I don't get it...' she said.

This conversation with Seth, it was like exploring a cave. Tunnels branched everywhere, opening entirely new caverns. They had no ropes or torches and a wrong step could be disaster. Turning back wasn't an option because it was pitch-black behind them, yet ahead those new caverns promised wonders. Beauty. Fragility. Joy. If only they were brave enough to push through the murky black.

'When I saw you sitting in the crowd at the growers' meeting that day, trying to hide, I knew I was right back at square one: a crowd of people and you were all I could see. Just like that day at the Vintage Festival.'

'That's nuts.' She put her hand on his shoulder. The muscles bunched and coiled under her fingers.

'So I'm driving out here. I'm standing outside your door, and I thought: don't fuck this up, Seth. I've fucked up so much when it comes to you and me. I want to start how we should have started years ago if everything else hadn't got in the way.'

'And all this came from Dottie Howlett's daughter?'

'What she said was the final straw. I already knew it, I think. I just didn't trust it.'

'And you do now?'

'I do. I've hated you for a long time Remy Roberts. I want to be sure I get loving you right.'

Chapter 21

They'd talked for hours, about everything and nothing, until slowly the periods of quiet lengthened and Remy's yawns outnumbered her words. She fell asleep curled with her back to Seth's chest, the quilt a blanket between them.

Seth's arm went numb in the night. He put up with the dead feeling for as long as he could, because there was something so perfect about watching Remy sleep he didn't want to disturb her. She snored—though he'd never tell her that—but close-up, her soft sighs comforted him. He loved that she slept deep and peaceful in his arms.

Eventually, though, he'd had to move and make his own space on the bed and when he slept, he dreamed of purring kittens.

He woke to a real, live kitten with large grey eyes and the first thing he did that morning was smile and kiss the kitten's nose.

'Good morning,' Remy said.

'Morning,' Seth murmured.

'Has anyone ever told you you snore?'

He laughed because she delighted him. She laughed—he hoped—simply because she felt like it. He hadn't heard that cascading, carefree sound from her in forever. Not since that day in the park years ago in the rain. He didn't want her to stop laughing. Ever.

'Come on, crazy lady, let's get up before I can't let you.'

***

It was a stunning late summer morning, blue sky and not a breath of wind. A veil of dew dusted leaves and grass, making spider webs wink with water diamonds. Morning sun spun through the window, turning the floors a creamy gold.

By the time Seth had the kettle boiled and coffee made, Remy had joined him. She wore well-worn denim jeans and a fitted turquoise shirt with an open collar, showing a silver pendant bouncing on a slim chain. Her hair was loose and he didn't think he'd ever seen her look more beautiful.

It was fun sharing her galley kitchen and he touched her often as they passed back and forth. She popped hot toast out of the toaster and juggled it to him, and he slathered the squares in dobs of butter and homemade jam. Fig for him. Mulberry for her.

They took toast and coffee to the patio, where the dogs trotted up from the back of the garden hunting for a thrown crust.

'She's looking at me like I'm up to no good,' Seth said to Remy, who had Breeze at her feet, staring at him balefully.

'Yeah, well, Occhy's looking at you like you're some kind of stud, so I wouldn't worry, hero. You can't win 'em all.'

Eventually, she sighed and stretched. Her hair tousled down her back in wheaten ripples.

'I don't want to work today,' she groaned, stretching her feet on the warm bricks, flexing her toes.

'Then don't. You're your own boss. Have a day off.'

'I really can't. Unfortunately I have the type of customer who expects me to live up to my work commitments.'

Shit. He'd known her second job would come up but he hadn't expected he'd have to deal with it so soon. He didn't want to come on too strong, but he couldn't pussyfoot around it either. He hated the idea of what she did for extra money. He'd hated it five years ago. He loathed the thought now.

'You can help me if you like. If you don't have other plans.' Her eyes twinkled.

'You need sound effects? Heavy breathing? I don't think so.' He reached for his coffee cup, scraped the toast plate over the table, clearing up.

Remy put her hand on his arm. 'Seth?'

'What?' His gaze dropped to where her fingers curled around his forearm, so pale against the dark hairs on his skin. 'I won't pretend I like what you do, Rem. I'm not that kind of bloke.'

Her fingers gripped tighter. 'Seth?' She said again, tugging.

He put the cup on the table. He couldn't stay angry. He was too happy to be with her.

'I haven't made a single sexual phone call for money since the day you heard me on my porch. I don't do it anymore, okay? I stopped straight away. I'm talking about a different job.'

'Oh.' He felt like an idiot. 'Alright then.' And after that: 'What do you need me to do?'

'For starters, we better call in to your hotel so you can change into something old and comfy. You'll be getting your hands dirty.' She made a show of looking him up and down. 'Leave the Armani on the hanger, okay?'

***

At the back of the Mulberry Mews aged care units in Oakbank was a communal garden: a long rectangle about the size of two cricket pitches side by side, bordered by a high slatted dark-metal fence with openings at regular intervals for white-painted metal gates. There were benches at the short sides of the rectangle with half-oak barrels on either side holding big magnolia trees. At the base of the trees, colourful flowers huddled.

Remy had parked as close as possible to the laneway, but getting all the gear into the garden still required considerable manoeuvring with a sack-truck and brute force. So far, Seth had carted four bales of pea straw, a stack of newspapers, four rubbish bins filled with compost and a variety of spades and tools from Remy's Rodeo along an alley which had the most crooked dog-leg he'd ever seen. He'd got so much straw under his shirt he'd taken the damn itching thing off, which meant he was half-naked in jeans and boots with Remy and a bunch of old people.

The old ladies loved it. They said the Mews hadn't had such eye-candy in the garden for years, and they giggled behind their hands: teenagers all over again.

The old men, on the other hand, kept asking what they could do to help. He could hardly set them to carting bales of straw or hammering pallet timbers, or upending bins of compost because it might have caused an early heart attack, so he settled for letting them rake up any vagrant straw outside the area Remy had designated for the residents' new vegetable patch.

It was ingenious really, these no-dig gardens. Remy had been telling him about them all morning as they'd loaded her ute with the things she'd need, then as they'd driven into Oakbank.

The new patch was about eight metres long and three metres wide. It was fenced by a border made from the pallet boards Remy kept in her stable. Now he knew what she used them for.

Seth's first job had been to cobble the border together while Remy laid wads of newspaper on the grass. 'To stop weeds,' she said.

Next came thick chunks of pea straw, laid as they broke from the bale. 'That's the base for the roots to grow into,' she said.

Then it was layers of compost. Homemade.

'I think you're prouder of your compost than you are of your jam,' he'd grizzled, as he'd lugged bin after bin along the alley. Those bins were the most cumbersome. He almost lost one off the sack-truck and a few of the old blokes had looked at him like they suspected he'd rolled up for work drunk.

Next came more pea straw. Then Remy clambered over the bed, scattering handfuls of blood and bone.

After that, one of the old blokes was allowed to water it in while they had lunch. A lady named Madge brought ham and salad sandwiches on a silver tray. They were cut in delicate white-bread quarters that made him feel like he was crashing a kid's birthday party. Another brought chocolate and cherry teacake, and someone offered him lemonade.

By then it was about two o'clock and the old codger with the hose had watered things into a landslide.

'Okay,' Remy said, licking chocolate crumbs from her fingers. 'Great job, Ernie. Turn the water off now.' Then to Seth she said: 'Now we get to the good part.'

'Great,' Seth said, envying her enthusiasm until she hit him with a hundred-watt smile that got his inner batteries all fired up.

Winter in the Hills got pretty cold, which was why autumn was so important to get vegie seedlings established while the soil retained its warmth.

Carefully Remy pricked out the broccoli seedlings and made holes through the layers of compost and straw. She packed the holes with more compost and planted straight in. Next to her, Seth did the same with the baby spinach.

He'd put his itchy shirt on while they ate lunch, probably to stop Madge and Lucy ogling his chest, but it had come off again now. The small of his back gleamed with sweat and Remy could smell him whenever they came close. She'd never minded the honest smell of a day's sweat on a blue-collar man, and she sure didn't mind it now.

Sunlight gleamed on his body, and outlined the hairs on his chest, and Remy had a hard time keeping her hands to herself.

'What are you smiling about?' he asked, poking her in the ribs, poking again when all she did was giggle, leaving fingerprint smudges on her shirt.

'It's a secret, is it?' Poking again as she tried to push his hands away.

'I say, Remy?' Old Ernie began.

Remy stood up in the straw, straightened her back. 'What's up, Ern?'

'Are you sure you've got that bean trellis in the right spot there? Won't it shade everything else?'

'Ern, this isn't England, remember? You're in the southern hemisphere now,' said Lucy, between characteristic quick blinks. Lucy had been a spectator from start to finish.

'Luce is right, Ernie. They'll be fine, love,' said Madge.

Ernie scratched his head. 'Bugger me, I'm an old duffer. I forgot about the different hemispheres.'

Bless him. Remy had seen photos of Ernie with his wife, Peg, at Peg's funeral a year or so back. He'd been a dashing young man in his day. An egg farmer. A good footballer.

'Shows what I know, mate,' Seth said, standing up from the bed of straw. 'I didn't even know what hemisphere we were in made a difference.'

'You always got to check which way the sun moves. No point putting all the tall stuff where it gets all the sun and shades everything else out. My dad told me that about tomatoes. I never forgot it,' Ernie said.

Seth stepped out of the straw and kept chatting. Ernie forgot about being an old duffer and started telling Seth all about the gardens where he grew up in Somerset, and Remy was grateful to Seth for his sensitivity.

Sensitivity. Now there was a new thought.

Remy dug in the poles for the bean trellis—making a teepee and lashing the overlapping tops with twine—then planted the bean seedlings at the base where they would climb.

'Job done,' she announced, stepping back. 'Can you water them in, Ernie? Just a light spray.'

'Think I'll manage that alright.'

'It'll be so exciting to have our own vegies. They taste so much better than what you get at the shops,' Madge said, giving Remy a hard squeeze.

'Not so expensive, either,' Lucy added.

Madge kissed Seth on the cheek and Lucy giggled behind her hand, then Remy and Seth packed up the tools.

'I'll be back next weekend to check on everything,' Remy said, poised at the metal gate leading to the front of the Mews. 'Water them every second day, Ern. Just lightly, if it doesn't rain.'

'Got more chance of winning Lotto than getting rain, I reckon,' Ernie said.

Chapter 22

They'd stopped at the bottle shop on the way home from Mulberry Mews where Seth bought a bottle of French champagne that was now in Remy's fridge. He had a shower and shave, dressed in clean clothes, hung out his towel and fed the dogs.

The sound of the shower running in Remy's ensuite helped cover the growl of his stomach. It had been a hell of a long time since the ham and salad sandwich at lunch.

Pizza ingredients covered the kitchen bench. He contemplated getting a few started. He didn't cook much, but how hard could homemade pizza be? Remy had set out jars of pesto on the bench, olives, a wedge of pumpkin, tomatoes, zucchini and a knob of mozzarella cheese.

To distract himself from the food, he wandered to the big Baltic pine bookshelf on one side of the fireplace. The top shelf held fantasy books, sword and sorcerer stuff like *Lord of the Rings* and a series of books by Raymond E

Feist. One of the Feist paperbacks was so worn it was held together with an elastic band.

The second shelf sported a stereo system and speakers and either side of that was a collection of old glass bottles. Seth picked up one of these and turned it in his hand—Seppelt's red wine vinegar. His phone buzzed in his pocket as he went to put the bottle back.

He checked the caller ID.

Funny, he'd anticipated this call from Ailsa all week. Now he had her on the phone, all he felt was pity. For him, for her, for all the time with Remy he could never get back.

'Hi, Ailsa. How are you?'

'Seth, darling. I'd be better if you'd tell me these rumours about you and Remy Hanley aren't true.'

'That might depend on what rumour you're talking about.'

'Rina said you kissed her.'

'Kissed Rina? I can tell you definitely, that rumour's not true.'

'Kissed *Remy,* Seth. You know what I meant. Please don't play games. I'm not in the mood and not a fool.'

From Remy's end of the house, the hum of a hairdryer replaced the spray of the shower.

'I'd never call you a fool, Mother. A meddling old woman maybe, but not a fool.'

Stunned silence greeted him, but Ailsa recovered fast. 'I'm going to forget you said that, Seth. I'm going to put that comment down to whatever lies she's been filling your head with.'

'I'll be in Perth later this week. I'll come to see you then. I'm not doing this now.'

'Seth, don't you dare hang up. It's not me who—'

He disconnected the call and turned his attention back to Remy's bookshelf, his gaze angrily roving the shelves.

The bottom rung held photo albums. He pulled the first one out. It was a thick, material-covered album, and as he flicked through it, he found photos that he assumed were Remy's mother's. Many were similar to pictures his parents had: black and white photos of beaches around Margaret River, a photo taken on the Busselton Jetty, a day trip to the caves.

He was about to put the album back and see if he could find one of Remy's—he wouldn't mind seeing a picture of Remy in her school uniform—when one of the photos caught his eye. He was having his second look, his third look at it, when the sound of the hairdryer stopped.

Seth put the photo album back, feeling a bit guilty for snooping. He crossed back to Remy's fridge, took out the bottle and popped the cork over the sink.

'Oh I love that sound.' Remy's voice floated to the kitchen from the front bedroom.

'I'm pouring you a glass now.'

He found a couple of champagne flutes in a cupboard and was filling them with the frothy liquid when Remy walked into the living area.

Seth put the bottle on the timber countertop and exhaled on a whistle.

Her hair was loose and straight and not quite dry, tumbling to the small of her back. Her feet were bare. A gold chain glittered on her ankle. Her jeans were tight. Her t-shirt was white. He shut up before his inner poet added:

and he took her to bed to spend the night.

'What?' she said, hesitating as she crossed the floorboards, glancing at her front like she thought she'd find tomato sauce spilled all over her shirt.

'Nothing.' *You look beautiful* didn't cut it. Beautiful didn't come close. 'You look amazing, Rem.'

'Thank you.'

'That sound you can probably hear is me kicking myself for wasting five years before I got around to telling you how incredible you are.'

It took a moment for his words to get through, as if he spoke in code that didn't compute. Then she smiled. She was still smiling when she threw herself into his arms.

As kisses went, Remy thought later, it wouldn't have won a prize for finesse.

Her jump was overeager and he wasn't ready, and really, she was lucky his arms were strong and his body was built to take flying leaps from eager women because if he'd been any less solid, she'd have knocked him into next week. As it was, he let out a kind of *oomph,* and stumbled until his backside found some support on her kitchen countertop. Her nose bumped his cheek. Her hair was in her face, in her eyes. Her knee bunted his shin and she thought her tooth might have cut his lip.

'Don't you fuckin' dare kill me before I get this kiss,' he muttered against her mouth, and that started her laughing, until the midnight gleam in his eyes ignited a yearning in her belly and all her giggles died, like he'd robbed them of air.

He smoothed the hair from her face. Clamped one fist around the strands at the back of her head and brought his forehead to hers. His scent was so familiar. Her soap. Her house. Dog. Underpinned by a scent so uniquely Seth, it brought tears to her eyes because nothing else, *no one* else, would ever smell like this. Not exactly like this. Ever.

'Don't kill me, before I get ... *this.*' His lips touched hers.

This time, it was slow and perfect, until it was ragged and amazing and Remy was standing on the tips of her bare toes with her whole body leaning into him and their breathing the loudest thing in the room.

'Kill me now. I'll go happy.' He set her on the soles of her feet, looking a bit like a guy who'd been given the world, with a cherry on top.

***

'I've got a confession to make,' he said later, as she sliced pumpkin for the pizzas and swiped homemade pesto across a pitta bread base. He'd switched from champagne to red wine and he spun the liquid and watched it trail legs inside the glass.

Remy could smell the wine from where she sliced. 'What did you do now?'

'I snooped in your photo albums while you were in the shower.'

'Some of those albums are my mum's. They go a long way back. I'm storing them.'

'Can I show you something I found?'

It sparked her curiosity. 'Sure.'

Seth moved to the bookcase, squatted at the bottom shelf in a way that did incredibly hot things to his backside in jeans. *Breathe, Remy.* He pulled out one of the fattest albums—an old one she'd covered in scrapbook-style material a decade ago or more—and brought the tome back to the countertop.

He flicked through a few pages. 'There aren't that many pictures of you as a baby.'

'We didn't have much money for developing photos. They cost a bomb back then.' Would she ever be able to make an admission in her life about money, or lack of it, without feeling embarrassed?

'There's not many of your father either,' Seth said.

'He was never home.'

'This one.' Seth turned the album on the bench so Remy could see it right way up and tapped the picture.

Black and white, faded with age, it was an image of a group of six young men and women on the beach. Remy had always loved it for the bathers the women wore. Sixties-style bikinis. It was a lovely, candid shot of happy people: her mother having fun.

'Mum called that place Trickle Beach. It's not far from Kilcarnup. It was our favourite spot for picnics when I was little. Four-wheel drive track though.' She pointed Lexie out to Seth.

'I thought that must be your mum. She's so much like you.'

Seth indicated the man in the photo who had his arm around Lexie, his outstretched hand buried in the sand beside her. 'Do you know who this is?'

Remy shrugged. 'Mum said he was some guy they met at the beach. He was there fishing. That's her friend Janice, she was a nurse. This guy was Lance. That's another couple of nurses Mum worked with. I can't remember their names.'

'That guy is my dad,' Seth said. 'That's Joe. He called this beach Joey's Nose—not after himself, by the way.'

'Really?' Remy peered closer, looked at Seth a couple of times. 'I asked Mum once if she knew your parents. She said she did, but she didn't let on much. She said it was a small town and everyone knew everyone.'

Seth turned the album back to face him on the bench, flipped through another few pages, but there were no more pictures of Joe and Lexie.

'I'll have to ask her about that next time I speak to her,' Remy said.

'Do you talk to your mother much?'

'Every few weeks.'

Seth replaced the photo album in the bookshelf. He detoured to the fridge to refresh Remy's glass. She had the oven preheating, fan running, and it added that background hum of white noise to the room, along with champagne bubbles, slicing, dicing and the kitchen hustle of drawers opening and closing, plastic chopping boards sliding on timber.

'I've never thought of putting pumpkin on a pizza,' Seth said, watching her chop.

'It's good. This one is fetta, pumpkin, oregano, caramelised onion, olives.' Behind her, the oven clicked that it was up to temperature. 'Going in right now.'

Seth's mobile phone buzzed a couple of times as she cooked. The third time he checked the device and Remy saw him frown.

'What's up?'

'It's that journalist from Channel 7. Jennie Grey. She's been chasing us for an interview the last few days.'

Remy stopped spreading mozzarella over the second pizza. 'Us?'

'She wants to come up here and take some photos of us at home and interview you.'

It hit the pit of her stomach like a lump of lead. 'Interview me? The media?'

'Don't worry, Rem. I'm putting her off.'

'Why would anyone want to interview me?' She grumbled. 'You maybe, sure. But me? I'm nobody.'

'You're not nobody, and don't worry about it. *The Advertiser* is her direct competition, and I've been in the papers a hundred times. I think she's just looking for a different angle out of those snippets in the paper. Don't worry. I'll look after it.'

Remy sipped her champagne, glad the food wasn't far away. She was starting to feel light-headed and that dizzy feeling wasn't helped by thoughts of journalists and cameras.

'You know what I've really loved about living in the Adelaide Hills?' She said.

'What?'

'I love that no one knows me. I love how anonymous I am here, especially how it was in the beginning. Do you know that in five years, I can only remember one time when I ran into someone I knew in the supermarket in Mount Barker? It's not like living in Margaret River.'

'That might change, if you're serious about being with me.'

'Yeah. I'm kind of afraid of that.'

'Can you handle it, Rem? I mean, without freaking out. Because if it's an issue we should probably stop right here.'

She wished her stomach didn't give that awful lurch at the thought of stopping right here. The last thing she wanted to do was *stop right here.*

'Maybe stop after pizza, hey? I'm starving.' She tried for a tone that said she was good with it, but her hand shook and mozzarella cheese missed the pizza topping and skittered across the counter. Seth reached for her wrist, held firm enough that her gaze flicked to his.

'I don't want to stop. I'm all in, Rem. I'm so far into you I couldn't find my way back if you gave me a torch.'

Her arm jerked in his hand, she couldn't help it. All of a sudden it was like the heat in his skin would burn her up. *Hell and Tommy,* what was she supposed to say to that?

The oven timer buzzed. So she said: 'Pizza.'

Chapter 23

Remy Roberts shouldn't be allowed to eat pizza. It wasn't fair. Watching her pink tongue curl around a melted strand of mozzarella cheese was its own special kind of torture, and don't get him started on the way she licked her fingers, or what it did to him when she pulled off an olive and popped it in her mouth.

She didn't even know she was doing it. He loved that about her.

Another thing he loved on her was that ankle chain. He'd linked silver jewellery and Remy in his mind all these years, but that dainty damn slink of gold on her foot had him rewriting his own preferences.

He'd like to see her wearing only that, nothing else. He'd like to kiss his way round it, nibble at her skin.

'Are you done? There's another half if you want it,' she said.

'As far as food goes, I'm all full up.'

He'd made her blush again. She stood to clear the plates, and he said,

'Remy,' once, to make her stop, and then: 'come here, beautiful.'

Her first response was so primitive, it made her ache. When he said her name, when he held his hand out to her, she wanted to climb into his solid, strong chest and burrow there forever. She wanted to feel his big arms haul her so tight, she'd never be let go.

Except this time she didn't need shelter or protection from a storm. It wasn't raining and nor did she want to hide away from the world. If she was going to be with Seth, it would be as equals. Partners.

So she smiled at him, let go of her shyness, banished her fears of not being pretty enough or rich enough or good enough to keep him. There was honesty in his eyes when he called her beautiful, a raw need that dismissed her doubts.

'I don't think so,' she said, backing away with her hands filled with pizza plates and her smile filled with promise. 'You come here.'

He was out of the chair in a flash, stalking across the floorboards. She barely had time to put the plates on the kitchen counter before he caught her to him, pressing her back, moulding her body to his.

He picked up a thick handful of her hair and rubbed it through his fingers, lifting it away from her neck. 'You've been driving me crazy every second I've been inside this house. You're all over it, everywhere around me.'

His lips found her neck and she sighed, tilting her head to give him access, wanting more of his mouth and his hands and just *him...*

'Hold on,' he whispered as his breath grazed her skin. His hands gripped her hips and he picked her up, setting her butt gently on the kitchen bench. 'I think that's safer.'

So their second kiss started perfect, straight off the bat. No bunted shins, no split lips. Then Remy whispered, 'bugger being safe, Stud,' and opened her mouth to let him in.

***

She woke to the sound of the curtain being pulled aside in her bedroom and the very first thing she did was blush.

Hell and Tommy, what a night.

She didn't want Seth to know she was awake. She wanted a few precious seconds to relive those recent hours. It started on the kitchen bench. It ended in her bed. She was pretty sure somewhere in the middle they'd christened the couch.

'I know you're awake, Rem.' He pulled the curtain completely open and bright light flooded into the room.

'That's *so* not nice,' Remy groaned, twisting away from the light.

'Never said I was nice.'

She giggled.

He pulled the covers back and they fought for a bit, stark naked, until all the bits of her that wobbled during wrestling games caught his attention, and made the part of him that might have wobbled not wobble at all.

Seth wrapped her up in the quilt and stopped her struggles.

'You don't fight fair,' she grumbled.

'I don't want to fight at all. You killed my fighting mood. Come share a shower with me.' He kissed her fingers, entwining them in his.

'You've only got three minutes. I'll have the eggtimer on you.'

'Jeez. Can I handle the pressure?' He tugged her arm.

The ensuite had been built beneath the low sloping roof of what had once been a verandah. Seth's head didn't fit beneath the shower-rose, so he had to bend his knees. Thirty seconds into their wash he gave up, dropping to those awful pink and beige tiles.

Remy squirted shampoo in her hands and lathered his hair. The shower spray washed the foaming suds away. He took the soap and rubbed her stomach, breasts, hips, thighs, making circular swirls all over her skin.

Remy leaned back against the wet wall and closed her eyes, shivering where the tiles were cold. Then he made her so hot with his hands, she needed the cool to keep her standing straight. Somewhere, late in the second minute or early in the third, his tongue replaced his fingers.

'Like that. Oh, just like that,' she muttered, opening her thighs wider.

She really didn't think she could go another round this morning, she ached all over in the very best of ways, but then Seth's tongue delved deeper, shooting waves of pleasure through her, and she changed her mind.

Gripping his shoulders, she held on hard, felt it build; roll, then rock through her, and as she shuddered to her climax, she shouted his name.

He kissed her belly button, held her through the tremors. 'That's gotta be some kind of record.'

'Don't sound so proud. You've got about fifteen seconds before I turn off the water and call the show and the shower over.'

Seth stood up beside her. 'Rem, all I need is ten strokes.'

She laughed and closed her hand around him: 'Let's see how many times ten goes into fifteen.'

Chapter 24

They took the dogs for a run in the vineyard after breakfast so Remy could inspect the fruit. Seth took measurements and they both agreed, by the end of the week Remy's grapes would hit the sweet spot.

Seth squinted at the gum trees lining the road and in the pockets of bush surrounding the vineyard. 'You ever get any problem with birds?'

'Yes,' she said. 'But not so much since the drought. There aren't as many birds around and the trees have had enough blossom.'

'No nets?'

'I netted the first two years. Then fruit prices dropped so much it wasn't worth it.'

Unspoken between them was the fact the big wineries such as Lasrey had been first to start cutting the prices they paid.

'It's business, Rem,' was all Seth said.

'I know.' She stepped nearer the vines. Turned with a handful of grapes to face him. 'Doesn't mean it doesn't suck.'

He nodded to concede the point. 'I'll talk to Rina tomorrow, get her to schedule your place in for the end of the week. I'll pick up the tab for your fruit pick.'

'You don't have to do that.' She frowned and he hated it, and when the frown turned to suspicion, he hated it more.

'I know I don't have to do it. I want to,' he said.

'I bet Montgomery Wines isn't paying picking costs for any other growers.'

'This is different. It's not Montgomery paying it, it's *me* paying it.'

'I'm not a charity case, Seth. I never asked anybody for a free ride in my life.'

'It's not charity. It's no big deal. Don't turn it into one.' He tweaked her ear. 'Sometimes you're allowed to just say yes, okay?'

He could read it all over her. Indecision. Discomfort. He tweaked her ear a little harder. 'You want to pay back Ailsa's money, don't you?'

'You know I do.' She flicked her head and he let go.

'You need every cent from harvest to do that, Rem. This just takes out a baseline cost for you.'

'Then it's kind of a matter of which of the Lasrey's I owe, right?'

She was so bloody stubborn. 'Why is this different to the way you help those old folk by building them vegie gardens on your own time? I can do this for you, Remy, and it's no big deal. It's helping out a friend.'

Her mouth set in a determined line. 'It's not the same. We're talking thousands of dollars, not a few bales of pea straw and a stack of old newspapers nobody else wants.'

'You want my mother out of your life, this is the way to do it. If you want to IOU me, that's fine.'

Her shoulders twisted from him. 'I'm so tired of owing people money.'

He held his hand to her and kept his voice soft. 'I don't want to argue. I don't want to ruin the weekend. I'm just trying to do the right thing.'

Remy took a step toward him, then another. Beautiful, liquid steps. And her hand felt warm when she put it inside his.

'I don't want to argue either.' She came close and kissed him, and he forgot about who would pay the grape pickers.

Seth wrapped his arm around her shoulders, and together they walked down the hill.

At the bottom of the valley, Occhy and Breeze chased ducks by the dam. When he glanced at Remy, her gaze was on the dogs and she was smiling at their antics. So natural and gorgeous when she relaxed like that, she stole the breath from him. Made him feel like the luckiest bastard alive.

Gently, he pulled her to him, and leaned to press his lips to her temple. Remy put her hand in the back pocket of his jeans and squeezed.

'Don't touch what you can't afford,' Seth said.

So she did it again and he chuckled. Then her hand dipped beneath the waistband of his jeans. Found skin. Her silky finger traced the dent at the top of his arse. Did it again, in that spot she'd discovered he liked sometime in the night. His laugh morphed into more of a groan.

'I wish I could stay here all week with you. I'd teach you not to tease.'

'What's stopping you? You're the boss, Stud. Play hooky with me.'

For all of five seconds he thought of doing exactly that. Turning off his phone. Leaving his laptop in its case. Shutting out the world. He never *did* get his game of Sixty Seconds.

Tempting.

Then he imagined what Rina would say if he vanished the week before vintage. She'd have a fit. She'd send out a search squad.

'I wish.' Seth sighed and let reality wash away the thought of his body pinning Remy's to his Margaret River office wall.

'I have to get back to Margaret River before vintage here cranks up, Rem. I need to sort a few things out at the office and I'll have to spend a day in in the Great Southern. I need to see my mother too. To say I have a few questions for her is putting it mildly.'

Remy's playful smile faded, and it made him feel like he'd switched a light off on the day.

'It's not for long. I'll be back.'

'It's okay. You're CEO of a big operation. I get that. I do.'

'About this payment for the grapes—'

'You mean the pickers.'

'I mean the grapes, Rem. Forget the picking. Me meeting your picking cost is nothing.'

'Only to you,' she grumped. Her fingers stopped stroking and her hand came out from his jeans. 'So what about the payment?'

'If I paid you in advance, would you write out the cheque to Ailsa so I can take it back with me?'

'The grapes aren't even off the vine yet.' She stopped walking.

He stopped too. 'It's only a week and they will be. They're not going anywhere.'

'What it if rains? What if there's a tornado?'

'You're insured, aren't you?'

She was quiet.

He was incredulous. 'You're not insured?'

Remy swung away from him defiantly. 'I can't afford insurance. It's like netting against bird damage. You show me the grower who can afford all these other "what if" costs when grape prices are so damn low. Some things have to give. And anyway, forget about insurance, how can you pay me for grapes that aren't picked? That's just stupid.'

How difficult was it to give money to this woman!

'I have to go see Ailsa this week. I can take the money for you—God knows I have enough questions for her about what she did to you, *and* to me—wouldn't you like to know that I gave her that money face to face? Wouldn't you want to know what she says?'

'Ye-es,' she said, although not one hundred per cent happily. 'But you don't even know what the tonnage rate is yet. How will you work out what I'm owed?'

'What did you tell me you need to pay Ailsa out?'

'Twenty-two thousand. I've got seventy-eight in the bank.'

'So if I make a payment for twenty-two, we're good?'

'What if my fruit isn't worth $22 000?'

Seth heaved an exasperated sigh. 'If I find I'm short, you agree Occhy can live at your place rent-free till you've paid off your debts.' Then a thought struck him and he winked, 'or—and I'm an idiot for not thinking of this before—I take it out of your body.'

He thought she'd been about to protest, but his words killed any argument before it could fall from her lips.

Remy cocked her hip, tossed her hair from her face. 'And what happens if my fruit is worth *more* than $22 000?

'I'm good for the balance, Rem. Or you could always take it out of *my* body.'

'With an offer like that, how can a girl refuse?' She laughed, happy again, and the world was a better place. Remy clapped her hands, then rubbed her palms together. 'Okay, let's do it! It's about time I got that monkey off my back. I've been using Ailsa's money as a fallback long enough. It'll be good to have it gone.'

'We'll go into your bank tomorrow, get it worked out.'

'Okay. It's a deal.'

She held it together for all of two seconds. Then she squealed like a happy banshee and ran from him, tearing down the hill. The dogs saw her coming and bolted toward her, jumping all around her, muddy paws going everywhere, like it was the best time in the world.

Watching the three of them, Seth thought the dogs had it right. Being with Remy was the best time in the world.

***

Jennie Grey rang Seth's mobile just before noon and he'd run out of excuses to put her off. As journalists went, Jennie wasn't one of the worst and if he had to put Remy in front of the media an interview with Jennie would be a soft start. So he told Jennie to come around 2.00pm.

As it turned out, he needn't have worried. Remy and Jennie discovered they had gardening in common, and the reporter had been on the property for all of five minutes before Remy invited her into the back garden to take a look around.

Seth was dispatched to make the two ladies a cup of tea and get a glass of water for the cameraman, Clive.

Relegated to tea lady at the ripe old age of thirty-five.

He watched them from the living rooms windows while the kettle boiled. Remy would point out a plant and Jennie would bury her nose in it, or touch it, or pluck it, or rub it ... whatever one did to release the scent.

He wanted to get back out there. Remy was too honest to be left with a journalist for long. Jennie could be getting all sorts of juicy scoops for her story and Remy might not even know what she was giving up.

That thought had barely popped into his head when it stopped him, mid-dunk, with a teabag dangling from his hand.

Remy was too honest.

For five years he'd been thinking of all the reasons why Remy was a liar and a cheat, why she was an actress and a scammer, and suddenly he thought of her as too honest.

He chuckled to himself as he squeezed the teabag and threw it in the compost bucket she kept under the sink. Picking up the cups, he curved his middle fingers around the glass of water, and went outside.

Seth found the two women just in time to hear Jennie say to Remy: 'I don't know how you picked which brother to date. They're both gorgeous.'

He opened his mouth to stop things before they got way out of hand, but he shut it just as fast, because he had to know Remy's answer.

She laughed. 'They are both gorgeous. I've seen a photo of their dad when he was young and you can see where the hot genes come from. Blake was only ever a friend. We used to hang out at the beach a bit. There wasn't really ever any choice. It was always Seth for me.'

'So it was love at first sight?'

Seth held his breath. Remy might have too.

'I guess so. I can't speak for Seth, but for me no one else ever came close. We've had a lot of bumps on the way, though.'

'And it never worried you that he was the boss?'

Again, there was that careful consideration as she framed her answer, and then she said: 'Sometimes, yes. We weren't supposed to establish personal relationships in the workplace at that time—it was considered an OHS risk. Typical me, I had to pick the biggest name in the company to fall for. I knew if a relationship between us caused any trouble, it wouldn't be the CEO who got sacked.'

'And that's kind of what happened then, isn't it?' Jennie asked, standing up from where she'd picked a sprig of basil or mint or whatever it was from the herb garden, squinting at Remy against the sun.

'Kind of, yes,' Remy said. 'But I had a problem in the vineyard when I worked there. I damaged one of the company's premier vineyards because I made a mistake mixing a spray. That's why I lost my job.'

There she goes again, too honest, Seth thought.

'There was a bright side with what happened to me, though, Jennie: it taught me a lot about chemical safety in a vineyard. These days I'm as close to organic as I can get. I don't use herbicides or fungicides, I plant the mid-rows here with a native cover crop and I slash it a couple times a year. I make compost tea for the vines. It's healthier for everyone.'

Jennie Grey opened her mouth for another question, but Seth chose that point to interrupt: 'Tea's ready, ladies.'

***

By the time the news people called it a wrap it was getting late. Seth and Remy were in the patio deckchairs nursing a beer, watching the dogs play.

Seth would catch an afternoon flight out of Adelaide to Perth the next day, and the thought of spending a week apart had both of them subdued.

The dogs kept them entertained, although for reasons all her own, Breeze was snappy at Occhy for the first time since he'd come to stay.

'Do you ever wonder what would have happened if you and Blake had got together?' Seth said at one stage.

'No.'

He took a long sip of his beer, drained it. From the deckchair beside him, Remy lifted her legs and crossed them comfortably over his knees and Seth had to adjust his weight on the seat to compensate.

'At work, we used to say you were the storm cloud and Blake was the sunshine. Blake looked for the best in people all the time; he was so uncomplicated. He was easy to be with,' Remy said.

'Not like me?'

'God, not like you. You were so intense. You still are. You had everyone running scared. I couldn't believe it that day when you came out of nowhere and volunteered to plank walk with us. That was the first time I'd seen you laugh. Do you remember that? Blake was shouting at us where to put our feet. Left. Right. Left. And you and I cracked up.'

He chuckled. 'Yeah.'

'I'll miss you tomorrow night,' she said. 'I know you have to go. But I'll miss you.'

'Me too.' He ran his hand down her thigh, over her knee, up again. 'Can we talk about what happens when I get back?'

'What happens when you get back?'

'I was hoping you might invite me to lodge here, you know—' he lifted her hand and put her fingers to his lips, kissing the tips—'me and my dog.'

'Yeah, sure. I can find a kennel for you. The nights are getting chilly though.'

'Crazy lady.' He tightened his grip on her hand and eased her off her deckchair into his lap. 'I want you, Rem. I want to be with you.'

'Wow.' She ducked her head shyly, all jokes gone from her, and a heartbeat later, she snuck her hand around the back of his head and bent to press her forehead against his. 'That would be great.'

So it wasn't a profession of undying love; but as Remy went, Seth counted it positive, and hell: if she wanted to show him how much she loved him a thousand times a day rather than tell him, he was good with that.

Who couldn't be good with that?

Chapter 25

Remy's mother called Monday morning while Seth and Remy were at the bank. Remy had to cut Lexie off with a promise to call back.

They ate a quick lunch at the cottage before he left to collect the rest of his things from the Oakbank Pub and settle his room bill. From there, he'd go to Montgomery Wines for more meetings and then, to the airport.

'I gotta go, Rem, or I'll never get on the plane,' he said, holding her tight, pressing his body to hers. 'But I'll be thinking the entire time of the day I get back.'

She wanted to tell him she missed him already. She wanted to tell him she loved him. Instead she kissed him until both of them were reeling.

'I'll call you when I get to Perth. It's a three-hour drive south. I'll need you to keep me company at least some of the way.'

'Drive safe,' she said, catching his bottom lip and sucking it between hers.

'Oh, bugger the plane. How 'bout we sit you up here like this for a minute,' and he lifted her onto the kitchen bench.

***

When Remy rang her mother, Lexie answered the phone super-fast. That wasn't like her. She was a bit of a bumble when it came to new technology and she was still getting the hang of her first mobile phone.

'Hi, love,' her mother said. She sounded like she'd been running.

'Hi to you, too. What's happening? Where are you?'

'We're in Cairns. We've been up to Port Douglas today. It's so beautiful up here.'

'I'm glad you're taking your time. It's a big country, there's no need to rush around it.'

'We've been in Airlie Beach and the Whitsundays for a while and we hadn't been catching much news, but then in Cairns this morning we had a lazy coffee and Bernie saw this article in the weekend paper about you and Seth

Lasrey. I almost had a heart attack. What's that all about?'

'Don't stress out, Mum. Seth and I are seeing each other.'

'What do you mean: seeing each other?'

'Well, you remember that I told you Max and Sue sold Montgomery Wines?'

'Yes. That was ages ago.'

'Well, the company that bought Montgomery was Lasrey Estate.'

'Yowza,' Lexie breathed.

'That's kind of what I said. So, long story short, Seth has been in South Australia for the last month, and we've kind of got friendly all over again.'

'Are you sure, love? Everything went so bad so fast last time. I don't ever want to see you in that kind of pain again. His mother's not in Adelaide too, is she? Please tell me she's not.'

'I haven't seen Ailsa. She's still in the West.'

She felt Lexie's sigh of relief all the way from Cairns.

'What about that Rina woman?'

Remy groaned. 'No such luck.'

'What makes you think this time around is going to be any different?

He's still a Lasrey. You're still a Roberts. The two of you really don't meet in the middle.'

'You said when I was little that I could be anything I wanted to be when I grew up. You said I was as good as anyone.'

'What about that French woman last time? The wine heiress? You were a wreck when you thought the two of them were engaged.'

'Yes, but that was a false alarm and I'm older and wiser now. I can look after myself, Mum.'

'I know you can, love. Sometimes I wish I'd been able to do more for you when you were young. I should have left your father a long time ago. Bernie's shown me that. I didn't have to put up with your dad all those years and struggle on like we did.'

'You did the best that you could. You took your marriage vows seriously. You meant it when you said the bit about as long as you both shall live.' It surprised Remy to find she was getting teary. She and Lexie didn't open up about their emotions much. 'Oh, look, Mum. Enough of the soppy stuff.

Tell me, has Bernie bought you the ring?'

'He said he wants to get it in Darwin. Don't ask me why.'

Remy had been about to ask *why Darwin,* so she changed tack. 'Mum, Seth was looking through some of your old photo albums yesterday. He showed me a photo of you at Trickle Beach with a group. He said his dad was in the photo. Joe.'

'That picture's ancient, Rem. That was before Joe and Ailsa got married.'

'You two looked pretty friendly,' Remy pressed.

'I don't know about *friendly,* Ailsa and Joe were engaged, and her parents were all set to buy the land where they planted vines. It was a wedding present.'

'So you and Seth's dad, never ... you know.'

'Remy, it was 1968. It might have been the swinging sixties but I was never much of a bed-hopping hippie.'

'Not even a sneaky kiss?'

Lexie hesitated too long. 'Maybe a few sneaky kisses, but that was it.'

'Did you ever regret not ... pursuing things with Joe Lasrey?'

'A little. I won't lie. I let Ailsa and all her money scare me off too easily, but I thought I was doing the right thing. You can't take back the past, Rem. You can't change it. If I'd never met your father, I would never have had you. You were always the best thing about my marriage to Wayne.'

'Thanks, Mum.'

'Anytime, love. You know that. I did always wish I'd done a bit more than kiss Joe. He was pretty dishy back then.'

'I hope Bernie's not listening.'

'Even if he was listening, he'd be fine. Everybody has a past. He and I are old enough to know that.'

'He's a keeper, is Bernie,' Remy said.

'I hope Seth is a keeper too, Rem. I really hope so. Be careful, love.'

'I will. Thanks, Mum. Stay safe. Whatever you do, don't follow any sign to a place called Wolf Creek.'

***

It was while she was getting dinner ready later that Remy got her first inkling of just how much she'd kissed her anonymity goodbye when she kissed Seth hello.

She was slicing chicken for a stir-fry, listening to the six o'clock news on the TV in the next room. When she heard her name in a promo for *Today Tonight,* she almost chopped her thumb into the pot along with the meat.

Tonight our own Jennie Grey brings you the story of an inspirational love that has lasted five years, travelled two states, and could have almost wrecked the relationship of two brothers ... It's the story of an Adelaide Hills grapegrower and her wine tycoon boss, and an Aussie surfing superstar ... and it's coming up on Today Tonight *straight after the news...*

The voiceover cut away as Remy rushed around her galley bench to see what was happening on screen. It was a picture of Blake at the beach, clutching his surfboard under his arm. He laughed and the camera zoomed in on him as he said: 'Yeah, nah ... my brother totally stole Remy from me.'

Remy slumped to the arm of the brown couch.

'Hell and Tommy.' Why would Blake say that?

***

Seth spent most of his first five minutes in Perth adjusting to the light. No matter where he travelled in Australia, Perth was always brighter. Adelaide, for all its status as the wine capital of the country, still had a big country town feel about it. Perth and Adelaide used to be on par before the mining boom. Now, millions, no *billions* of dollars in development had flooded into the WA capital and it was a whole lot faster, bigger and noisier than Adelaide.

There were two messages on his phone. One from Blake. One from Remy. They'd both have to wait.

He caught a taxi to Blake's flat and used his key to get his car out of the garage. With a two-and-a-half hour time difference between Adelaide and Perth he hadn't lost much with the flight. In South Australia, Remy would have had dinner and she'd be in front of the television or with a book about now. Here, it was still peak hour and most of the city had only just knocked off work.

His car started like clockwork, even though it had been sitting in Blake's garage for six weeks. Seth was looking forward to blowing out the cobwebs on the drive south to Margaret River, but first he had a twenty-minute drive to Ailsa's place in Fremantle.

Her hand flicked the blinds as he parked in her driveway and she opened the door before he knocked, welcoming him in. He bent low to kiss her papery cheek.

Ailsa's home was a modern courtyard-style building, built one street back from the Esplanade in the old part of town. It smelled of tea-tree oil furniture polish and perfume. Most of the hanging space on the walls was covered with paintings: still-life fruit, portraits and landscapes. Ailsa spent most of her time in the city these days and was patron of several art galleries.

The sofas were white and overstuffed, the furniture plush, the timber polished and the whole place gleamed like over-bleached teeth. An open *Country Life* magazine lay across an ottoman that matched the chairs.

'Come and make yourself comfortable. I'm having a brandy. Would you like something, dear?'

'No, thanks.'

'Suit yourself. Won't you at least sit down?'

'I've been sitting for the last three and a half hours on the plane. Standing's fine.'

He needed more than brandy to get comfortable in this place. It was everything Remy's cottage was not. He couldn't wait to leave. First, he had a few things to get off his chest.

Ailsa wore pale blue pants and a matching jacket, navy sandals with low heels. Her face was, as always, heavily made-up and her grey hair, nearly white now, salon-perfect. She poured a generous shot in a brandy balloon and added ice.

'So,' she pouted theatrically. 'Judging by the way you hung up on me last time we spoke, I don't suppose you came to tell me you dumped her?'

'No.'

'Just like your father,' Ailsa contemplated the ice in her drink. 'Loyal to a fault.'

'You say that like it's a bad thing.'

'You spent a weekend with her five years ago and she ruined you for anyone else. When I think of poor Helene coming out here and what you put her through...' Ailsa trailed off.

Seth did feel bad about Helene. The French woman got caught in his rebound. He'd been so angry about what Remy had done—what his mother *said* she'd done—he'd had no emotional space for Helene in his life at that time. All he'd had was work. The angrier he got, the more he stayed away because it wasn't Helene he most wanted to see when he came home. He and Helene never had a chance.

Remy said he'd got hard over the years. He'd definitely been hard on Helene. She'd wanted to love him and he pushed her away.

He rubbed the short hair of his scalp. His hair felt aeroplane-itchy and he wanted a shower. 'Helene and I parted friends in the end and she's happy now. She's married. They have a baby on the way. You should send her parents a card and congratulate them.'

'I already did,' Ailsa said, taking a sip of her drink. 'That should be you, you know. We could be Lasrey-Bouchard now, if it wasn't for that gold-digging tramp.'

'Be very careful, Mother,' Seth warned. 'I told you that before. One more slur like that I'm out of here, and I won't be back. Not once has Remy ever done anything that made me think she was after my money.'

'Apart from blackmailing $100 000 out of us, you mean.'

'That blackmail line is bullshit and you know it.' Remy's cheque was in Seth's wallet and he took it out. 'Here.'

'What's this?'

He crossed the room and gave the cheque to her. Had to stop himself throwing it at her. 'Remy says she always thought of it as a loan.'

'A loan.' Ailsa took a beat to examine it. Then she put her glasses on and inspected it again. Then she laughed. The sound was all raw around the edges, no warmth.

'Well how about that,' she said, more to herself than to him. 'How much of this is yours?'

'None bar an advance on this season's grape cheque. She'd been saving to give it back to you.'

'Well, that's not something you see every day.' She folded the cheque in the gutter of the *Country Life* magazine, took a sip of her drink and said nothing.

'Tell me what really happened between you and Remy five years ago, Mother.'

'Darling, that story's old. I've explained it to you so many times.'

'Well, give it to me once more, for the hell of it.'

His mother's mouth closed into a stubborn red scratch. 'What does *she* say happened?'

'I'm asking you.'

Outside, a horn blared as a driver took issue with another at the traffic lights. Seth wished it was as easy to let off steam around his mother. Conversations with Ailsa were a bit like trying to drive the wrong way down a one-way street: something was always going to hit you.

'I told you. She admitted to not paying enough attention to her work. She offered her resignation and I accepted it. It was only afterward that she tried the sexual harassment blackmail idea on for size.'

'What did she tell you I did that qualified as sexual harassment?'

Ailsa looked out the window, took her time about bringing her gaze back. 'She said you kissed her...'

'I didn't kiss her, so she didn't say that.'

'Well, what *did* you do?'

'That's not your business, Mother. That's not what this is about. Remy says she never made any blackmail threat at all. She says you paid her to resign and stay away from me and from Blake.'

'That's absurd.'

'Or you're lying.'

'How can you say that to me, Seth?' She clanked her glass on the coffee table. Her fingers curved around the arm of her chair like claws.

'Why didn't you tell me Dad knew Remy's mother?'

'She told you that?'

'I found a photograph in an album. It was one of Lexie's. Rem didn't know who the bloke was, but it was Dad. I'm sure.'

'Joseph loved her,' she said, so softly he wasn't sure she'd said anything at all. 'We were engaged when Lexie came to Margaret River, but we hadn't got married yet. He was going to break it off with me. My parents had already picked out the land they were going to buy us for the vineyard. If your dad left me, he wouldn't have got anything. He'd never have had the chance to set up his own winery.'

'So he chose you? Not Lexie?'

She shook her head at him without really seeing him. 'I went to see Lexie after her shift finished one day—she was working at the hospital. I asked her if she really wanted to see Joseph rot in a dead-end teaching job if he married her, never doing what he loved because they would never have been able to afford it. I asked if she was prepared for him to end up resenting the ground she walked on when I could give him everything he'd ever dreamed of. I told her if she loved Joseph, she'd see what choice was best for him. She'd let him go.'

'And she did?'

'She did. The problem was, Joseph wanted the vineyard every bit as much as he wanted Lexie, and she didn't fight for him. She didn't have as much fight in her as her daughter did, that's for sure.'

'As her daughter does,' Seth corrected, trying to imagine how Remy had felt facing off against his mother in the boardroom years ago. She was a formidable woman and Remy had been just a girl. A very scared girl with a big debt hanging over her head who thought she'd killed a vineyard and was about to lose her job.

Ailsa sighed, but she was committed to her story now and the brandy had warmed her up. 'Joseph went on a binge a few years later when Wayne and Lexie got engaged. He almost left us then. I threatened him with everything: losing you boys, losing the winery. He loved you kids, of course. He just never loved me.'

Seth looked at his mother and tried to conjure feelings of warmth. It was damn hard.

He could only ever remember his father looking at her with the type of resigned tolerance thirty-odd years of marriage to a woman like Ailsa must bring. He wondered if Joe ever looked at Ailsa the way he looked at Remy now? He doubted it. But they must have been happy enough? They had two sons, the business, each other. 'Dad wouldn't have stayed with you all those years if he didn't want to be there.'

'Yes he would, if it got him his vineyard.' Her eyes turned flat and hard. 'Do you know that he had affairs? The first one was with the bit of fluff we had managing cellar door. She's the reason I pushed so hard to get that workplace policy in place.'

'This is all in the past, and Dad's not here to defend himself. If it's true, I'm sorry he hurt you that way.'

'What do you mean *if* it's true, Seth? Of course it's true.'

'You've told so many lies I don't think you know the truth.'

'Anything I've ever done, I've done because I love you. You and Blake. All I ever did is try to look out for you. Rina does that too.'

'What's Rina got to do with it?'

'Rina understands where the company is vulnerable. She helps me watch out for it.'

Riddles. 'We don't need looking out for. We never did. I've lived and breathed Lasrey since I left school. It's all I've ever done, and it's made you a nice retirement income. Better than nice. Maybe now it's time to give some of it back.'

The comment shocked her so much, her feet slid off the ottoman. 'Give what back? Give it to whom?'

'Give back to the community. We can afford to bump up our sponsorship programs. We can do more than just increase the amount of vineyard assets we hold.'

Ailsa picked up the copy of *Country Life* and thumbed the cheque inside it. There was a set to her chin that he recognised well.

Seth strode to the open window and took a deep breath of air infused with salt and sea, so much nicer than Ailsa's stuffy sitting room. Behind him, Ailsa said: 'A journalist rang me asking about you and that girl. She knew Remy worked for us once. She knew about the vineyard incident.'

'I know. I was with Remy when they did the story.' He turned back into the room to meet his mother's eyes. There was a smugness about her expression that triggered his next thought. 'You tipped the press.'

'No darling,' Ailsa smiled.

'Then who?'

'Rina.'

'Bullshit.'

'Rina does whatever I ask. She always has.'

Seth searched for any sign of a lie on Ailsa's face, but couldn't see it. His mother was certain of Rina's support. Sure of it.

'You asked Rina to go to the media?' Seth demanded. 'Why?'

'They were digging for dirt on you and Remy. They would have found out the gory details eventually—or plain made it up. Rina told them the truth.'

'All media commentary comes through the CEO's office, Mother. You know that. It's part of our board policy.'

'Darling, you're right. I forgot. Think of it as an oversight.'

'Oversight?' Seth gave up trying to find any semblance of warmth for his mother. He had none, and he hadn't had any for a very long time. 'Has it ever crossed your mind that it might be nice to have a couple of grandkids running around this place? Little people who might carry on the Lasrey name?'

Ailsa sprang forward. 'Oh, dear God. Please tell me you haven't got her pregnant already!'

Christ. 'She's not pregnant.'

'That's alright then.' She settled again. 'That would be just like her. That's how they trap men like you. First the baby. Then the ring. Then half the house.'

Seth was at Ailsa's feet in a flash, snapping up the *Country Life,* extracting Remy's cheque.

'What are you doing?' Ailsa stammered. 'Don't!'

Seth tore the cheque in half in front of her eyes. 'You never thought you'd see that money again, Mother, so you won't ever miss it. I know someone who can use it and who needs it, far more than you ever did.'

He ripped again, then a third and fourth time, and dropped the fluttering pieces on the floor. Not putting past Ailsa to somehow cobble the pieces with tape or glue, he kept a couple segments in his fingers.

'Have you gone completely mad?' Ailsa said.

'You say all the decisions you made were for me and Blake; well, that's bullshit. Everything you've done, you've done for yourself.'

'You've got it all wrong,' Ailsa called as he left the room. 'I never—'

Seth let himself out of the apartment.

***

Seth started the car, pulled into traffic and felt better with every revolution those tyres made on the road.

Years ago he'd told Ailsa that no man ever went to his grave wishing he'd spent another hour at work. Life was too short to put up with his mother's crap.

He rang Remy as he drove south. With the phone on hands-free, he replayed the conversation with Ailsa for her benefit while sunset crept over the dunes separating the freeway from the coast. He edited the nastiest parts but even so, Remy's snorts, sighs, and sounds of disbelief said it all.

'No wonder she wanted me gone,' Remy said when Seth told her about Joe loving Lexie. 'Every time she looked at me, any time she saw my name on the staff board or in the files, she would have been reminded of my mother. When I stuffed up the vineyard spray that day I gave her the excuse she needed.'

'I'm so through with that woman,' Seth said. 'Tomorrow I'll call our lawyers and see what I need to do to restructure the company without Ailsa in it. There's Rina too. She's in this up to her neck.'

'It's sad, Seth. That's all I feel.'

'Yeah.' He pictured Ailsa's face as he'd dropped the pieces of torn-up cheque on her carpet. She hadn't been sad. She'd been livid. 'Let's talk about something else.'

'Okay, well ... have you seen the news today?' Remy asked. 'Jennie Grey's story was on television here tonight.'

'I didn't see it. I've been in the air and then with Mother. What happened?'

'It was a good story, really. The promo spun me out a bit though. They were talking about how ours was a love story involving two brothers, and then the microphone cut to Blake on the beach and he said: "Yeah, my brother totally stole her from me."'

'Shit,' Seth groaned. 'I'll shove Blake's surfboard down his throat.'

'Well, what you don't see until the story runs in full is that Blake actually says: "Yeah, my brother totally stole her from me" ... and then he laughs like it's a huge joke and says: "nah, not really. Remy and I were only ever good friends. I saw her first though. I'm not ever gonna let him forget that."'

'I still think I might kill him,' Seth muttered.

'The last thing he told them was that he'd always thought you and I would be great for each other,' Remy teased.

'Okay. I'll let him live.'

They talked about the week ahead. Remy had plans to hire a bobcat to level the backyard so she could make a start on laying pavers. Occhy's rent money had gone toward the load of paving sand she'd need, and the bobcat.

'Why don't you wait till I get back? I can help.'

'Can you drive a bobcat?'

'Not really, but I can push a wheelbarrow and I can level sand.'

'Well *I* can drive a bobcat. Zac knows a guy who can get me a bobcat for a few hours on the cheap. If it pans out, I'll have the job done by the time you get back.'

'Sounds good.' He checked the clock on the dashboard. They'd been talking for a solid hour and the time flew. He'd have to hang up soon though, his battery was running low.

'Hey,' she said. 'I meant to tell you and I've kept forgetting: I found out why Breeze is being such a bitch to Occhy.'

'Why?'

'She's in heat.'

Seth couldn't say anything for a few seconds, but he could picture how Remy had probably blushed. 'What does that entail, exactly?'

'It entails a bloody big pain in the arse. It means I have to keep her and Occhy separate for up to a fortnight if we don't want little American Staffies in a couple of months. I've never been through it when I've had another dog on the property.'

'And we don't want little American Staffies?' He added the question mark, just in case she had her heart set on puppies.

'We don't,' Remy said super-firmly. 'I'm too young to be a grandma.'

'Well, I'm probably old enough to be a granddad, but whatever you want to do is fine by me.'

'So, I'll have to chain Occhy up outside the gate. I don't have any other way to keep them separate. But I don't like the idea of keeping him on the chain.'

'Chain him up at night maybe, but leave him off in the day. He won't go anywhere if there's a bitch in heat right under his nose. Poor horny old dog.'

They talked some more then said goodnight. Seth drove with the moon outside his passenger window, full and milky in the sky. He followed it through Bunbury and Busselton and it was high by the time he drove up the gravel driveway into the log cabin that, other than Remy's cottage, was the only other place he'd ever thought of as home.

Chapter 26

'This looks excellent,' Remy said late the next day, hands on hips, surveying the newly-laid pavers.

They'd been hard at it, she and Zac, but the effort was all worth it. Now there was a nice neat paved edge running along the back of the cottage, separating garden from house. She had room to put a bench there with pots either side, and she could move her outdoor table out into the middle of the pavers rather than where it had been all this time, shoved up hard against the wall.

She had all that space over near the fence to do something with too, now that there were no longer stacks of brick pavers making the place ugly. Maybe a pizza oven or an outdoor fire pit. Remy closed her eyes. She could see Lexie and Bernie in the garden this spring, colour all around.

All she had left to do was get a section of brickwork fixed where age had crumbled the corner of the cottage under the gutter. After that, it would be perfect. If anyone deserved a wedding day of perfection—second time around, surrounded by the people she loved—it was Lexie.

The best thing about today had been spending it with Zac. She'd hardly seen him since he'd busted Seth kissing her on the verandah. Zac didn't drop by anymore with eggs or the mail and she'd missed him. She didn't have enough friends in her life to lose them over something silly as that.

When Seth got back, she would take Zac up on that beer, get him over. It'd be fun.

Remy went into the house for two stubbies of Pale Ale and returned, handing one to Zac. 'Thanks for helping me out.'

'That's cool. I wasn't doing much. It looks good.'

'We did it heaps faster than If I'd tried to do it all by myself.'

'You don't have to do everything by yourself you know, Rem. There are people around who'll always lend a hand to help.'

'Yeah. I know. I don't like asking. You know me.'

Remy dragged a couple of her deckchairs out into the middle of the new paving and they both sat.

Breeze was with them, looking disgruntled. Occhilupo wasn't particularly happy either, having been banished to the other side of the gate for the last twenty-four hours. Both dogs had been whining on and off for most of the day, which had made the noise of the bobcat engine a relief because it drowned them out.

'Did you ever sort out that trouble with the carpenter about your roof?' Zac asked.

'Nope. I let it go. I didn't want to have to talk to him about it. I just wanted it to go away.'

'Sometimes with bullies, you get to the point where you have to stand up to them to get them to fuck orf,' Zac said.

'Zac Williams' words of wisdom, hey?'

'Something like that.'

***

That night, she rang Seth. She told him about the landscaping. He told her about sacking the winemaker in their Great Southern winery, and about approving the purchase of a $200 000 technology spend on a new software system across the company.

'Makes my day kind of boring in comparison,' she said.

After that, the silence stretched. Remy shifted on the couch, pulling some pillows in behind her back.

'Are you on the couch?' Seth asked.

'I am.'

'Which couch?'

'The brown dog-eared one in the reading nook. You know, as opposed to the other brown dog-eared one in the living room. I sit here sometimes and think about what the Menzels used to do in this room. They wouldn't have had power then and they probably had a kerosene lamp. Maybe they sat and read, or sewed.'

'Maybe they spent a lot of time in bed. Didn't you tell me they had a carload of kids?'

Remy laughed. 'Three boys. Maybe a horse and cartload.'

'I like picturing you in your house,' Seth said. 'It makes me feel closer to you.'

'What about you? Where are you?'

'In my office.'

Silver-grey. Natural light streaming through the windows. Stainless steel machinery far below.

'A few years ago the painters came through because marketing wanted to give all our offices a corporate makeover. I didn't let the painters in my office. It felt like they might paint you away if they touched one of these walls.'

'I was only there once,' Remy reminded gently.

'Yeah, but you made one hell of an impression,' Seth said huskily, and his voice brought the memory of that afternoon flooding back.

'Are you busy?' Remy asked; she meant, do you have time to talk?

'I'm always busy. There's always stuff going on. What's up?'

'I was thinking it might be fun if you told me a story.'

'What sort of story?'

'A sexy one.'

He laughed. 'That's your thing, not mine.'

'Not anymore. Go on. It's just you and me here, give it a try.'

'I'll feel like a dick.'

'Give it a try,' she pressed. 'I promise I won't laugh.'

'Shit.' He stalled for a second. 'Give me a clue. My mind's blank.'

'It's nearly nine-thirty here, I'm ready for bed.'

'You said you were on the couch. I thought you were reading.'

'Work with me, Seth.'

He sighed. She could imagine him pulling his hand across his scalp. Not all guys were into phone stories, she knew that, but she wanted him and he wasn't here to put her hands on. Plus she'd never done this before—from the other side—and she was curious.

'Let me shut the door,' he said.

Remy settled into the cushions, squeezing the phone against her ear. If she held it tight enough, it drowned Occhilupo's plaintive whines. Breeze had given up whining. She looked fed up with the entire thing and just wanted her playmate back. Another week or so should make things safe.

'Okay. I'm here,' he said.

'Go.'

'You're going for a job interview today,' he began.

'Recruitment fantasy. Boss and employee. Lovely. Go for it.'

'Remy?'

'Yeah?'

'No commentary.'

'Okay.'

He started again: 'You have a job interview today.'

'What's the job?'

'Administration.'

'Administration?'

'You wanna be a rocket scientist, go to the NASA sex fantasy website and find your storyteller there.'

'Sorry. Keep going.'

'So it's a job interview at a lawyer's office in the city. You've been shopping today, and you're running late.'

'I'm breathless?'

'Remy. You're not making this easy for me.'

'Sorry.' She giggled and he swore and she said: 'Seriously, I'm sorry. I won't heckle.'

'You introduce yourself to the receptionist and she asks you to take a seat. It's nearly five o'clock. The receptionist tells you that you're the last interview for the day. You're interested in how many other people have been interviewed.'

'Are you sure I'm interested in that?'

'Remy.'

'Sorry. But seriously. What am I wearing? What's the interviewer's name? Where am I exactly? I'm a chick, Seth. Details matter.'

'*Christ on a stick.* Okay. So you're wearing a short black skirt. It's cut above your knee. It has a wave in it so that it flounces when you walk. You're wearing sheer black stockings and a white shirt. Your flatmate calls it your pirate shirt because it has big floppy sleeves at the wrist but the rest of the arm is tight. You feel good when you wear it and you chose it because you're going out clubbing later. It's a Friday night.'

Remy was quiet. He was getting into it now, she could tell. She'd never thought he'd go for it, and she intended to enjoy this for everything it was worth.

'So, the receptionist dials her boss and lets him know that you're there. About thirty seconds later the door of his office opens. You stand up and introduce yourself. He shakes your hand.'

'What's his name?'

'Reginald.'

'Seth, you're killing me here. *Reginald?*'

'He tells you to call him Reg.'

'Hell and Tommy.'

Seth ignored her. 'The receptionist says she's leaving the office now and wishes him a good weekend. He asks her to lock the downstairs on her way out and he asks you to come into his office.'

'Now we're getting somewhere.'

'You sit where he indicates and cross your legs. Then you think that's showed off a bit too much leg and you uncross them, folding your feet under your seat. You put your handbag on the floor. His office is modern with a bloody big desk, and he has pictures of naked women on his walls.'

'Photographs?'

'Nah, prints. Modigliani's.'

'Modigli-who?'

'Never mind. Good nudes. Not trashy.'

'Nice.'

'His eyes watch your legs while you're working out where to put them. You always liked your legs. They're your favourite feature. Reg asks about your work history, and your education. He asks you those questions like where do you see yourself in five years, and then he throws in a curve ball. He asks you to describe yourself in three words.

'You say: "Honest. Loyal." And you have to think about the third one. While you're thinking about it, you notice he has nice eyes. He's got a good body, short black hair, and you think he's pretty hot. Your last boss had bad breath and sweaty hands, but this guy is confident and classy. You think you could work under him quite happily.'

'Oh please,' Remy sighed. 'Work *under* him, seriously?'

'"Impudent" is the third word you choose. You say: "That's me, Reg, I'm honest, loyal and impudent. My mouth always gets me in trouble." He smiles. He has a nice smile. His chin has one of those Clint Eastwood clefts you always liked. He says: "Girls don't get in trouble for using their mouths around here. It's kind of an advantage."'

Remy giggled.

'What did I do wrong now? Aren't you supposed to be swooning?' he said.

'Seth, I love you for giving this a go for me, but you aren't that good at it.'

'Does that mean I can stop now?'

'You've got some porn star lecherous boss about to jump my bones at a job interview. Yeah, I think so. Quit now while you're ahead.'

'I'd so much rather play with you in person than over the phone, sweetheart.'

'Don't feel bad. I don't think I could remember how to make a fantasy phone call after all these years, either.'

'That's a good thing. I don't ever want you to have to do that again.

Unless it's to me. You can have a speed dial to me, okay?'

Speed dial to Seth. 'That sounds like it could be good fun.'

'Truth is, Rem. Just talking with you on the phone is enough. You have the most beautiful voice. I could listen to you all day. You can read the dictionary to me and I'd get a hard-on.'

The promise in his voice made her shiver.

Normally, this would be her time to make a wisecrack, but she didn't want to break the mood. The moment felt too important. He felt too important.

'I miss you,' she said.

He let out a breath. 'I miss you too, Rem. I'll be home Saturday.'

Chapter 27

By Wednesday, Rina Stein had a dilemma. She had about eighty hectares of vineyard all coming into the sweet spot, with Easter right round the corner. Immovable object meets irresistible force. Try telling a fruit contractor they might need to work Good Friday or Easter Sunday, and see how far it got you. Then try telling a grape to slow how fast it got ripe.

Adding to Rina's quandary, one of those vineyards was Remy Roberts'. Usually, grapegrowers made their own arrangements for picking their fruit, but for his own reasons Seth had agreed to pay for the pickers at Remy's block. So now it was Rina who had to do the work to lock it in. *Good old Rina,* she grumbled. *Rina will fix it.*

Seth said he thought Remy's fruit should be ready Thursday or Friday.

Rina's mood darkened as she drove along Red Gum Valley Road, slowing because she knew the driveway must be coming up soon and the trees were thick.

Seth said the property wasn't far after the turn off to Quarry Road, on the left. Rina slowed further, checking her rear-view mirror for traffic, trying to ditch the feeling she was being watched, and she shouldn't be here. She had every right to be here. Seth was Remy's viticulture liaison officer but Seth wasn't here and that meant Rina had to cover. If he wanted the fruit off this week it was up to Rina to check it met specification.

She almost missed the driveway and had to brake hard to make the turn.

Rina picked up speed as she wound alongside a dry winter creek, hoping Remy wasn't home. She didn't want to have to make small talk with her. She didn't want to see her. Remy always looked at her funny, like she *knew.*

Slowing as she neared Remy's house, she let out a big sigh of relief. She couldn't see any other cars or people. She parked under a huge ugly pine tree at one corner of the house, picked out her plastic bags and labelling equipment, and climbed out.

It was a pretty enough property, if a bit wild for her taste. She liked gardens how she liked her pubic hair: all clipped and trimmed, with nice neat edges. Remy's garden looked like David Attenborough might pop out from behind a bush at any moment with some rare bug clinging to his finger.

A huge block-headed dog trotted out to the front of the property, barked a couple of times like it didn't trust her being there, but it didn't come off the verandah and she was glad. If it had, she would have been back in the car and out of this place. Bugger those grapes.

Then she looked more closely at the mutt on the steps.

'I know you,' she muttered.

It was Occhilupo, and Occhy being here meant whatever Seth had going on with Remy was more serious than the kiss the newspaper was crowing about. If his bloody dog was strutting around like he owned the place, what did that mean? Was Seth living here too? *Already?*

How had that all happened so fast? How had she missed it? Ailsa would be furious.

Hurt and disappointment cannoned into the black rock of emotions she thought long buried when it came to Seth. The wave of it sent Rina slumping back in the driver's seat. She felt sick, cold all over although the sun on her legs was warm, and *God* she felt stupid. Unbelievably stupid that she'd missed what had been happening right in front of her eyes.

All the signs were there. They were the same as the signs of five years ago: Seth smiling more, frowning less, leaving work early, getting in late. There were times she'd tried to ring him and his number rang engaged for an hour. Then last weekend he hadn't come to the winery at all.

There were other signs too. Rina had overheard Maggie Castle tell Lewis Carney that Seth seemed more relaxed.

He was relaxed because he was in love. With Remy. *Again.*

It took several minutes of steady breathing with the driver's door open and her head on her knees before Rina felt able to move.

On the verandah, Occhilupo yawned. Huge yawn. Lots of teeth.

Her brain started working again. She shouldn't jump to conclusions. Seth's trip back to Lasrey headquarters in WA had been a spur-of-the-moment decision so he could take care of that idiot winemaker at their Great Southern winery—Bainbridge. It was natural Seth wouldn't take Occhilupo with him, and he knew Remy liked dogs.

For someone supposed to be taking care of the animal, Remy wasn't doing much of a job at it, Rina thought. Occhilupo could wander. He might get hit by a car on the road. He could bite someone. There were sheep in the neighbour's paddock. He might chase them.

I should call the ranger.

'Come on, Occhy,' *you big ugly dog.* 'Come on. Let's get you back behind the fence.' She approached the dog and brought him around Remy's verandah to the back. He licked the back of her hand and she wiped his nuzzle mark distastefully on her uniform pants.

When she reached the gate, she saw another dog in the yard. Smaller, but still a living wall of muscle and teeth. Why couldn't people get normal dogs?

Little fluffy ones that couldn't take your leg off in a gulp.

Why didn't this one get out if Occhilupo had?

Not my problem.

When Rina opened the gate, Occhilupo arrowed through the gap—nearly tore the gate out of her hand—and both dogs raced to the back of the garden. There was a fair bit of snapping and snarling and growling. Rina hoped she hadn't done the wrong thing. What if they killed each other?

Again. Not my problem.

Shutting the gate, she trudged away from the house and up into the vineyard to take her fruit samples, cursing Remy as she walked, feeling twitchy as hell the entire way, as if the vines had eyes.

No matter what happened to Remy, the girl had the knack of bouncing back. She was like a fucking spring. *Boing. Boing. Boing.*

Rina passed a pump shed near the dam. It wasn't a big shed. Not big enough for vineyard equipment or chemicals. She wondered where Remy kept stuff like that and decided they must be in sheds closer to the house.

Moving quickly, Rina expertly collected grapes for her maturity sample, putting the berries into plastic bags and labelling them for measuring in the lab at the winery later. Some she sampled, using her tongue and her winemaking skill as her only instruments. Remy's fruit burst with flavour. As sauvignon blanc went, this was damn good. If it wasn't perfect now, it would be very soon. The fruit was right in that so-called sweet pocket winemakers loved.

There'd been talk of big rains coming—an early break to autumn. The news was full of it because of fears it might ruin the horseracing picnic carnival they held near here every Easter. Apparently it made the racetrack heavy, or dead.

Rina thought about that for a while as she stood in Remy's vineyard with sunshine all around and clouds of frustration and jealousy in her head.

It would be a shame if a rainstorm caused Remy's fruit to split ... but, if it rained, it rained. Rina had been blamed for a lot of things in her time, some right, some wrong.

She couldn't be blamed for the weather.

She made a note in her diary: 'slight acid on tasting. Test again Saturday.' When she got back to the winery, she'd calibrate the refractometer ever so slightly wrong. It would give the sample she'd taken a false read. If she got her measurements right, the readings would show Remy's fruit as being not quite ready. If a storm came at the weekend, this fruit would still be on the vines.

Remy wouldn't have any fruit worth selling. 'Petty, but poetic,' Rina said to herself.

Glad to be done with Remy's place, Rina hurried down the hill. She put the fruit samples in the coolbox. The snapping and snarling from the rear of Remy's cottage showed no sign of abating. Again, Rina hoped she'd done the right thing. Maybe she should ring the ranger anyway?

Who cared if it got Remy in trouble? She should take better care of Seth's dog.

***

Remy spent Wednesday morning working on a garden for a lady who lived in Birdwood—a paid job this time—and on the way home she'd called into Mulberry Mews to check the seedlings she and Seth planted. Call her sentimental, but she had a vested interest in the garden they'd created together, thriving.

Lucy and Madge offered her tea, and Ernie decided he should do a spot of watering. They were in the garden keeping Ernie company when Remy's phone rang.

'This is Brian Stratton from the Mount Barker ranger service. I'm looking for Remy Roberts?'

'This is Remy,' she said, with the kind of sinking feeling you get when you expect to hear bad news. Why else would a ranger ring? 'What's happened?'

'Remy we have a dog registered to you, it's an American Staffordshire Terrier, tan and white bitch called Breeze?'

'Yes, that's right.' *What's she done now?*

'We've had a report of a brindle male dog loose on your property.'

'I'm looking after that dog. He wouldn't hurt a fly,' and then she added: 'Who reported it?'

Madge's and Lucy's ears pricked. Ernie missed it. He was too busy watering.

'I can't tell you that, sorry. I assume it must have been a delivery person, or a meter reader, or a neighbour—although usually a neighbour calls the dog's owner directly. Anyway, apparently the dog wasn't aggressive but the caller didn't like that it was running loose. They were concerned about it getting hit if it wandered onto the road, or that it might chase sheep, so the caller said they shut the dog in your backyard.'

Remy's heart sank. 'Oh no.'

'Is that problem?'

'Normally both dogs would be in behind my fence, Brian. But my bitch is on heat and I've had to separate them. That's the whole reason the male was outside the gate. If he's inside now...' She left the sentence unfinished.

'Leaving the male untethered is probably not the smartest thing to do anyway. If the female is on heat, other male dogs could come from miles around. If they run into an untethered male you could have all kinds of trouble on your hands. Maybe I better take a drive out there.'

'I'm on my way home now, Brian. I'm twenty minutes away.'

'Okay. Because someone rang it in, I'll still have to come out there, so I'll be there soon.'

'Okay.'

'Thanks for your cooperation. If you're looking after that male dog for any length of time, he should get registered here too, okay?'

Remy had no idea if Occhy was registered in Western Australia. She assumed he was. 'I'll check with the dog's owner. Thanks, Brian.'

She hung up.

The ranger was right. She hadn't thought of the problems that Occhy might pose if other dogs came to her property. The Williams had working kelpies. They'd be no match for a dog like Occhilupo if it came down to a fight. Not that Occhy was a fighter.

She'd have to tell Rina to make sure the picking contractors knew not to bring dogs on to her property when they came to pick her grapes. Not while Breeze was on heat.

'Always stuff to think about,' she muttered.

'Dog trouble, Remy dear?' Madge said.

'You can say that again.'

'I knew a couple who used to breed dogs in Strathalbyn. When their little girl was in season, every dog in town would hang outside their front gate,' Lucy said.

'Is that right, Lucy?' Remy said, wondering what age oldies got before their hearing wasn't so sharp.

Ernie, bless him, just kept watering.

***

Remy drove on the speed limit from the Mews. A couple of times she passed semi-trailers carrying crates of grapes and had to pull over to the side of the road. Because she was in a rush, the delays chafed, and it felt like the journey took longer than normal.

At the front of her house, she parked and turned off the engine. The second she climbed out of the car she heard a shrill, choked-off sound that made her wince in sympathy.

Maybe Breeze cornered a possum, or a cat? But it didn't quite sound like that.

Remy sprinted toward the nightmare now billowing out of control in her imagination. Breeze caught by the collar somehow, slowly strangling; Breeze with her paw impaled on a rose bush. Unlatching the gate, rushing through, calling as she ran—she burst through the middle part of the garden, passed the stable, and stopped in her tracks.

Both dogs were near the silver birch trees, Occhy with his front legs up on Breeze's back, humping like his life depended on it.

'You horny bugger,' Remy said, dropping to her knees in the thick mulch by Breeze. She didn't growl. She didn't want to startle either animal into any false move.

The fright and pain in Breeze's brown eyes and the panic in her squeals cut at Remy's heart. She stroked Breeze's tan and white head, held her collar and tried to offer comfort, knowing how important it was to keep her still. She could hurt Occhy if she tried to pull away. Remy put a hand on Occhy's collar too.

There was a book on Am Staffs in her bookshelf. It had a chapter on the whole breeding thing, but it was a while now since she'd read it. Occhy was heavy and Breeze wouldn't stand still, and her shrill cries never stopped.

'Well, that looks like fun.'

Remy spun around. Coming fast out of the shade near the stable strode a man in a fawn-coloured uniform.

My hero. 'You must be the ranger. I'm Remy.'

'Yep. I'm Brian. You look like you've got your hands full.'

Remy was being pulled in two, trying to hold the animals from where she sat. 'Can you help me? I have no idea what to do.'

The ranger squatted near the two dogs. 'Let's try this.'

He took Occhy's hind leg and raised it over Breeze's back. It left the two dogs standing, still linked, back to back. Or arse to arse, for want of a more technically correct term.

'That doesn't look like it should be anatomically possible,' Remy said, but she could see Breeze calm immediately. The awful squealing stopped.

'Success,' Remy said to Brian.

'Yeah, maybe. You never know with dogs. The whole thing's pretty hit or miss.' He was quite serious.

'I just meant I was glad she's calmer now. I don't really want her to have puppies.'

He looked at her like she was a parent of a wayward teenager, caught with his pants around his ankles and his girlfriend on the bed.

So, this is awkward.

'I guess this is all in a day's work for you, hey?' she asked him, because surely conversation was better than silence at a time like this. Perhaps he saw this sort of thing all the time. Perhaps he sat on the grass beside two dogs fucking, trying to *un-see* what was happening, every second day of the year.

'This is a bit out of the usual. We see some very strange things.'

I can only imagine. 'How long is this supposed to take? They've already been at it ten minutes.'

'It could take twenty. It can take half an hour. It's over when it's over. Then he'll have a cigarette.'

Remy laughed out loud and they settled in to wait.

***

Later, she called Seth. Infuriatingly, he thought the whole thing was funny. 'Love was always going to find a way, Rem.'

'Love didn't have anything to do with it. Just some nosey meter-reader do-gooder who would be better off keeping their nose out of it, and your bloody horny dog taking advantage of mine when she's vulnerable.'

He chuckled. 'It's too late to worry about it now.'

Remy gave up. Seth was right. No harm was done.

'I'll call my vet tomorrow and see what he says I should do. I really don't want puppies.'

'I think mini Occhy and Breeze would be kind of cute.'

'For a tycoon, you're such a softie.'

Chapter 28

When Remy hadn't heard from Rina by lunchtime on Thursday, she rang Montgomery Wines. Rina wasn't there. She left messages on her voicemail for Rina to call her back. She waited an hour but Rina never called.

Remy knew she could have complained to Seth, but if their relationship was going to work, she couldn't run to him every time something didn't work out as she'd planned. He had a corporation to run.

So she tried Lewis Carney.

He was under the pump—they had a lot of fruit coming in—but he made time to go into the office and check the schedule for her.

'You're not on the list till next week, Rem,' he said eventually. 'Tuesday.'

'That can't be right, Lewis. There's rain forecast for the weekend. If we wait, we could lose the lot. It's ready right now.' She made him check the schedule again.

'I'm telling you, Rem, you're listed for Tuesday. There's a note here that

Rina sampled your block yesterday and you're at 11.6 Baume ... oh shit!'

'What?' Whatever had happened, it sounded dire. She hoped to heck it wasn't anything to do with her grapes.

'Rem—I can't talk. I got grapejuice going everywhere. I'll get Rina to call you back.'

'Lewis!' He was gone. She was talking to thin air.

Remy hung up, more confused than ever. She ran through her options, but there weren't many. She didn't want to call Seth. Rina wasn't answering her calls. Lewis had his hands full.

She had to work this out herself. Remy knew her vineyard, and she'd been taking samples every second day for two weeks. She didn't believe Rina's measurement was correct. No way.

Five years ago she'd been young and naive and she'd let Ailsa scare her off. It wouldn't happen again. She knew her own vineyard and she knew it was ready to be picked. This time, she'd stand up for herself. All she needed was a little help from her friends.

With that in mind, Remy ran out the front door to the Rodeo and went to find Zac.

***

On Friday morning, a row of cars lined the driveway beside Remy's vineyard. They belonged to Bryce and Sheila Williams, Zac and two of his mates, along with seven-month pregnant Zac's pregnant Clea and her husband, Levi.

They were there because they were her friends and wanted to help, except for Zac's mates. They were doing him a favour because he'd offered them each a side of lamb for their freezers.

'Thank you, Bryce. I owe you big time for this,' Remy said to Zac's dad.

Bryce jammed his hat on his head. 'You'd do the same for us at a pinch if we needed it. Don't worry about it.'

Sheila added, beaming: 'It's our pleasure.'

Remy demonstrated how to handle the secateurs and snipped off a few bunches. She showed her motley pickers where to look for the empty crates she'd already laid along the vine rows.

'When your crate is full, leave it in the centre of the row and I'll come along on the motorbike and pick it up, okay? Please don't anybody hurt their back trying to lift anything that's too heavy. Zac and I will handle it.'

Zac had donated his farm quad-bike to the cause.

'Okay everybody? Any questions?' She looked hard at Clea. 'Make sure you don't overdo things.'

'I won't,' she said at the same time as Sheila added: 'She won't, Remy. I won't let her. I haven't waited this long for a grandchild for him or her to be born in a vineyard.'

'You're not bloody kidding,' Bryce put in. 'At least get over the fence, Clea, if it comes to that. Let the little bugger be born on a sheep farm or I'll never live it down!'

They laughed and got started. They were purposeful, and they were positive. It was a good thing because Remy wasn't feeling particularly positive at all, but contrary to her wildest dreams, the picking went well and they got through more that day than she'd thought possible.

Other than Zac's two mates and Clea, who'd been told to take it slow, the other four fronted for work on Saturday. Clea came later to keep up the supply of coffee and tea and lunch.

Bryce complained a bit about his back, but they were in good spirits as they picked up the vineyard rows where they'd left off the night before.

Glancing skywards, Remy sent a quick prayer to the universe that the rain would stay away, and they'd get finished. No one from the universe answered, but for the moment at least the sky was clear and rain seemed a world away.

***

The Qantas flight landed midmorning Saturday in Adelaide. It was about fifteen minutes late because there'd been fog in Melbourne and flights across the country had been delayed. Seth got through the terminal fast, collected his luggage fast, and sent Rina a text to let her know he'd landed. Rina had his car and she would come pick him up.

He took his luggage out to the front of the terminal and waited. Soon enough, the Lasrey Estate black ute dodged past the taxis waiting to pick up passengers and nosed into the kerb. Seth heaved his bags in the back and opened the passenger door.

'Howdy,' Rina said.

'How's it going? Thanks for picking me up. Hope I haven't spoiled your Saturday.'

'Lewis is working today, it's not a problem.' She checked her driver-side mirror and eased out from the kerb, picking up speed.

The roads were clear and Rina was through the city, heading up Glen Osmond Road to the Freeway. By the time she pulled off at the Hahndorf exit and started driving along Onkaparinga Road, they were pretty much all caught up with what was going on for Lasrey in the West and at Montgomery here in South Australia. Rina seemed relaxed and Seth figured it was time.

'What favours are you doing for Ailsa?' He asked.

Rina's hands twitched on the steering wheel and she glanced hard at him. 'What do you mean what favours?'

'Did Ailsa ask you to give the media that stuff about Blake?'

'They already knew about Blake but I don't think they put two and two together about "our" Blake being Blake Lasrey, world surfing professional. Once they knew that, they got interested real quick.'

'I bet they did,' Seth said, as his lip curled. 'What else has Ailsa asked you to do for her?'

'I'm a director, Seth. So is she. I'm happy to keep your mother informed. We talk a lot about the winery business. It would be strange if we *didn't* talk.'

He pointed to his left. 'Slow down, the driveway's just up here.'

'I know where the driveway is.'

'What do you do for her? She said you know where the company's vulnerable and you understand? What did that mean?'

'Jesus, Seth. What is this? I don't know. I think about the company all the time ... opportunities, strengths, weaknesses, threats.' Rina slowed the car and turned into Remy's driveway. The second she made the turn, she crouched lower in her seat, peering over the steering wheel as Remy's vineyard lay ahead. 'What the hell?'

The place was buzzing. Cars lined the driveway. Remy's Rodeo sat several metres into the vineyard paddock with the trailer-gate down. Half a dozen crates made a neat stack in the back.

Remy was on the quad-bike, guiding it out into the vineyard with a stack of empty crates roped on the back. Breeze trotted behind.

'What does she think she's doing?' Rina muttered, lips zipped tight.

'Looks to me like she's picking her grapes.'

Rina chugged past a massively pregnant woman who was holding a flask of tea or coffee in one hand, fanning herself with her hat in the shade of the bushes near the house. He hoped to heck she wasn't picking grapes. That baby looked like it might be born any time.

Rina had to slow to navigate the driveway, made narrower than usual by the line-up of cars at the side. When they reached the cottage, Seth got out of the car and dumped his travel bag on the front step. Rina started making sounds as if she was heading straight home. Seth wasn't finished with her yet.

'Hold on. I want to talk with Remy and see what's going on.' Seth strode toward the vineyard without looking back.

Rina called out, but he didn't stop.

Remy's blonde ponytail bounced as she navigated the bumps and gutters in the paddock, slower this time as she rode downhill. Those were full crates on the back.

Breeze trotted behind. He waved, and Remy deviated toward him. A beautiful big smile grew on her face and he knew something similarly goofy was spreading across his own jaw. She was magnificent, his woman. He was the luckiest man alive.

Across the vineyard, one by one, heads popped up to watch. Seth didn't care about the audience. Let them stare.

Remy let the bike engine idle a few metres before she reached him. Once it stopped, she stood up on the pedals, took hold of his shoulders to steady herself and kissed him full on the lips, in front of everyone.

A whoop went up from the vineyard.

Remy blushed and it was so sweet, and he felt such relief to have her in his arms, he kissed her again. Slower this time, tasting sunscreen and watermelon wrapped up with heat and longing. The combination knocked the breath out of them both.

'I've missed you,' she said and he nodded, holding her close.

'Me too. It's scary how much.'

One by one, those curious heads in the vineyard withdrew from above the canopy and left them alone. Seth could see Rina picking her way across the paddock toward them.

'I had to organise my own pickers, I hope you don't mind.' Remy said, lifting her foot over the bike so she could stand beside him.

Seth kissed her hair. 'Why would I mind?'

'Well, you said your team would do it. But I couldn't get hold of anyone and Lewis said my block wasn't on the schedule till Tuesday. Tuesday can't be right. Plus they're forecasting rain.'

'The fruit's not ready,' Rina said, still five metres away, watching them warily.

Remy snorted through her nose. 'I know my own vineyard and I'm telling you it *is* ready. It's *perfect.* Here, try this.' She reached into the crate behind the quad-bike and pulled out a bunch of grapes.

Seth picked off several berries and put them in his mouth. Flavour burst on his tongue. Lovely, balanced fruit flavours.

Seth turned to Rina. 'We need to help Remy get this off before it rains.'

She looked away. 'All our pickers are busy.'

'Where?'

Rina glared at him. 'One contractor is at Robert Linke's place, another at Alf Flack's, or maybe Harman's place.

'Those vineyards aren't worth half what Remy's fruit is worth to us.'

Rina stood her ground. 'This vineyard isn't *ready.'*

Seth held out the bunch of grapes. 'Try these. Tell me they're not ready.'

Reluctantly, Rina put two berries in her mouth. Sweet taste or not, her face was all sour. 'I agree, this bunch is good, but that's not to say there isn't variability across the field. My sample average on Wednesday came in well under spec. The lab results prove it.'

'You were here Wednesday?' Remy interrupted.

'Yes,' Rina snapped, giving every bit of attitude back. 'I did the tests myself. I wrote it all up on the whiteboard schedule. I've got the diary notes to prove it.'

'Were you the one who called the ranger about Occhilupo?'

Rina hesitated a moment too long. When she realised that, she appealed to Seth. 'Occhy wasn't even tied up. He could have got lost. Someone might have stolen him. I was worried.'

'Forget about the dogs, both of you,' Seth said, as Remy went tense as a plank beside him. 'No dog was hurt. No harm was done.' *He'd deal with that later.*

'Remy? How you going with those crates?' Bryce called from the vineyard. 'We need more empties.'

'I gotta go,' Remy said. 'I gotta get these emptied. You sort this out. Just let me know what's going on, okay?' She put the quad-bike in gear, turned in a wide circle and headed for the Rodeo.

Seth turned to Rina. 'Get this done. Make it happen.'

'My samples said—'

'I don't care about your samples. You must have calibrated wrong. This fruit is perfect.'

'Fine,' Rina spat. 'I'll fix it. I don't know why I'm surprised. You've *always* given her special treatment.' She spun on her heel.

'Leave my car at the winery. I'll collect it later.'

'Fine,' she said.

'Rina?' Seth said, softer now he'd got his own way. 'Thanks for picking me up at the airport.'

She didn't answer.

***

Bitch. Rina's footsteps hammered the word as she trudged toward the car.

It was that same fucking thing all over again. No matter what obstacles you put in her way, Remy always bounced back. *Boing. Boing. Boing.*

It wasn't fair.

Everything she'd done for Seth over the years. All those times she'd had his back. All the overtime. All the hours. Commitment. Dedication. Loyalty.

Worth nothing because Remy was the only woman he'd ever want. Remy could do no wrong. Even near-killing a vineyard couldn't convince Seth the girl was bad news.

Remy-bloody-Hanley/Roberts. Whoever she was.

Rina reversed out of Remy's cottage, drove back down the driveway, navigating cars, people, quad-bikes. Fuming.

As the bonnet of Seth's car reached the last vehicle, Rina stepped on the accelerator.

She only saw the pregnant woman at the last minute because she caught movement out of the corner of her eye as the woman waved at her from the shade. Automatically, Rina jerked the steering wheel, correcting to the left.

She saw a flash of tan and white at the edge of her vision. Then she felt and heard a bump. The flash hit her left front tyre and all Rina's anger vanished.

She braked, and braked hard. A cloud of dust engulfed the car.

Looking in the rear-view mirror, horror filled her throat.

She could see Remy and Seth, both of them running toward her. She saw the pregnant lady with one hand clutched across her chest, pointing at the ground, white-faced.

And she saw a scrap of tan and white fur on the gravel drive. It wasn't dead. It was moving. It might have tried to wag its tail.

Or was that the wind blowing the dog's tail? The dust made everything hard to see?

Had she killed Remy's dog?

Rina shoved the door open and leapt from the car.

Chapter 29

'Seth? Where is she?' Remy asked, so upset she couldn't walk across the waiting area at the Adelaide Hills' vet, she had to run.

He'd been sitting on a chair, but he stood up to meet her and she skidded into his arms.

'They're operating on her now. She's going to make it, Rem. They said she'll be fine. It might slow her down for a while. That's all.'

'Are you sure? You're not just saying that? *Hell and Tommy.* She got run over, Seth.' Her eyes were savage, wild and wide.

'I know.'

'I only let her out because she'd been cooped up in the yard all week. I should have left her there ... She was safe there.'

Breeze's yelp was a sound Seth would remember till the day he died. Both he and Remy had run toward the lump of beaten tan and white fur on the road.

'Seth, I can't afford ... I don't have pet insurance...'

'I've got this, sweetheart. We'll sort it out.'

She leaned into him and Seth pulled her close. *Some homecoming.* It was barely two hours since he'd got off the plane.

'Thank you for helping her. God, I'm so glad you were there,' Remy said.

Seth put her away from him so he could look at her face. Her hair was everywhere, long since fallen out of whatever elastic had held it in. Stress creased her brow and her eyes were dark with worry.

'Rina didn't do it on purpose, Rem. I'm sure of that.'

'I know,' Remy said. She believed it. Shocked as she'd been, she'd seen Rina's face. It had been ashen. Drained. Stunned. Rina hadn't even been able to stutter an apology. Her mouth wouldn't form the words.

Rina had been first to get to Breeze. She'd almost spun the ute into the ditch as she'd skidded to a stop. Squatting on the gravel, oblivious of the cuts the rocks engraved in her knees, Rina's hands had fluttered at her sides, useless.

Breeze had tried to wag her tail, as if to reassure the woman who'd run her over, caused her all this pain.

'She's a beautiful dog,' Remy said, eyes welling. 'She knew we were trying to help her. She didn't bite or growl at all when we put her in the car, and it must have hurt.'

Seth pulled her close, rubbing her back and her shoulders and any part he could reach. Gradually she quietened and not long after, the vet nurse came out to tell them Breeze was doing fine. They'd keep her overnight and if she was doing well in the morning, she'd be going home with a splint on her front leg, a quilting club's supply of stitches, and a bucket around her head.

'I'm getting some pink bling to hang off the bucket,' Remy sniffed.

'You do that,' Seth said, feeling his love for Remy flow over him like a wave. For the first time that afternoon, he let himself breathe the scent of her hair.

Remy stirred restlessly. 'I've got to get back. I don't want to leave, but if

I don't get that fruit off ... I've left them all out there working.'

'Rina promised she'd take care of it. She feels awful about hitting Breeze. Even if she ends up out at your place herself tonight with a set of secateurs, she'll make sure it gets done. You stay here and I'll go back out to your place. It's almost two o'clock. I'll call you to let you know how it's going.'

'Thanks, Seth,' Remy said, giving in gratefully. 'I'd like to be here when she wakes up. Breeze never liked the vet. I don't want her to be scared.'

'It takes a lot to scare an Am Staff, Rem. Don't forget that. It takes more than a lot to bruise one. They're super tough.'

'They are. You're right.' And for the first time since he'd heard her cry out when that terrible thump and yelp filled the air, the stress in Remy's face relaxed.

***

With the help of her neighbours, and thanks to Rina, they got the fruit off before the rains.

Remy's harvest officially came in at 12.5 tonnes of sauvignon blanc fruit. The $3200 per tonne Seth paid brought her a small buffer on top of the $22,000 advance.

It wasn't much, but it was better than so many other growers had. The Adelaide Hills wasn't so bad, but in the Riverland and the Barossa there were grapegrowers who hadn't found a buyer for their fruit for years, and who'd had to cut their grapes and let them fall to the ground. Some didn't even do that, they let the fruit wither on the vine.

There were grapegrowers walking off land they'd tended for generations, and others selling for a price less the cost of ripping the vines out. Some just let the weeds take over. The wine industry had a term for it: mothballing. All over the country vineyards were being put in mothballs, left with zero or no input costs while growers waited for fruit prices to recover.

With true Am-Staff fortitude, Breeze recovered far faster than the viticulture industry. She was also pregnant, they discovered on one of her return check-up visits at the vets.

'Love will find a way, grandma,' Seth said when she told him the news, putting his arms around her and nuzzling her neck.

'Love had nothing to do with it, granddad. It's just your very horny dog.'

***

After Breeze's accident, Seth and Remy were happy to take the autumn days as they came: slow and steady with plenty of time to learn each other. Sensual days and nights filled with food and wine, love and laughter.

On one of those nights, Remy commented that Ailsa had yet to present the $100 000 cheque.

Seth bumped the heel of his hand on his forehead and swore. 'Sorry, Rem. I never told you that part, did I? I ripped the cheque up when I saw her in Perth.'

'You ripped it up?' Remy's jaw dropped.

'Yeah. In front of her greedy damn eyes. She pissed me off to the point where I thought fuck it, she doesn't need it. I tore it into pieces.'

'I can't believe you didn't tell me.'

'I forgot about it.'

Remy felt a bit faint. 'How do you forget about a $100 000? I've had years where I wished I could forget about that money and I never could. *Hell and Tommy.*'

'Ailsa didn't deserve it. It meant nothing to her except maybe a few more paintings for her walls.'

'But ... what do I do with it? What will I do about it? I can't keep it.'

'I did have some thoughts.' Seth stood to top up Remy's red wine, and stayed there, balancing the bottle in his big hand. 'I thought about using the money to seed a community-based program building vegetable gardens for the elderly. I was thinking here in the Hills, the Barossa, McLaren Vale—the wine regions for starters to give back to people who've been part of our community.'

Remy nodded, thinking about how it could work, seeing it in her head.

'It's a more structured version of what you're already doing. I thought we could get the TAFE colleges and schools involve somehow. We could provide the equipment and we'd resource it, and they could provide the labour. Kids get to learn about gardening and the community's health improves.'

'We could call it The Munch Program,' Remy said.

'Munch?'

'I wanted to call my business—my vegie garden business if I ever did get it off the ground—Munch, or something like it. It sounds foodie. It sounds healthy. It's short and sweet. Munch.'

'I was thinking about calling it The Lasrey/Roberts Community Garden Program for the Elderly,' Seth said, smiling.

'Munch is very catchy.'

'Compared with my mouthful, it is.'

'It's a lot of work, Seth. I don't know how to even get something like that started.'

'Margaret Castle was a schoolteacher once. She said she was sure schools would leap at the chance to get involved in something like that. It has great core fundamentals, she said, as long as it doesn't cost the Education

Department any money. If it costs them, they'd run a mile.'

'If the $100 000 was seed money...' Remy began, before Seth finished off: 'Lasrey can add it to our annual sponsorship budget. We can kick in more each year. Other corporations might get involved once it's up and running and we've got a model to show them.'

'I like it,' Remy said. 'I love it. It's a great idea. What do we do next?'

'I'll take the concept to our next Lasrey board meeting and we'll go from there. Meanwhile, it might as well stay in your account. Don't go to Hawaii without me, okay?'

'Bugger. You read my mind.'

***

On Easter Saturday, Seth took Remy to the Oakbank Racing Carnival. She'd been before, but never to the corporate tents. Whenever she'd gone to Oakbank it had been with Zac and Clea and a handful of mates. They'd parked in the middle of the racecourse, set up their barbecue and drunk cheap champagne while the boys cooked bacon and eggs.

She'd worn jeans. When the trumpet sounded and the new race was about to run, they'd rushed to the bookies to place two dollar bets, then to the rails to watch the horses thunder by.

Oakbank with Seth was all kinds of different.

She needed a dress and good shoes, but she drew the line at any kind of hat and refused to tote a handbag around all day, or carry anything called a clutch. Instead, Seth carried her money and a lipstick in his pocket.

'Are you having fun?' he said, returning to her side with a fresh glass of bubbles.

'It's good. I think I like it better in jeans.'

He smiled at her and she knew he was thinking of how much fun he could have with her, *without* her jeans. She couldn't believe she'd once accused him of not smiling enough and she reached up on tiptoes and kissed him.

'Sorry to interrupt you pair of lovebirds.' Rina appeared beside them, not looking sorry at all. She wore a burgundy dress, much the same deep wine red colour as in her glass. She looked nice, Remy thought. The dress softened her bones.

After the debacle at the vineyard the day Rina had run over Breeze, the winemaker seemed to be making an effort to be nice, even if it appeared to be a struggle at times.

'Will you make a bet for me, Seth?' Rina asked him. 'I want Chess Of Gold in the next race.'

'Chess Of Gold?'

'Chest Of Gold. Sorry, looks like I'm slurring my words.'

'Sure. What about you, Rem?' Seth asked.

'I'm about fifteen dollars up for the day, so put it all on Vagrant Dancer for the win.'

He disappeared through the crowd, sharing a joke with Max Montgomery on the way. Max and Sue were Lasrey guests, along with Rina, Lewis Carney and his wife, Jackie.

'I bet you never thought last Easter that this is where you'd be right now,' Rina said when she and Remy were alone.

'Easter was earlier last year. I was picking grapes, from memory.'

Rina overbalanced slightly in her heels, and for the first time Remy realised the winemaker was very close to being drunk.

She tried to catch Max or Sue's eye ... or Lewis', someone who might come help her out of this conversation, but Sue was deep in discussion with the wife of the local politician and Max was studying the form guide.

'Do you want to sit down, Rina? I can get you a coffee if you'd like.'

'Coffee? God no. People will think I'm drunk.'

'Or a water?'

'Oh don't fuss. I'm fine,' Rina said. 'How's Breeze?'

'She's coming along, thanks. She's having puppies in another few weeks.'

Rina's mouth curled. 'Lovely. Just what the world needs. Puppies.'

Yes. Sometimes Rina's nice-o-meter struggled. 'You don't like dogs much, do you? Seth told me.'

'Dogs. Cats. Canaries. No, I don't like animals much. At least horses pull their weight. But you know I was sorry when I hit Breeze, right? I might not like dogs but I wouldn't want to injure one.' She shuddered.

Remy looked for Seth. He was the tallest man in the marquee and he wasn't hard to find, but she couldn't see him right now.

'We'll miss the start. Are you coming?' Remy said.

'Nah. Might sit for a minute. My feet are killing. Sorry. I didn't mean to be rude before. Maybe I have had one too many. I'm out of practice these days.'

Remy left her and Rina found a chair near the wall of the marquee where there was room to kick off her shoes and put her feet up.

That's where Seth found her a few minutes later.

'Had a few too many, Rina?' He asked.

It took her eyes a second to focus, before she smiled. 'Right as rain. Good to go again. Don't worry about me. I'll be fine.'

'Do you want me to call a taxi for you?'

'No. No.' She batted the question away. 'I'm fine. I wish everyone would stop fussing.'

'I'm not being much of a CEO if I leave you on your own.'

'Why? Are you worried some rich eligible bachelor will have his wicked way with me? That only happens to Remy.'

'Come on, Rina.' Seth reached for the wineglass and took it from her. 'Let's get you home.'

'Did you know Remy always bounces back, whatever happens? Even her name sounds like a spring. *Remy. Remy. Remy. Boing. Boing. Boing.*' She giggled.

'Have you got your shoes?' Seth was tired of it. The race had started and he was missing watching the excitement on Remy's face as she listened to the race, as she cheered her horse on and jumped about if the race got close.

A great cheer came up in the grandstand. The horses were in the home stretch. Out in the crowd, he could have sworn he heard Remy call clearly: 'Go Dancer. *Go* Dancer!'

Rina spun her shoes. Then she put the heels on the grass and slipped her feet into them, very carefully, one at a time, and did up each buckle.

'You know, Rina. If you'd hurry it up, we might actually see who wins when they come round again.'

'Remy always wins. Doesn't matter if it's horses, grapes, dogs or men.' She sat back in her chair and Seth gave up any faint hope of seeing the end of the race. 'It's boring how many times she wins.'

'I'm getting you a coffee.' He stood up, but Rina grabbed his arm and tugged him back down.

'You asked me if my passport was up to date. Do you remember?'

'What? When?'

'That long weekend after Vintage Festival. You asked me about going to Bordeaux with you.'

The weekend I met Remy. 'Yeah. So?'

She made a sniffy little giggle and it choked away to nothing. 'I thought you were asking me to go to Bordeaux with you, but you weren't. You were asking me to go *instead* of you, so you could spend more time with Remy.'

She smiled at him, all sad and twisted with mascara bleeding, and Seth thought: *this is getting ugly.*

Slowly the crowd filtered back into the tent. The marquee, which had been hollow and echoing, refilled. Max led the way, Sue behind him. Then Remy, moving like she always did, even in heels: hips rolling easy as water sliding over glass.

'See,' Rina said in a small voice. 'She comes back and you don't see anyone else.'

'You missed it,' Remy said, glowing with excitement. 'Vagrant Dancer won!'

'Hoo-bloody-ray,' Rina muttered.

'Okay. I'm calling the cab. Remy can you watch she doesn't do anything to embarrass herself, or my company?'

'What would you consider embarrassing?' Remy asked him quietly.

'No dancing on a table. Anything to do with challenging the patrons in this tent to a drinking contest.'

'Okay.'

Remy sat in the chair Seth had left vacant and Rina said: 'Oh. It's you. How's your dog?'

Haven't we done this already? 'She's good thanks. Recovering well.'

'What about Seth's dog? You didn't get in trouble with the ranger?'

'No.'

'I would have looked after Occhy if Seth asked. He didn't ask. He never asks me for anything.'

Hell and Tommy, come on Seth, hurry up. This is getting ugly.

Sue Montgomery sat on Rina's other side and patted her leg. 'Had a few too many, love? We've all been there. Don't worry. We'll look after you.'

'Thank you,' Rina put her hand over Sue's. 'No one ever cares about me, not really. I should just leave. Even the horses I pick lose.'

'The horses most people pick lose, love. Don't feel bad about that.'

'Mine is still running,' Max Montgomery, who'd come to sit next to his wife, added.

'Her horses always win,' Rina said, pointing at Remy. 'She wins everything. Even when she loses, she wins.'

'I have no idea what you're on about, love,' Sue said.

'She's so nice. She's so unbelievably nice. I almost killed her dog—' she nodded pleasantly to a bemused Sue—'I ran it over ... and she forgives me.'

'It was an accident, Rina,' Remy said, embarrassed. *Seth? Where the hell are you?*

'Not like back home,' Rina said, head slumping toward her chest. 'No accident in the vineyard there.'

'Nah, sorry, love. I still don't know what you're on about. Here's Seth. He'll sort it out.' Sue stood and touched the side of her head, indicating Rina as she passed Seth with a touch on his arm. Remy heard Sue whisper: 'Think your winemaker's had a few too many, love.'

Seth took his turn in this game of musical chairs. 'Taxi is on its way, Rina. It'll be here in five minutes and you're only ten minutes from Max's place. You could walk there.'

If she wasn't pissed as a newt, Remy thought, but what she said was: 'but not in those shoes.'

Rina's head snapped up, but her eyes were glassy. 'Stop being nice to *me.* I don't deserve it. I've never been nice to you.'

'What are you talking about, Rina?' Seth asked.

It all came out in one big, dirty rush. 'I thwapped the adjuvant. I took that axyl-whatsit bottle and put the oxflo-whatsitsname in. I wanted her to get the sack. I thought maybe, if she wasn't around ... you and me, Seth.' Rina's head lolled back. 'I'm so pathetic.'

Remy's head spun and it had nothing to do with alcohol.

'You're talking about five years ago, right? You're saying you changed the chemicals and that's why Remy sprayed the wrong stuff?' Seth's voice was calm, almost hypnotic.

'Yesh.'

'Did my mother know?' Seth asked. 'Did Ailsa ask you to do it?'

'God no,' Rina's hand struck the stem of her glass. Red wine slopped to stain the grass. 'Ailsa would have sacked me if I'd done anything that might harm her family's precious vines.' Rina touched Seth's arm, pinching his shirt between her fingers. 'I knew if I raised the alarm early, it would be okay. It happened once when I was working in the Hunter Valley years ago. One of the trainees mixed the wrong wetting agent. They mixed in a herbicide instead of the adjuvant or the wetting agent, whatever that stuff is. I would never have done it if I didn't know it was safe, Seth. You've got to believe me. That's how I knew it would be okay if I raised the alarm early enough.'

That's a helluva punt, Seth thought, but he didn't say it. He looked for Remy and found her, white-faced.

She was standing near one of the tables, gripping it like it was the only thing keeping her up.

'Are you sure Ailsa never knew?'

'Not about that. I never told her that. Not like the other thing.'

'What other thing?' Seth asked, calm as ever.

Rina put her hand over her mouth and groaned: 'Think I'm gonna be sick.'

They all got out of the way as she rushed from the tent.

***

'Never for a minute did I think anyone else could have done it, Seth,' Remy said later at home as they dissected the day. 'I can't believe it.'

'You and me both, Remy. We'd never know if she hadn't said anything.

She's got off scot-free for five years. I'm not sure why she owned up to it now.'

'I'd say the wine had something to do with it. Maybe after she ran over Breeze it all caught up to her and she just needed to let it out. I don't think Rina drinks much anymore. It must have really affected her.'

'You're very generous about people who've tried to hurt you, Rem. Next you'll be sending Ailsa a Christmas card.'

'Hey, steady on.'

He laughed and she joined him.

'I think you're angrier about this than I am,' she said.

'I'm mad at myself.' He turned to her. 'Here I am thinking I'm such a good judge of character. I got you so far wrong it's not funny, and I had Rina wrong the entire time.'

Remy put her hand on his thigh. 'She's good at her job. It's because of her you were able to spend that time in so much big-picture stuff. Rina took care of the details. Lasrey wouldn't be where it is today without Rina. You wouldn't either. Say what you want, but the two of you complement each other.'

He mumbled something indecipherable, but in a way that acknowledged what she said was valid. 'I still think there's more she's not telling me, but I couldn't get anything out of her in the taxi.'

'Forget about it,' Remy said, snuggling closer to Seth on the couch. 'I was so sure it was my error, you know. I couldn't think of any other reason except it being my stuff-up. The thought that someone would deliberately swap the chemicals never crossed my mind.'

'Rina relied on that. Rina knew Ailsa would point the finger at you. She gave Ailsa the excuse she needed to fire you, and she didn't need much of an excuse. She saw you as too much of a threat. Both of them did.'

Remy traced her fingernail on Seth's wrist. 'What will you do with Rina now?'

'I don't know. She must have offered me her resignation twenty times in the taxi.' Seth had ridden home with her to make sure she got there okay.

'I don't think you should accept it. Unless she's really genuine about it and it's not just a gut reaction. The chemical thing happened so long ago and only you and I, and your mum—if you tell her—will ever know about it. I've got over it. I've lived with it so long it doesn't matter to me anymore. It's from a whole other time in my life.'

'What about the grapes? She would have let your fruit ruin in the rain, if she could have. Can you forgive that?'

Remy thought about it. 'Something changed when she ran over Breeze. I think all this hate has been eating at her a long time. I don't think Rina's an evil person at heart. Maybe she had to get it all out.'

'That's profound.'

She punched his arm. 'Who knows what goes on in the head of Rina Stein? I give up.'

'Between me and my mother and Rina, we've ballsed up your life brilliantly. I'm so sorry.'

'It's okay. Truly. It's all okay. Everything happens for a reason, I believe that. I have a day like today at Oakbank with you ... I have you and my vineyard and my mum and my dog. I don't owe anyone a cent, except the bank. My life hasn't turned out too badly.'

'And you're about to be a grandma...'

She laughed and clinked her wineglass with his. 'Yeah. There's that too.'

Epilogue

The weekend after Lexie and Bernie tied the knot at Ivy Lodge in October, Seth took Remy out for dinner in Adelaide. He'd hired the executive apartment at the very top of a high-rise hotel in King William Street for the night.

They'd eaten on Gouger Street. She'd had a meal of whole chilli crab that had taken her about two hours to finish, and he'd loved every second watching her crack crab claws and suck the white meat from the shell.

He'd walked her back to their accommodation slowly—navigating the pavement in heels required her full concentration. It was eleven floors up in the elevator, a swift turn right into a plush carpeted corridor, and a juggling act to swipe his access card into the lock and keep his hands from roaming beneath Remy's dress.

What a dress. She'd finally let him buy her a new outfit for her birthday in July. She'd chosen a pink dress that was almost a match for the watermelon colour that had caught his eye in the park all those years ago. This one had a lace top and a short skirt that flounced as she walked and showed her gorgeous legs. He loved it on her. He loved it off her.

'Ooh. Look at this,' Remy said, as she walked into the apartment in front of him, picking up a bottle of champagne from an ice bucket on a low coffee table. 'I guess you spent enough hiring this place to earn a bottle of bubbles on the house?'

Seth grabbed the card. 'We did. But that bottle's in the fridge. This one,' he flashed the ornate card, 'is a gift from my mother.'

'Another one?' Remy almost fell off her heels. 'She's persistent isn't she?'

'This is true. She's trying very hard to say sorry.'

Since Ailsa had been told about Rina's part in the vineyard incident that got Remy sacked, she'd back-pedalled faster than a politician at election time.

'You know she's worried about a lawsuit, don't you? She knows how much that might dent her company dividend, because I'd be taking the damages straight out of her profit share,' Seth said.

'And here I was thinking she might like to babysit the puppies...'

Smiling wryly, he took two champagne flutes from the fridge where they'd been cooling and poured them each a glass. Beyond the windows a bird's-eye view of the city waited. Seth opened the rooftop access door and Remy followed him into a private oasis where a blue-tiled swimming pool shimmered with water lit by soft blue light. The water overflowed the pool's edge like a white curtain, sliding into a bed of pebbles beneath.

Remy knelt by the water, trailing her hand in a shallow ripple across the surface.

'You're so exquisite, Rem.'

She smiled at him over her shoulder as she stood up. 'Thank you.'

He lifted a silk strap from her shoulder, moving the material aside to kiss her creamy skin. She shivered in his arms, her gaze on the street.

'What do you think she's thinking?' Remy murmured.

'Who?' Seth didn't look up.

'See that lady over there?' She indicated with her chin.

This time he paid attention. There was a woman on a balcony on the opposite side of King William Street. She had a nice round face and soft features. Her hair was short and curly.

'What about her, Rem?'

'She looks sad. See how she's watching the people on the corner down there?'

'Don't ask me to think too much about other women when I'm here with you.'

Remy tilted her head, arching herself against Seth's caress, but she didn't take her eyes off the woman on the balcony.

'No one should be alone on a night like this,' Remy said. 'It makes me sad. When I'm so happy, you know? It makes me sad to see someone who isn't shining like us.'

He paid more attention this time. The woman wore a silky bathrobe. She had a glass tumbler in one hand that she put occasionally to her lips. Whatever she was drinking glinted in the light coming from the apartment behind her. There was something *Mona Lisa* about her, Remy was right.

'Put your hands over your ears, Rem.'

She giggled, but she covered her ears and once she'd done it, Seth let out a whistle that would have stopped traffic if they hadn't been so high off the road.

The woman on the balcony looked right and left, trying to find the source of the whistle. Seth waved, and after a few slow seconds, she looked up, seeing the movement. If he'd been closer, he might have thought she frowned, but then she waved instead.

Seth cupped his hands around his mouth. 'Are you okay?'

'Pardon?' The woman called back.

'Are. You. Okay?'

'Me?' She pointed at herself, looking over her shoulder just in case Seth had been talking to anyone else. 'Yes. I'm fine, thanks.' She had a nice voice and it carried easily above the city sounds.

'I'm about to ask this lady to marry me,' Seth yelled.

Remy stiffened, and he heard her gasp.

Across the street, the woman gave them a big thumb's up. She didn't look sad anymore.

Seth got down on one knee. He felt a bit silly doing this with an audience, but it felt right too, for reasons he'd really never want to try explaining. Maybe because the woman on the other balcony was smiling at them now and because he knew that made Remy happy.

He'd do a lot to make Remy happy.

'You told me once that talk is cheap, and that action speaks louder than words?'

'I remember,' she murmured.

'Will you give me a lifetime, where I can show you I love you every single day?'

'Yes, Seth. I will.'

A big burst of warmth filled his chest.

'What did she say?' The woman across the street called.

'Yes,' Remy answered, her voice ringing across the void. 'I said yes.'

'Congratulations.' The woman raised her glass. 'That's awesome.'

'What's your name?' Seth called, standing up, pulling Remy close.

'Gina,' she yelled.

'Thanks for being our witness, Gina.'

She laughed, like she found that funny. 'That's about the most fun I've had on this street on a Saturday night in forever. Thank you both for that. I hope things work out brilliantly for you.' She went inside, pulling the screen doors shut behind her.

'Now. Where was I?' Seth said, returning his attention to the strap of Remy's dress and the sweet curve of her neck.

Remy turned in his arms, smiling up at him. Seth picked her up and carried her over the threshold into the apartment. He let her down long enough to slip the pink dress from her shoulders and let it pool at her feet. Then he began making love to her all over again, starting where he'd left off.

Thanks for reading **So Far Into You.** I hope you enjoyed it.

Turn the page for a bonus story, **Angry Birds and Turtle Doves,** based one year after Seth and Remy solve the problems of love and the universe in *So Far Into You.* Sydney's hot. Adelaide's hot. And it's getting hot down under the tablecloth. This story published in 2015 by Escape, from the anthology *It Happened at Cafe Nix.*

If you'd like to know more about me, my books, or to connect with me online, you can visit my webpage <www.lilymalone.wordpress.com>, follow me on twitter <@lily_lilymalone>, or like my Facebook page <lily.lilymalone>

You can also follow me through my publisher's page here www.escapepublishing.com.au

Reviews can help readers find books, and I am grateful for all honest reviews. Thank you for taking the time to let others know what you've read, and what you thought.

If you liked this book, here are my other books: **His Brand Of Beautiful** and **Fairway To Heaven.**

This book was published by Escape Publishing. If you'd like to sample some more great books from my fellow Escape Artists, please read on.

Angry Birds and Turtle Doves

Strange, the difference a year makes.

Last time Seth Lasrey sat his backside in Cafe Nix, he'd flirted with the waitress, Tamsin, because she reminded him of Remy. It was something in the way she moved. That same willowy walk. Not exactly like Remy. No one moved like Remy. Remy's walk was easy as water sliding over glass.

That was February last year when he'd met with Max Montgomery and Montgomery's accountant. They'd all been in Sydney for the Sydney Wine Show where he and Max had signed the deal for Lasrey to buy Montgomery Wines, over a lunch of the best pork belly Seth had ever tasted.

'You always like to see the wine list first, Mr Lasrey. I remember,' Tamsin said now, materialising beside him.

'I do, and thank you, but I already know what I want.'

She paused, fixing him with green eyes that had probably seen every come-on known to woman or waitress and anticipated one right now: 'And what would that be?'

'Pork belly and a bottle of Bowen Estate Cabernet.'

'Ah,' and her eyes crinkled into a smile that held genuine warmth. 'Good for you. Nice choice.'

Tamsin eased her way back toward the bar and Seth pulled his phone and earpieces from his satchel. It was just after eight, Cafe Nix gearing up for another busy night. Most of the tables held couples. Some were groups, business meetings he suspected, or tourists. A stuffed koala poked out of an older lady's handbag and the young boy with her had an Australian flag tucked across his thighs.

It would be 7.30pm in Adelaide. They were in the middle of a heatwave there. Remy said last night it was expected to last another two days and she almost sounded disappointed. She loved the heat.

He'd bet she was wearing her shorts right about now. Her shortest shorts.

The Jessica Simpson/Daisy Duke denim ones that showed the curve of her arse when she bent over in the garden. Probably in tandem with her purple tank top: the one with material that could have hugged a pencil it clung so damn tight. If she'd been digging or pruning—and she was always digging or slashing at something, or getting him digging or slashing at the tougher stuff—there'd be a darkened purple vee in that sweet valley between her breasts. She'd be hot. Drippy. Sweaty. Remy.

He let his thoughts rest there for a few pleasurable seconds. Then he thought about her boots.

He couldn't picture Remy any other way. He'd lost count of the times in the last year he'd told her she should appear in adverts for Blundstone. It would have solved all her money problems in a heartbeat. Bugger the bank.

A junior waitress, not Tamsin, brought him a bottle of iced water. Seth loosened his tie, tugged it out of his collar, undid the top button, started to feel human.

He put the first of his earpieces in, watching Tamsin pick her way through the tables with his bottle of Bowen. She poured without stopping to let him test it. Another testament to her good memory. He'd never been one for testing wine in a restaurant. There were so many screw caps nowadays the odds of finding a corked wine were pretty much zero. He didn't like the wank value of it either.

Red wine flowed. Tamsin put the bottle in a Cafe Nix holder, smiled at him, and kept moving.

Seth swirled the liquid, buried his nose in the glass.

He and Max had drunk Bowen Estate last year too. Max had got himself so pissed over lunch he hadn't been able to back up in time for the Awards dinner that night. Montgomery's winemaker, Lewis Carney, had accepted the trophy for best white wine in show on Max's behalf.

Seth put his other earpiece in. The hum of conversation over cutlery receded. From his seat, he could see Sydney Harbour shining: the bridge lit up like half a lemon alight.

Remy rang at quarter to eight, Adelaide time. On the dot.

'Hey,' he said, 'cause he'd forgotten the cool greeting he'd planned the second the screen lit up with her name.

'Hey yourself. How's it going?'

'Hot.'

'Not as hot as here. It hit thirty-nine today. The dogs are licking an ice-cream container milk-ice block.' She laughed. God he loved her laugh. 'Can you hear them?'

Seth listened. A vague canine growling that could have been his stomach came down the phone. He smiled anyway. Remy and those dogs were his life. Two American Staffordshire Terriers: Occhilupo the male, and Breeze, and now their puppy: Judster. Juddy was the last of the six pups they'd had last year. The others had all sold to good homes.

'I miss you,' he said. 'Next time you have to come with me. You'd love Sydney.'

'I'd hate Sydney. I don't even like little old Adelaide. I don't like cities.'

'You'd like this restaurant. It has crab.'

'I'm so there. When are you taking me, cheapskate?'

He laughed. Loud enough to make the woman with the koala in her bag glance his way. 'Don't make me laugh, Rem. People are staring.'

'You're probably wearing odd socks.'

He inched an ankle out from the table. 'Nope.'

'I knew you'd check. Three days away from me and you can't even dress yourself with surety. How the mighty Seth Lasrey has fallen.'

Softly, because the woman with the koala was checking him out again, he said: 'I love you. I miss waking up with you in the morning. I miss listening to you snore. I'm not the same man without you.'

'I don't snore.'

He smiled. It was so like Remy. He declared undying love and emotion. She talked about odd socks and snoring. Remy's emotions were still shackled somewhere inside that lovely big heart she let slumber in her chest.

It used to bug him. Now he accepted it for what it was. Remy's father was a drunk. He'd died about six years ago in a car accident in Margaret River. She'd grown up listening to him make promises to her mother: that he'd stop drinking, that he'd be a better husband, that he loved her, that he wouldn't gamble anymore, that he'd change ... and it never amounted to anything.

She'd told Seth once she'd prefer to show him how much she loved him every day, than tell him. Words were cheap. Words didn't mean anything.

He took another sip of his wine.

'So what are you having for dinner?' She asked him.

'Pork belly.'

'Gee you have a hard life.'

'You're the one who makes it harder.'

'Bet I made it hard last night,' she said, voice lowering to that sexy purr she did so well.

'I'm not alone in my hotel tonight, Rem. I'm in a crowded restaurant. So we'd better not repeat the experience.'

'Are you sure? It sounds like it might be fun. You always said you wanted me to keep your number on my phone sex personal speed dial.'

'You wouldn't be so keen to get me all revved up if you laid eyes on the waitress. She walks like you,' Seth said, shifting slightly in his chair because even this much suggestion from Remy had his cock stiffening. No wonder she'd been good at her second job.

'You said nobody walks like me.'

'Well she goes close, Rem. She's got hair halfway down to her arse, like you. If I closed my eyes, and she closed her eyes, we could pretend.'

'Why does she have to close her eyes?'

'They're green. Only grey eyes work for me these days.'

'I think you just drew a line through ninety-five percent of the female population.'

'Then it's lucky I got you.'

'What about her legs. Are they like mine?'

Seth slowly tracked Tamsin across the restaurant floor. She was leaning over another table, pouring wine. Her tight black skirt crept up her thighs to a backside shaped like a double quarter peach.

He stifled a groan. 'You have no idea what you're doing to me here, Rem.'

'Yes I do.'

'You must trust me more than you trust yourself.'

'I do. I trust you with my life. That's the only reason I play the game.'

'You wait till I get home. You won't walk for a week.'

She gave him a giggle filled with promise, then said: 'How's the wine show going?'

'It's good. Judging was today. Presentations are tomorrow night.'

'I hope Chameleon wins.'

'Me too.'

Remy's grapevines provided the fruit for Montgomery Wines flagship Adelaide Hills Chameleon Sauvignon Blanc.

'I can't believe you and Rina weren't going to make Chameleon last vintage,' she said.

It was a gentle dig and he didn't mind. 'That was a different stage of our relationship, Remy Roberts. If you remember, I hated you then. I didn't mind at all the thought of bankrupting you and having you beg me for mercy.

On your knees.' The lady with the koala glanced at him and he turned away from her, lowered his voice further and said: 'with your skirt pulled up over your arse and your knees wide, so I could see your pussy spread for me.'

'Hell and Tommy,' Remy said, a little breathless. 'You are getting good at this.'

He felt a jolt of satisfaction and delight. His cock got a jolt of delight too. Not sure about satisfaction. But that was part of what made these phone calls when he was out of town fun, and he would get his own back on the teasing, they both would. Two days from now when he drove into her cottage on Red Gum Valley Road and wrapped her in his arms, because she was everything he wanted.

'Well if I'm on my knees ... you know where that leaves you vulnerable, Seth. You'd be standing before me...'

Jolt. Jolt.

'You'd be hard as a rock. That cock of yours would already be jutting from your pants, just waiting for my mouth to close over it, take you so far in.'

Jolt didn't cut it. He had no words to describe what this woman did to him.

A hand touched his shoulder and he spun. It was Tamsin with his pork belly in the crook of her arm, on a wide, white plate.

'Hold on,' Seth said to Remy, taking the earpieces out.

'I'm very sorry to interrupt you, Mr Lasrey. Your call looks most important. I didn't want to place the plate and startle you.'

'That's fine, Tamsin.' He leaned his upper body away, sliding his chair back all of two millimetres because he couldn't risk her seeing the tent in the front of his pants.

A smile curled the waitress' lovely lips. Was it a knowing one? Seth wasn't about to find out. He'd jump off the Sydney Harbour Bridge before he cheated on Remy.

Tamsin put the plate in front of him. 'I hope you enjoy your meal.'

'Thank you, I will.' He'd enjoy making a meal of Remy too, when he got home. Seth put the earpieces back in. 'Sorry about that, sweetheart. My pork belly just came.'

'Lucky it came before you did.'

She chuckled: a happy sound, like a glass jar of bouncing jellybeans. It made him chuckle too. They were quiet for a beat and then she said: 'I love you.'

Seth stopped laughing. 'Our phone calls never ended that way before.'

'I know. I'm saying it now.'

'I love you, Rem.'

'I know. You say it all the time.'

And normal service was resumed. 'So I'm hanging up now, before you kill my buzz.'

'Happy pork belly, Seth. Sleep well.'

'Goodnight, Crazy Lady.'

Seth unplugged his earpieces and tucked them and his phone in his satchel. The boy at the table with the woman with the koala gave him a grin that was missing two front teeth. 'Were you playing Angry Birds, mister?' The kid said.

His mother, or she might have been grandmother, said: 'Don't stare, Bradley Randy Bishop. It's rude.'

Seth laughed as he picked up his fork. 'No mate, I wasn't playing Angry Birds.'

'Definitely not Angry Birds,' the woman said to him. And she winked. 'Turtle Doves maybe.'

BESTSELLING TITLES BY ESCAPE PUBLISHING...

His Brand of Beautiful
Lily Malone

When marketing strategist Tate Newell first meets wine executive Christina Clay, he has one goal in mind: tell Christina he won't design the new brand for Clay Wines. Tell her thanks, but no thanks. So long, good night.

But Tate is a sucker for a damsel in distress and when a diary mix-up leaves Christina in his debt, Tate gets more than he bargained for.

What does a resourceful girl do when the best marketing brain in the business won't play ball? She bluffs. She cheats. And she ups the ante. But when the stakes get too high, does anybody win?

Falling in love was never part of this branding brief.

Fairway to Heaven
Lily Malone

It's going to take more than summer loving to heal old wounds, but a remote beach, old friendships and a bit of sunshine might just spark a second chance at love.

When Jennifer Gates drives to Sea Breeze Golf Club to kick off date-night with her boyfriend, the last thing she expects is to find Golf Pro Jack giving one of his lady students a private—and very personal—lesson in bunker-play.

Lucky for Jenn, her best friend gives her the keys to the Culhane family's beach shack on the white-pepper shores of Western Australia's Geographe Bay.

Jenn hopes a weekend on the coast with her young son will give her the space she needs to rebuild her confidence after Jack's betrayal.

But she's not the only person seeking sanctuary by the sea. Brayden Culhane is there too, and Jenn can't look at Brayden without remembering the tequila-flavoured kiss they shared on the shack steps years ago.

As long-buried feelings are rekindled, and a friendship is renewed, Jenn knows it is more than lazy summer days bringing her mojo back. Romantic sunsets, ice-cold beers and the odd round of golf can only go so far, because this time trusting Brayden with her heart won't be enough. Jenn has to learn to trust her body, too.

Wild Flower
Eliza Redgold

For centuries, fragrant orchids have made potent love potions, but in a world of technology, can they still wield their power?

Dianella Lee fights to conserve rare, tiny orchids on Australia's southern coast, one of the most biodiverse wildflower regions in the world. But her world of beauty and love is thrown into harsh relief when her family business is almost destroyed by her own mother.

Wade Hamilton has made it big in Silicon Valley, California in 3D computer images. He's about to make a huge, life-changing business deal and needs time out, not complications. But one glance at Dianella and her passion, and he succumbs to orchidmania.

Opposites attract, and orchids have their own magic, but when faced with distance, family drama and diverse priorities, what chance do a flower girl and a billionaire have?

I've Got You
Louise Forster

She's at risk of drowning in more ways than one—and he's the last person she expects to pull her out of the water.

Belle Fabrini is sailing through the Whitsunday Islands to see her grandfather, when she's caught in a freakish storm. Luckily, Kabe Hunter finds her and hoists her on board his yacht just before a huge wave threatens to end her life.

Belle hasn't seen Kabe since high school, a time she spent crushing on Kabe in a big way. Now he's sitting across from her in a tiny cabin wearing nothing but a towel. But Kabe has a reputation for loving and leaving gorgeous tourists, and Belle doesn't need any more complications in her life.

Kabe, however, has other plans. Belle has always been different, and it seems like only he can see through her happy-go-lucky façade to the pain behind. Belle is drowning in her secrets, but Kabe has no intention of losing her, now that he's finally found her again.

Connect with us for info on our new releases, access to exclusive offers, free online reads and much more!

Sign up to our newsletter

Share your reading experience on:

The Escapades Blog

Facebook

Twitter

Watch our reviews, author interviews and more on *Escape Publishing TV*